- HERGÉ -
★

THE ADVENTURES OF TINTIN

THE BLUE LOTUS

Little, Brown and Company
New York   Boston

Little, Brown and Company
Hachette Book Group
237 Park Avenue, New York, NY 10017
Visit our website at www.lb-kids.com

The publisher is not responsible for websites (or their content) that are not owned by the publisher.

First Edition: July 2011

ISBN: 978-0-316-13382-1
2011921034
SC
Printed in China

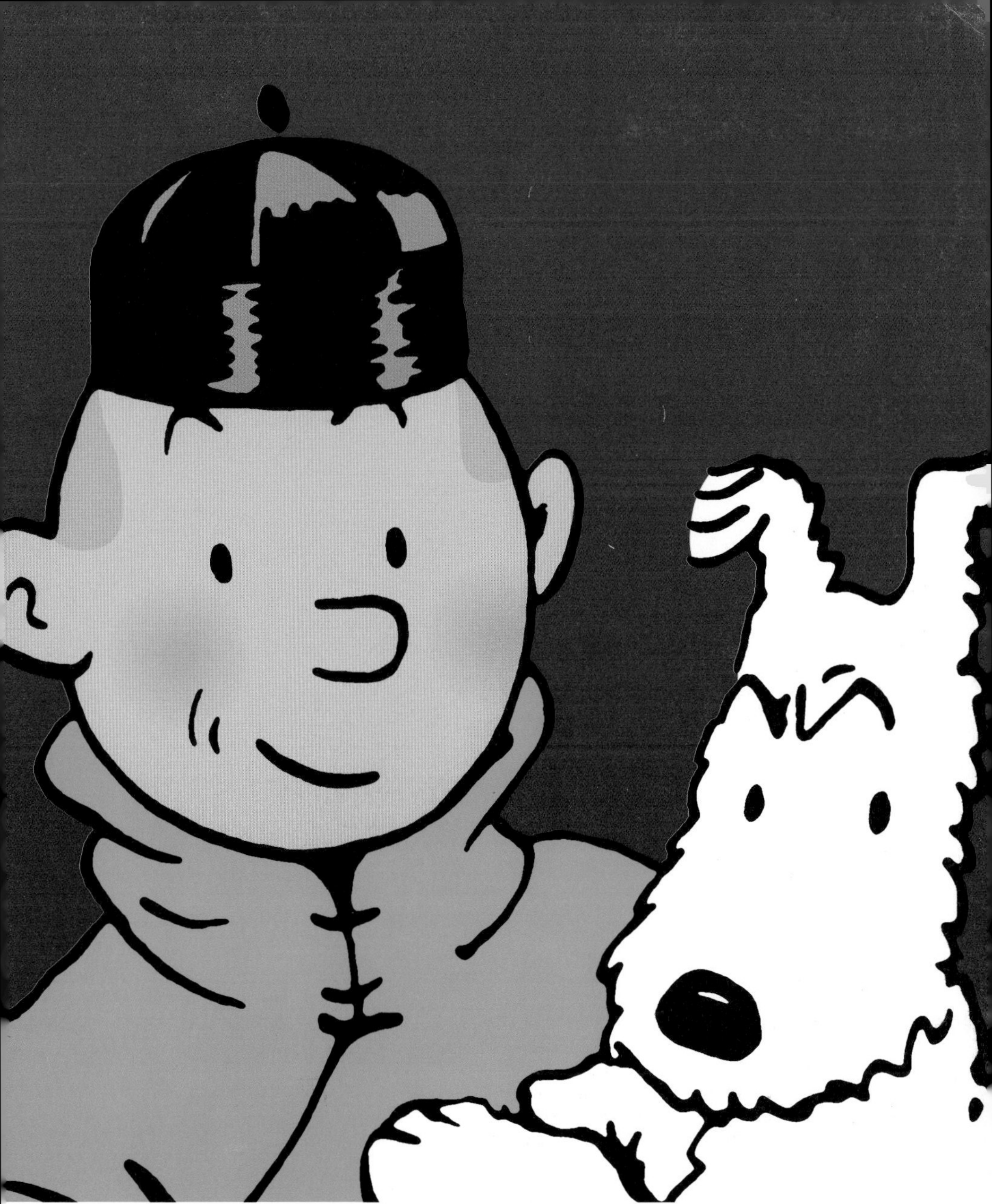

Tintin and Snowy

Courageous Tintin and his faithful dog Snowy travel around the world, hot on the trail of gangsters and dangerous criminals.

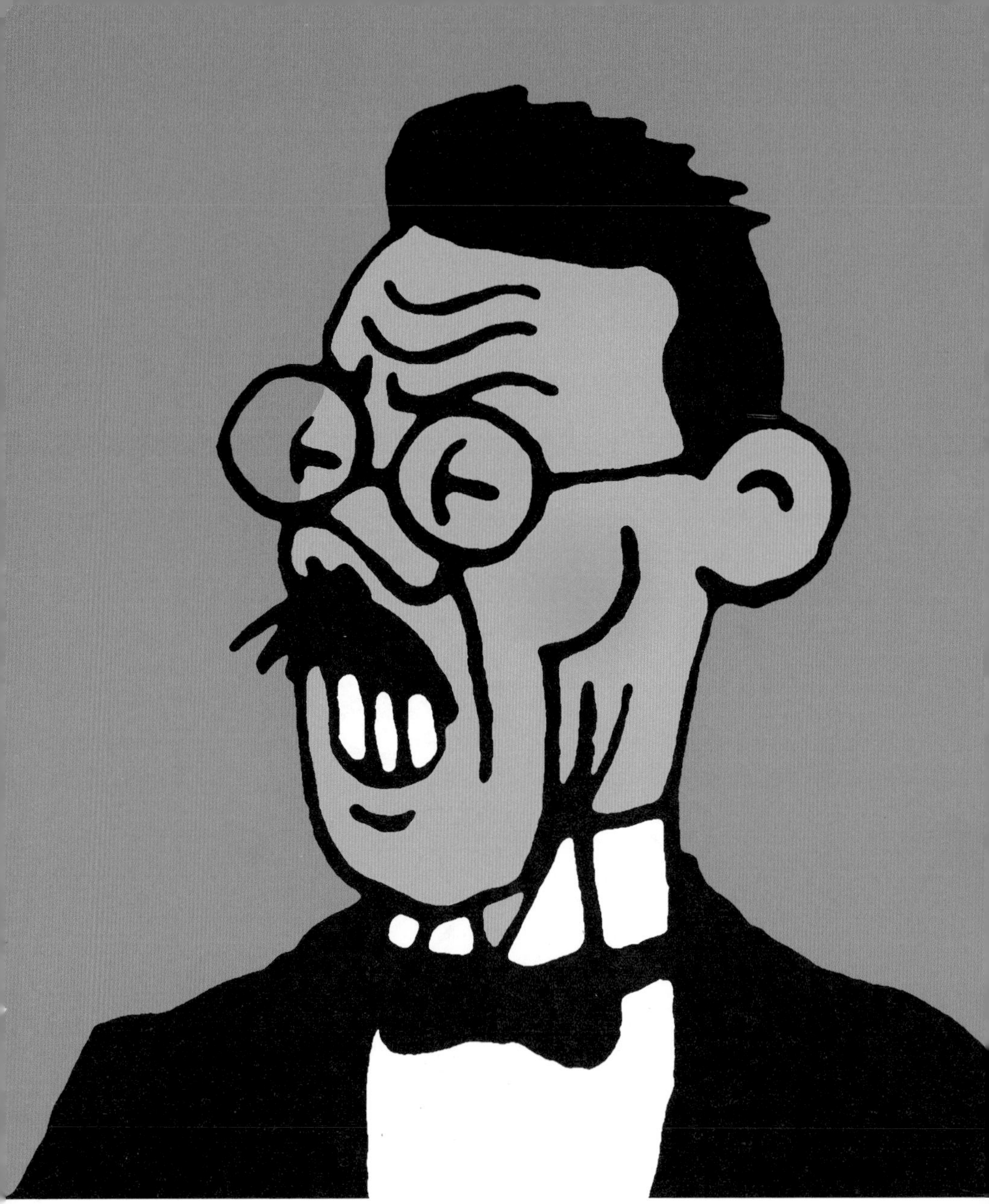

Mitsuhirato

A secret agent and smuggler masquerading as a businessman. Mitsuhirato is determined to get rid of Tintin once and for all.

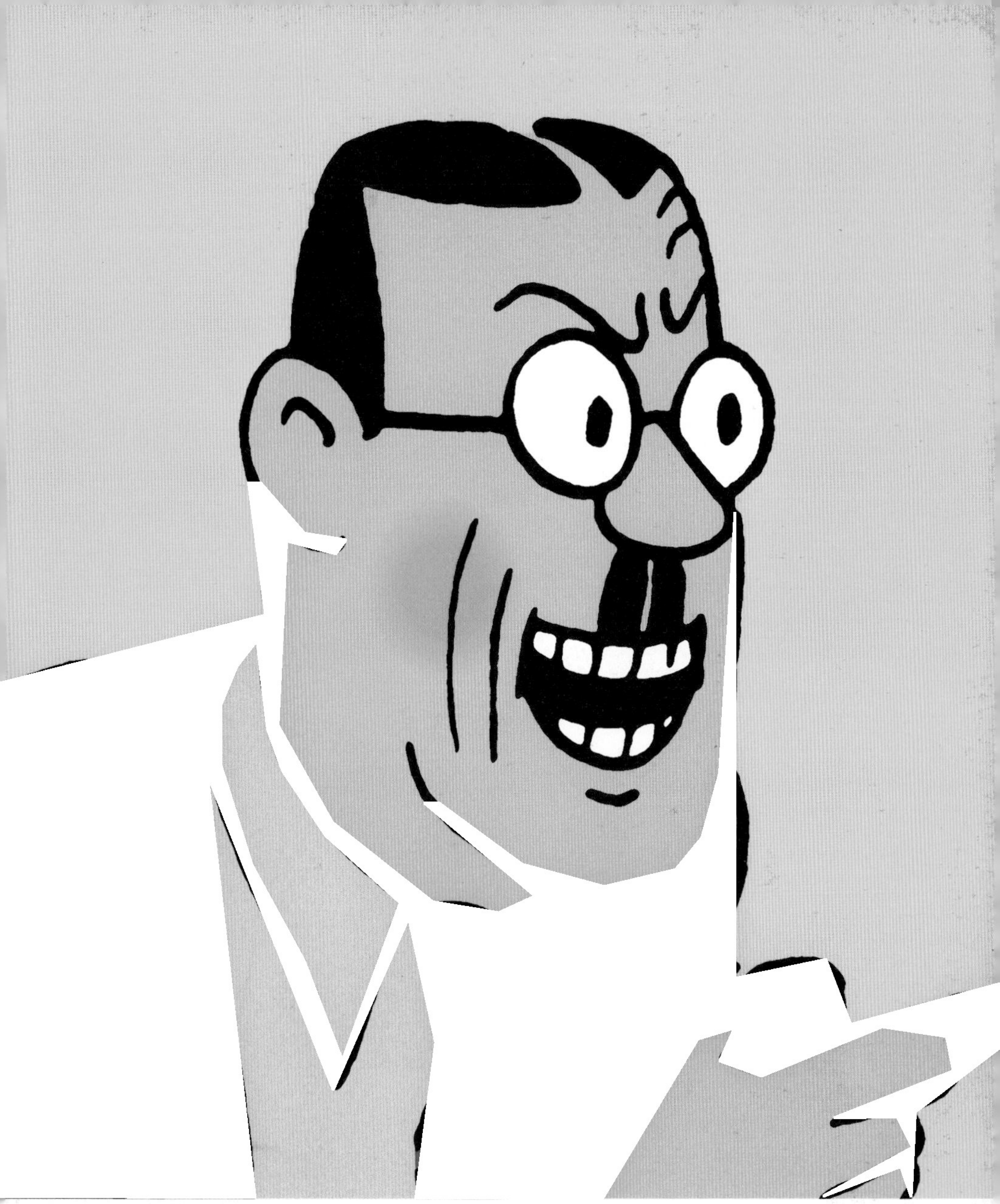

Dawson

The corrupt police chief of the Shanghai International Settlement.
Dawson will do anyone a favor if there is something in it for himself.

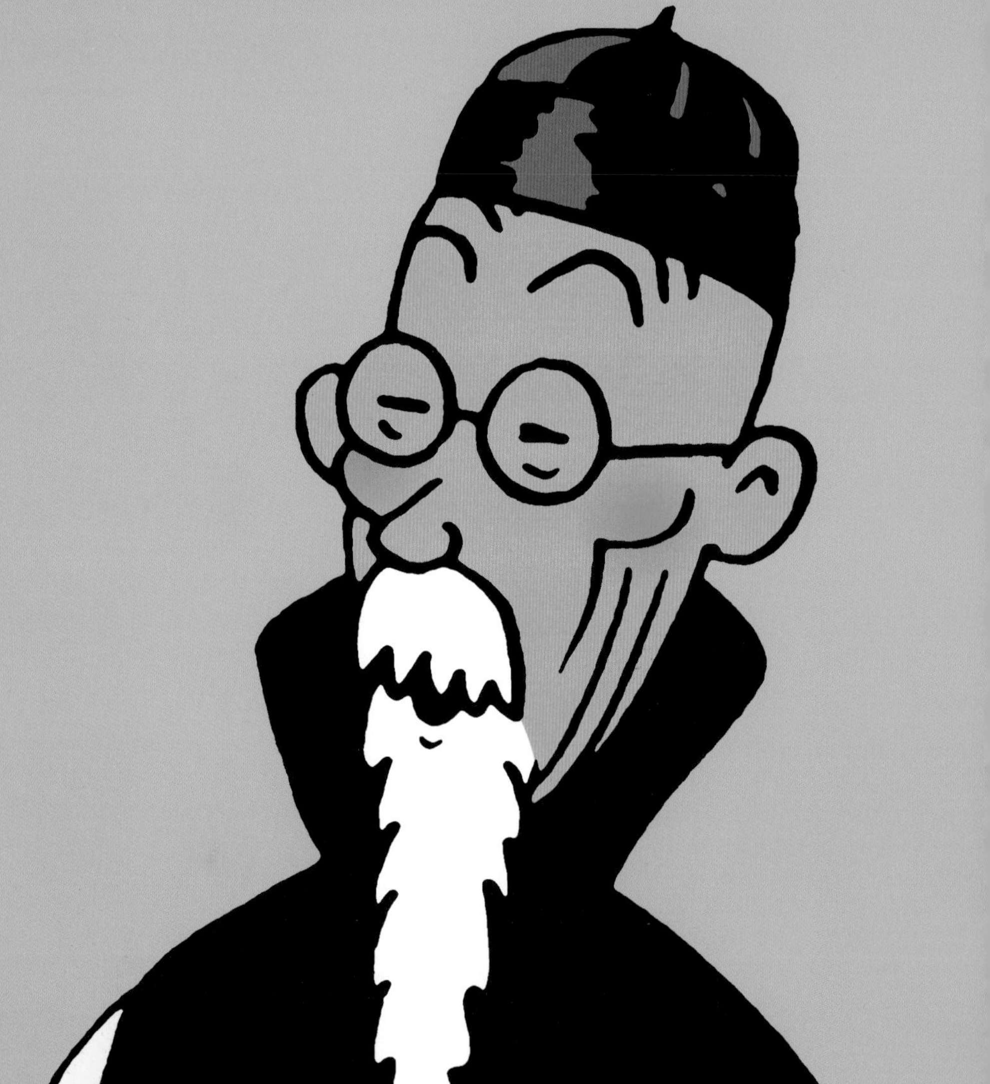

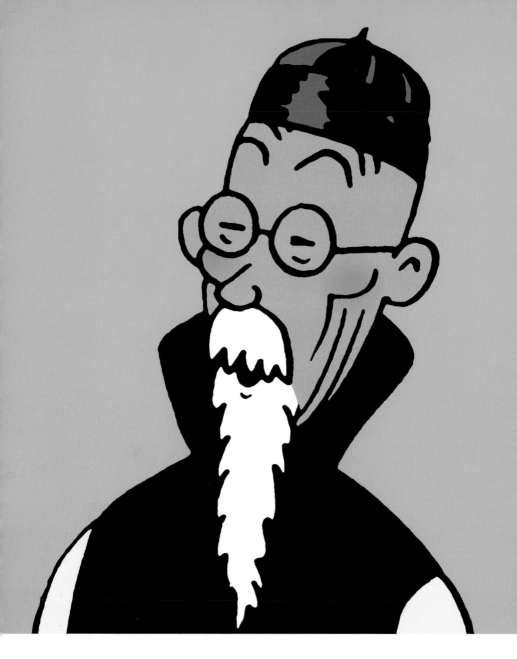

Mr. Wang Chen-yee

The noble leader of the Sons of the Dragon,
a secret society dedicated to fighting smuggling.

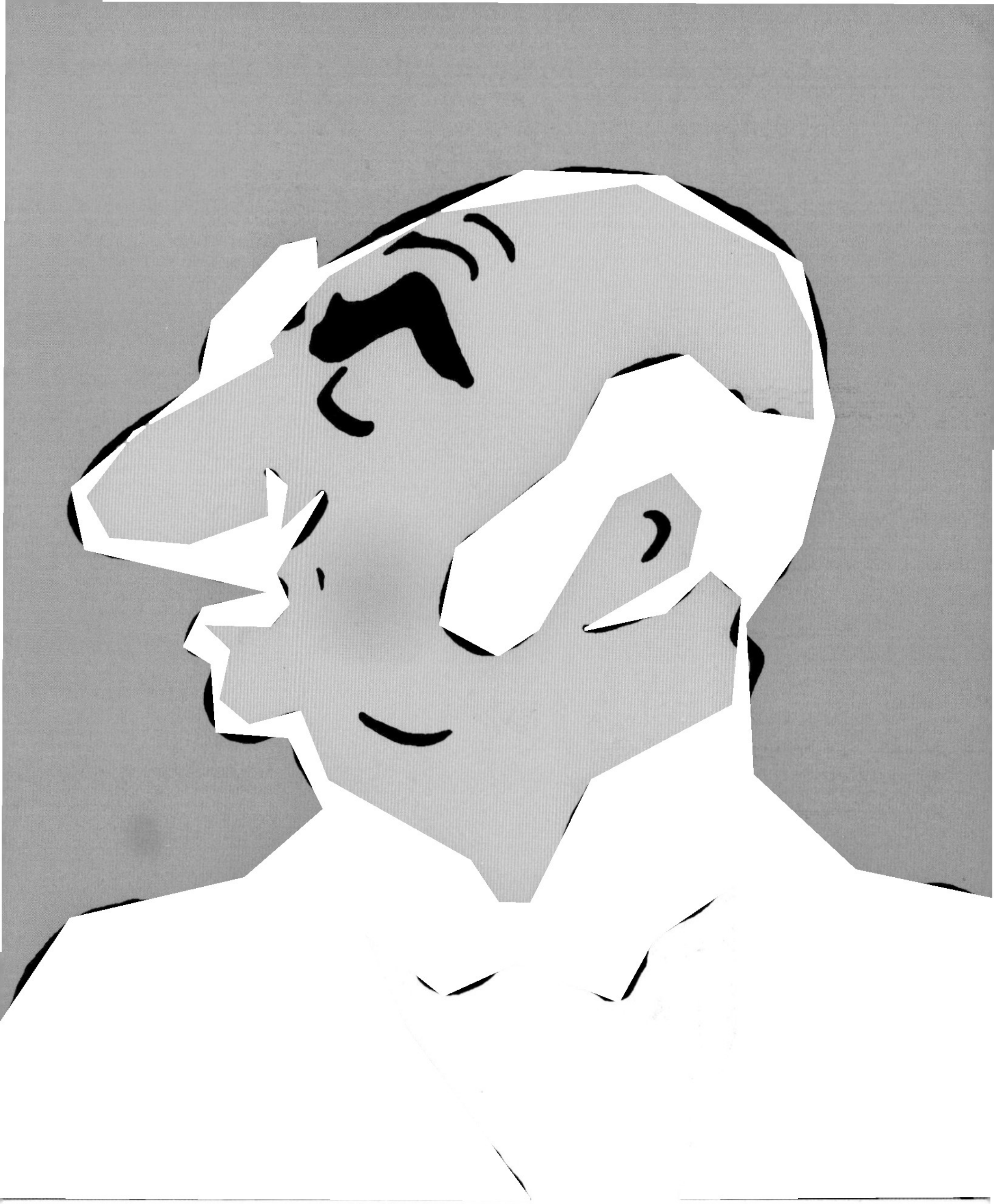

Rastapopoulos

At first it seems like millionaire film tycoon Rastapopoulos is Tintin's friend, but sometimes appearances can be deceiving!

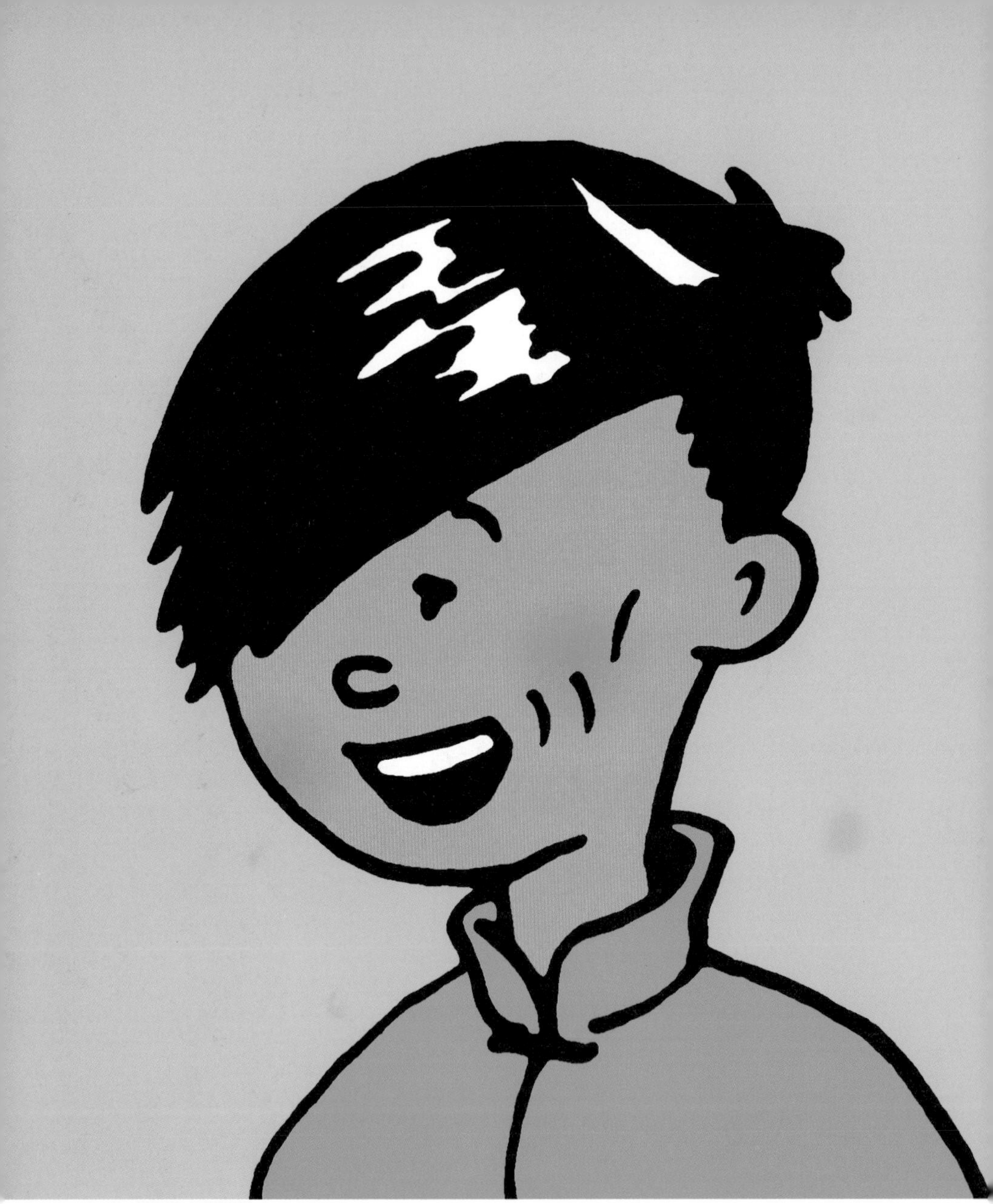

Chang

A young Chinese orphan who becomes Tintin's best friend, in this adventure and forevermore.

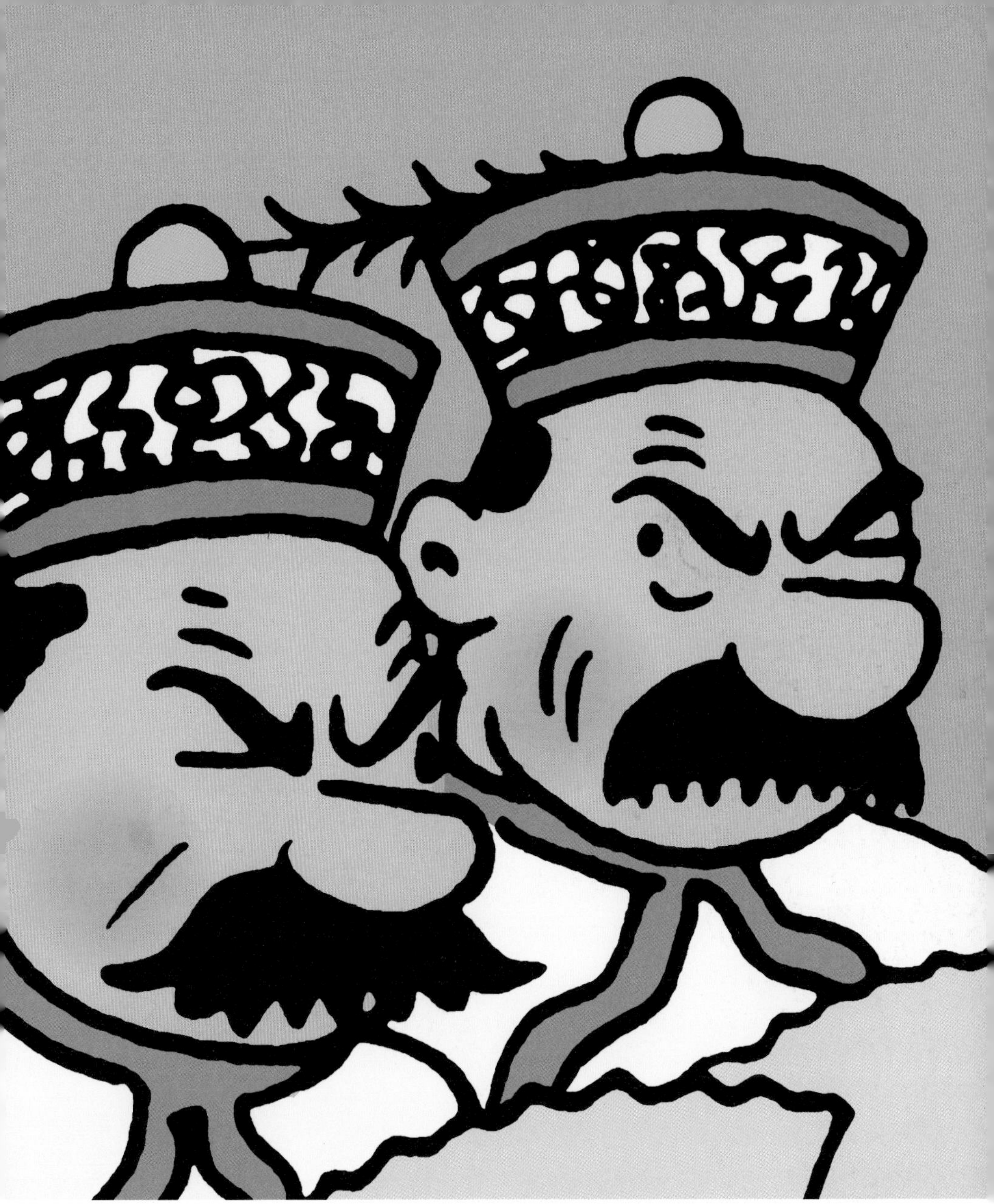

Thomson and Thompson

These clumsy police detectives will go to any length—
even hunting down and arresting Tintin—to obey their orders!

THE BLUE LOTUS

藍蓮花

TINTIN AND SNOWY are in India, guests of the Maharaja of Gaipajama, enjoying a well-earned rest. The evil gang of international drug smugglers, encountered in *Cigars of the Pharaoh*, has been smashed and its members are behind bars. With one exception. Only the mysterious gang-leader is unaccounted for: he disappeared over a cliff.

But questions have still to be answered. What of the terrible Rajaijah juice, the 'poison of madness'? Where were the shipments of opium going, hidden in the false cigars? And who really was the master-mind behind the operation?

CRR WHEEE

How can a dog get a wink of sleep? Not a minute's peace since he fell for short-wave radio!...

CRR WHEEE WHUIIT

There it is again. That's the station I've been trying to identify...

It doesn't make any sense... What can it possibly mean?

It must have some meaning ...but what?

My direction-finder shows WSW, ENE. In theory the transmitter should be along a line in the same direction, passing through Gaipajama.

Tintin Sahib, the Maharaja requests your presence.

Thank you. I'll come.

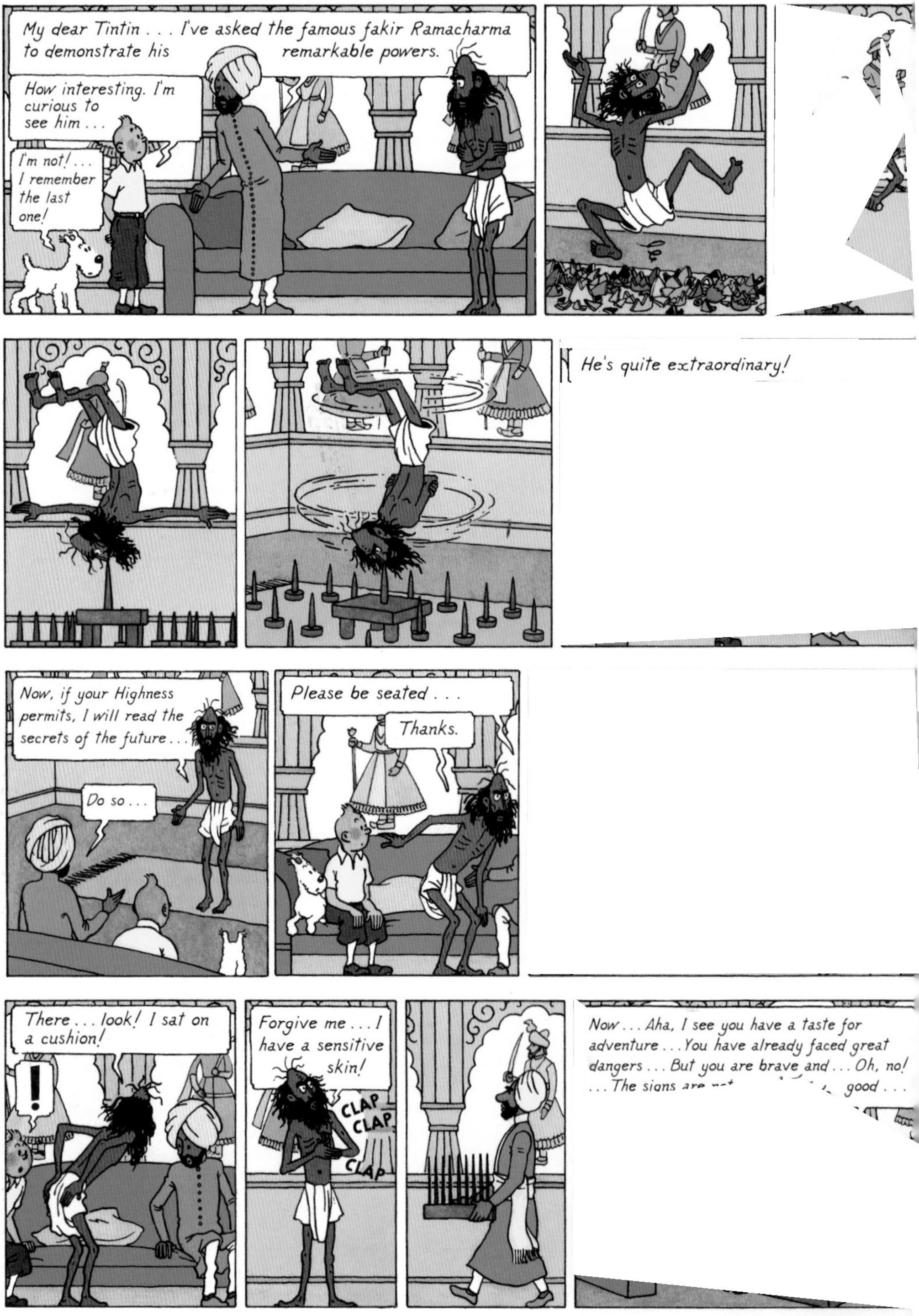

My dear Tintin . . . I've asked the famous fakir Ramacharma to demonstrate his remarkable powers.
How interesting. I'm curious to see him . . .
I'm not! . . . I remember the last one!
He's quite extraordinary!
Now, if your Highness permits, I will read the secrets of the future . . .
Do so . . .
Please be seated . . .
Thanks.
There . . . look! I sat on a cushion!
!
Forgive me . . . I have a sensitive skin!
CLAP
CLAP
CLAP
Now . . . Aha, I see you have a taste for adventure . . . You have already faced great dangers . . . But you are brave and . . . Oh, no! . . . The signs are
good . . .

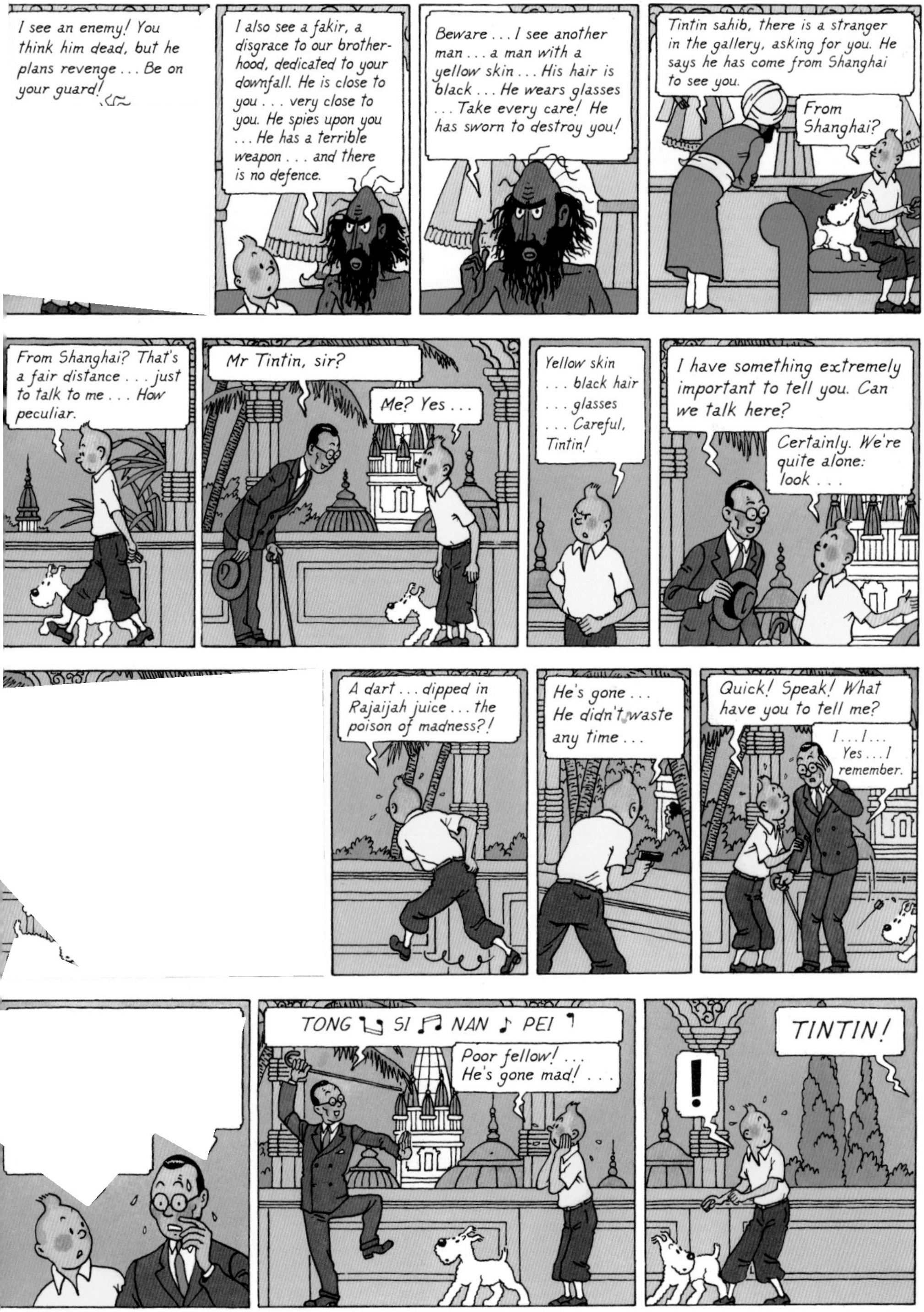
I see an enemy! You think him dead, but he plans revenge . . . Be on your guard!
I also see a fakir, a disgrace to our brotherhood, dedicated to your downfall. He is close to you . . . very close to you. He spies upon you . . . He has a terrible weapon . . . and there is no defence.
Beware . . . I see another man . . . a man with a yellow skin . . . His hair is black . . . He wears glasses . . . Take every care! He has sworn to destroy you!
Tintin sahib, there is a stranger in the gallery, asking for you. He says he has come from Shanghai to see you.
From Shanghai?
From Shanghai? That's a fair distance . . . just to talk to me . . . How peculiar.
Mr Tintin, sir?
Me? Yes . . .
Yellow skin . . . black hair . . . glasses . . . Careful, Tintin!
I have something extremely important to tell you. Can we talk here?
Certainly. We're quite alone: look . . .
A dart . . . dipped in Rajaijah juice . . . the poison of madness?!
He's gone . . . He didn't waste any time . . .
Quick! Speak! What have you to tell me?
I . . . I . . . Yes . . . I remember.
TONG SI NAN PEI
Poor fellow! . . . He's gone mad! . . .
!
TINTIN!

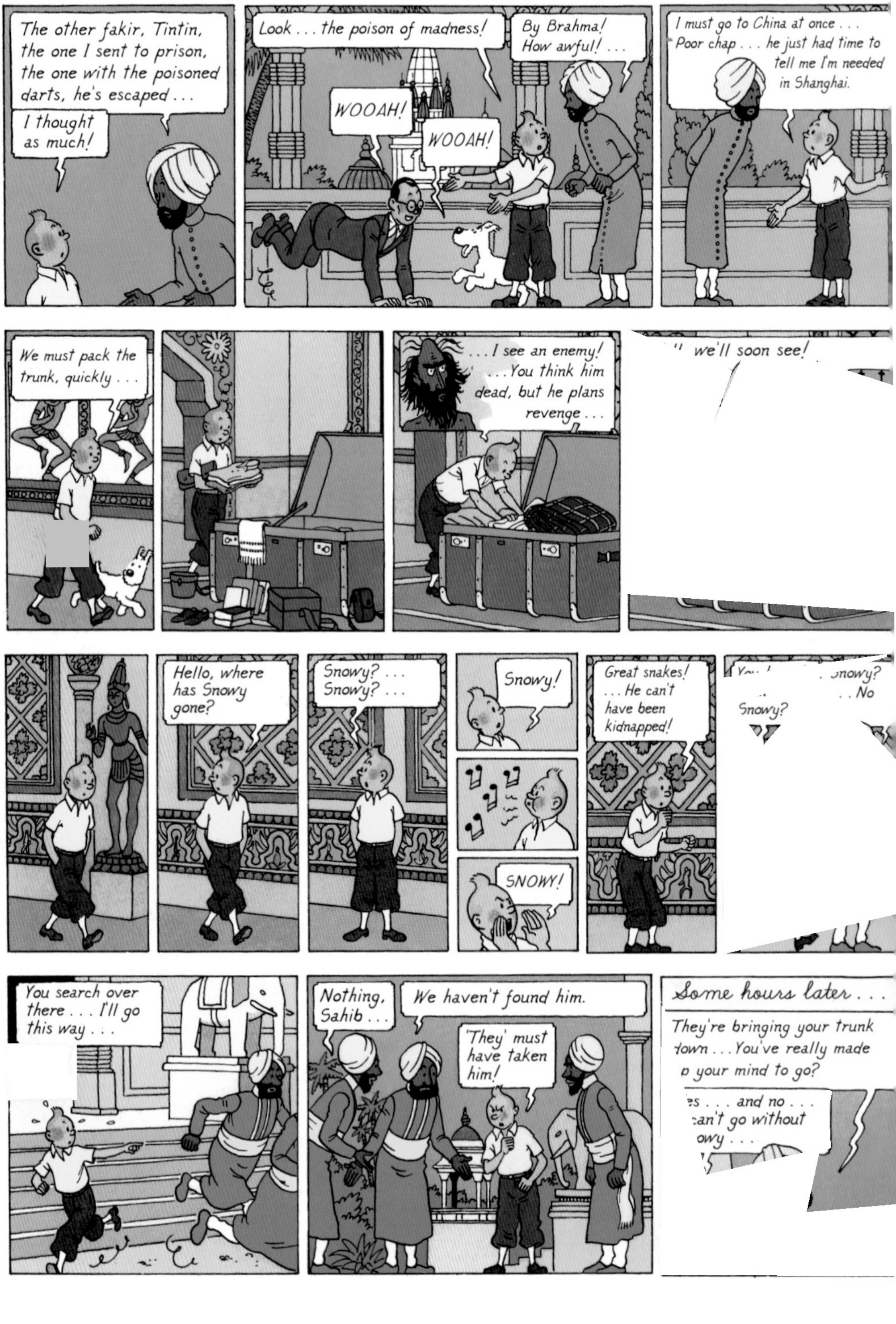

The other fakir, Tintin, the one I sent to prison, the one with the poisoned darts, he's escaped . . .
I thought as much!
Look . . . the poison of madness!
WOOAH!
WOOAH!
By Brahma! How awful! . . .
I must go to China at once . . . Poor chap . . . he just had time to tell me I'm needed in Shanghai.
We must pack the trunk, quickly . . .
. . . I see an enemy! . . . You think him dead, but he plans revenge . . .
we'll soon see!
Hello, where has Snowy gone?
Snowy? . . . Snowy? . . .
Snowy!
SNOWY!
Great snakes! . . . He can't have been kidnapped!
. . . No
Snowy?
You search over there . . . I'll go this way . . .
Nothing, Sahib . . .
We haven't found him.
'They' must have taken him!
Some hours later . . .
They're bringing your trunk
own . . . You've really made
your mind to go?
es . . . and no . . .
an't go without
owy . . .

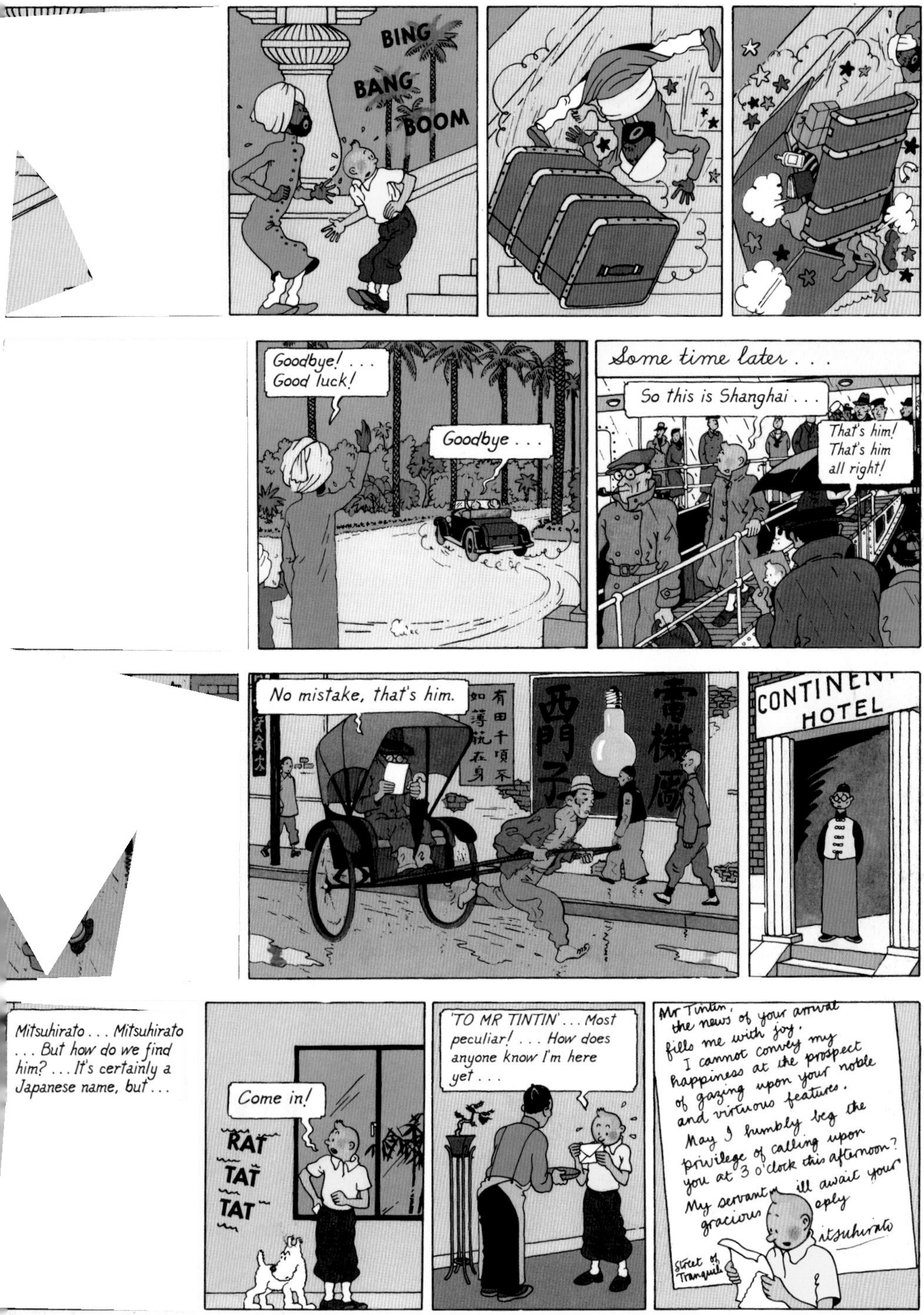
BING
BANG
BOOM
Goodbye! . . . Good luck!
Goodbye . . .
Some time later . . .
So this is Shanghai . . .
That's him! That's him all right!
No mistake, that's him.
CONTINENT HOTEL
Mitsuhirato . . . Mitsuhirato . . . But how do we find him? . . . It's certainly a Japanese name, but . . .
RAT TAT TAT
Come in!
'TO MR TINTIN' . . . Most peculiar! . . . How does anyone know I'm here yet . . .
Mr Tintin,
the news of your arrival fills me with joy.
I cannot convey my happiness at the prospect of gazing upon your noble and virtuous features.
May I humbly beg the privilege of calling upon you at 3 o'clock this afternoon?
My servant will await your gracious reply
Mitsuhirato
Street of Tranquil

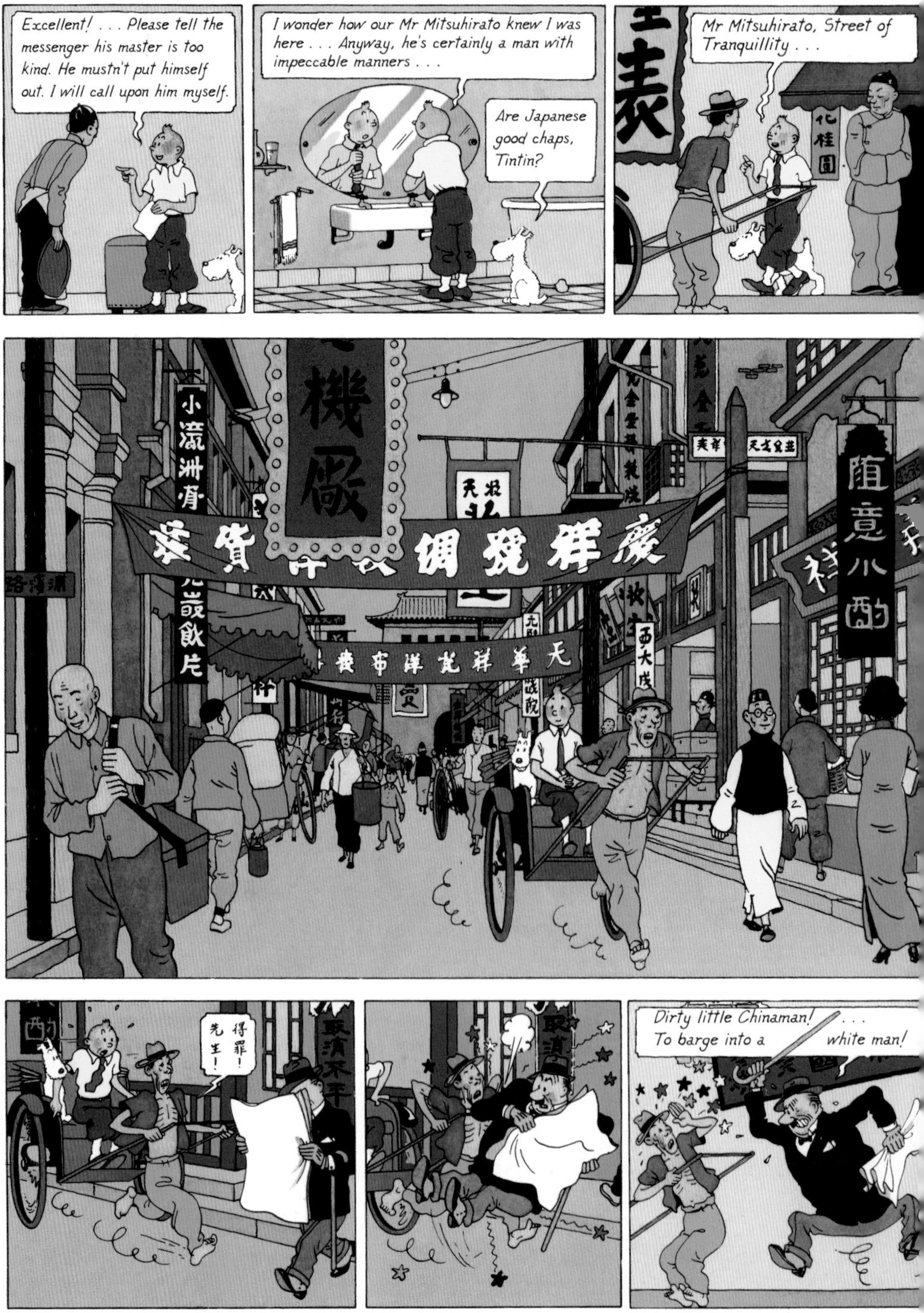

Excellent! . . . Please tell the messenger his master is too kind. He mustn't put himself out. I will call upon him myself.
I wonder how our Mr Mitsuhirato knew I was here . . . Anyway, he's certainly a man with impeccable manners . . .
Are Japanese good chaps, Tintin?
Mr Mitsuhirato, Street of Tranquillity . . .
得罪！先生！
Dirty little Chinaman! . . . To barge into a white man!

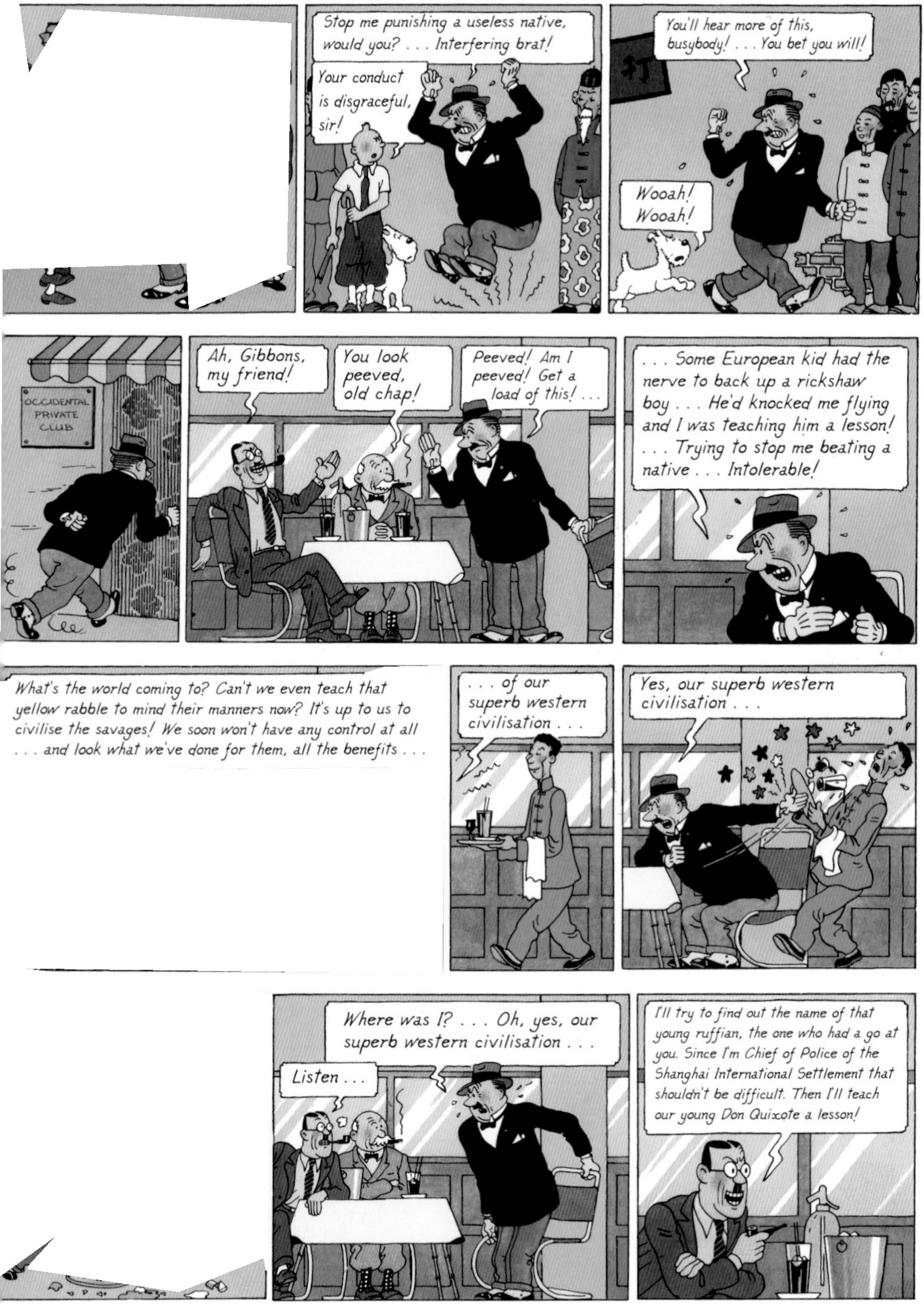
Stop me punishing a useless native, would you? . . . Interfering brat!
Your conduct is disgraceful, sir!
打
You'll hear more of this, busybody! . . . You bet you will!
Wooah! Wooah!
OCCIDENTAL PRIVATE CLUB
Ah, Gibbons, my friend!
You look peeved, old chap!
Peeved! Am I peeved! Get a load of this! . . .
. . . Some European kid had the nerve to back up a rickshaw boy . . . He'd knocked me flying and I was teaching him a lesson! . . . Trying to stop me beating a native . . . Intolerable!
What's the world coming to? Can't we even teach that yellow rabble to mind their manners now? It's up to us to civilise the savages! We soon won't have any control at all . . . and look what we've done for them, all the benefits . . .
. . . of our superb western civilisation . . .
Yes, our superb western civilisation . . .
Where was I? . . . Oh, yes, our superb western civilisation . . .
Listen . . .
I'll try to find out the name of that young ruffian, the one who had a go at you. Since I'm Chief of Police of the Shanghai International Settlement that shouldn't be difficult. Then I'll teach our young Don Quixote a lesson!

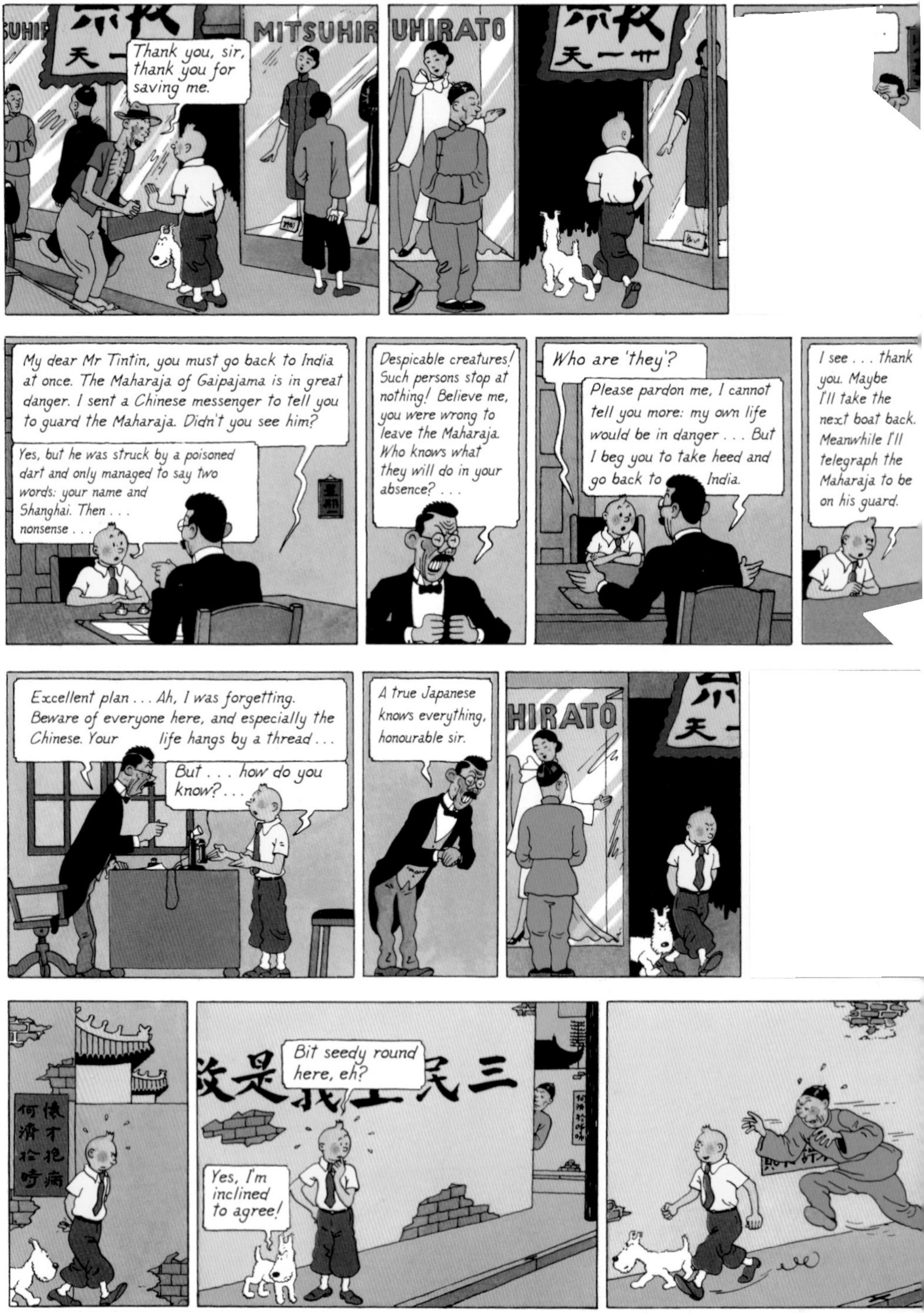
MITSUHIR
Thank you, sir, thank you for saving me.
UHIRATO
My dear Mr Tintin, you must go back to India at once. The Maharaja of Gaipajama is in great danger. I sent a Chinese messenger to tell you to guard the Maharaja. Didn't you see him?
Yes, but he was struck by a poisoned dart and only managed to say two words: your name and Shanghai. Then . . . nonsense . . .
Despicable creatures! Such persons stop at nothing! Believe me, you were wrong to leave the Maharaja. Who knows what they will do in your absence? . . .
Who are 'they'?
Please pardon me, I cannot tell you more: my own life would be in danger . . . But I beg you to take heed and go back to India.
I see . . . thank you. Maybe I'll take the next boat back. Meanwhile I'll telegraph the Maharaja to be on his guard.
Excellent plan . . . Ah, I was forgetting. Beware of everyone here, and especially the Chinese. Your life hangs by a thread . . .
But . . . how do you know? . . .
A true Japanese knows everything, honourable sir.
HIRATO
Bit seedy round here, eh?
Yes, I'm inclined to agree!

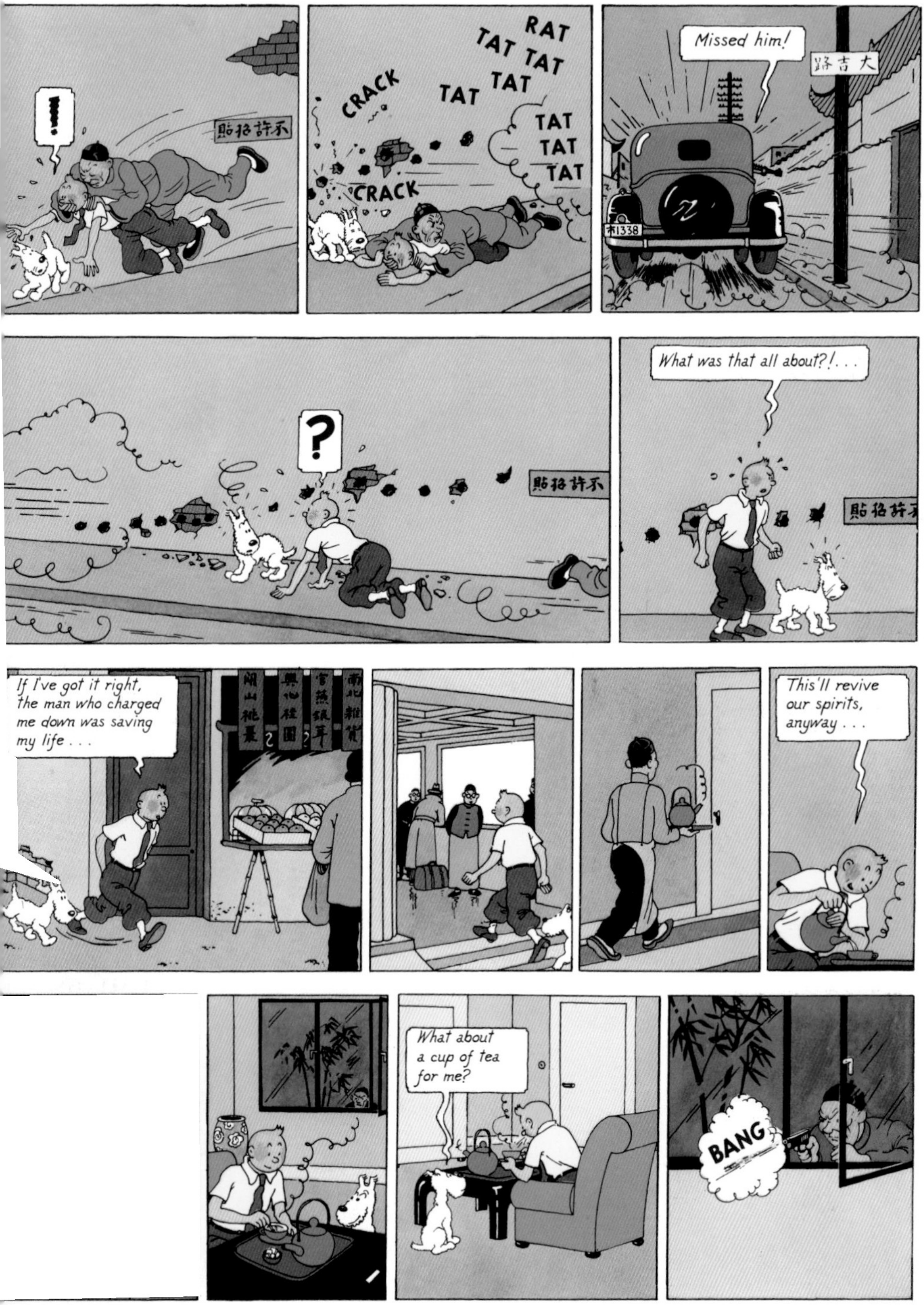
!!!
CRACK
TAT
RAT TAT TAT
TAT
CRACK
TAT TAT TAT
Missed him!
?
What was that all about?!...
If I've got it right, the man who charged me down was saving my life . . .
This'll revive our spirits, anyway . . .
What about a cup of tea for me?
BANG

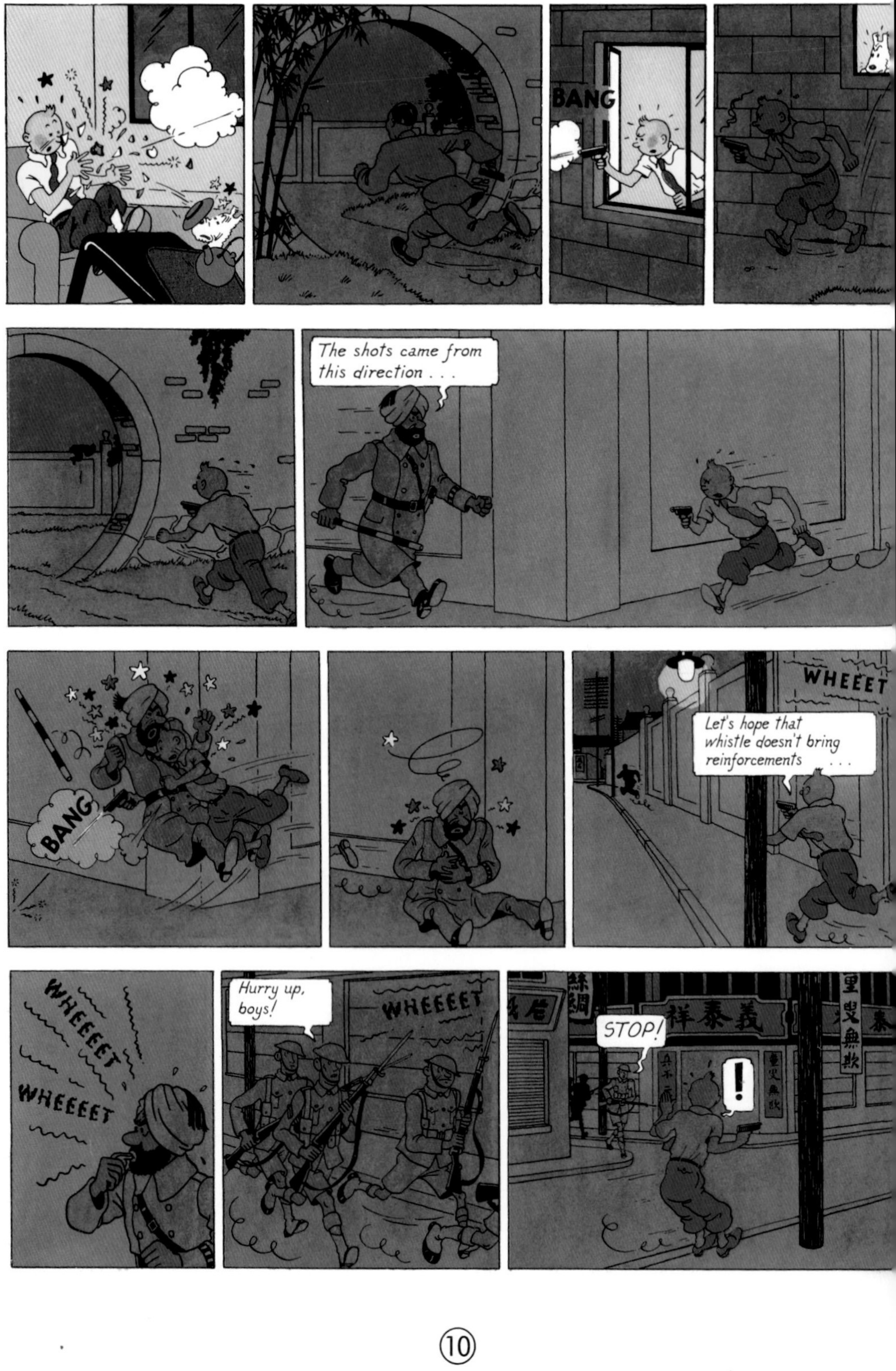
BANG
The shots came from this direction . . .
BANG
WHEEET
Let's hope that whistle doesn't bring reinforcements . . .
WHEEEEET
WHEEEEET
Hurry up, boys!
WHEEEEET
STOP!
!

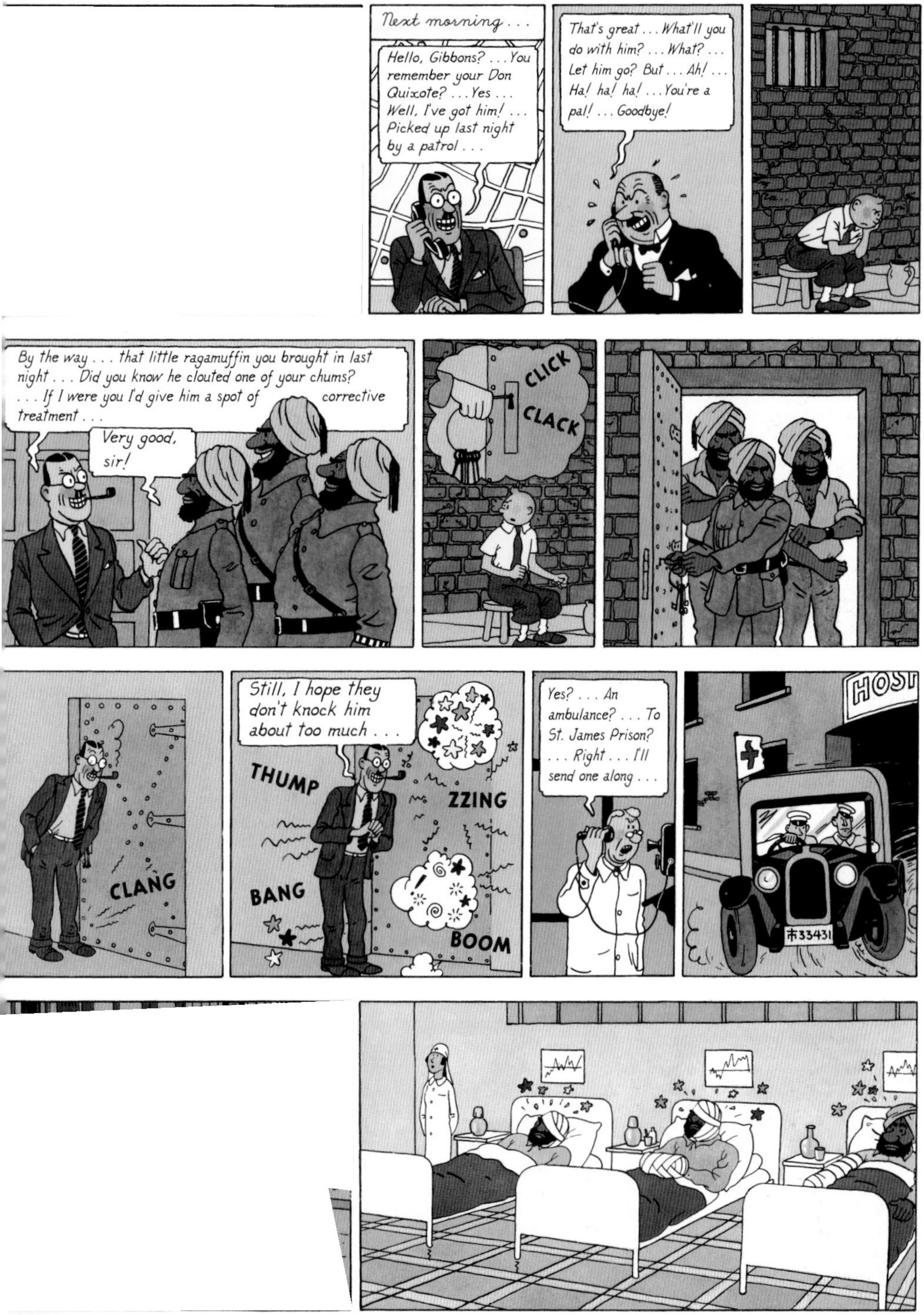
Next morning . . .
Hello, Gibbons? . . . You remember your Don Quixote? . . . Yes . . . Well, I've got him! . . . Picked up last night by a patrol . . .
That's great . . . What'll you do with him? . . . What? . . . Let him go? But . . . Ah! . . . Ha! ha! ha! . . . You're a pal! . . . Goodbye!
By the way . . . that little ragamuffin you brought in last night . . . Did you know he clouted one of your chums? . . . If I were you I'd give him a spot of corrective treatment . . .
Very good, sir!
CLICK
CLACK
CLANG
Still, I hope they don't knock him about too much . . .
THUMP
ZZING
BANG
BOOM
Yes? . . . An ambulance? . . . To St. James Prison? . . . Right . . . I'll send one along . . .
市33431

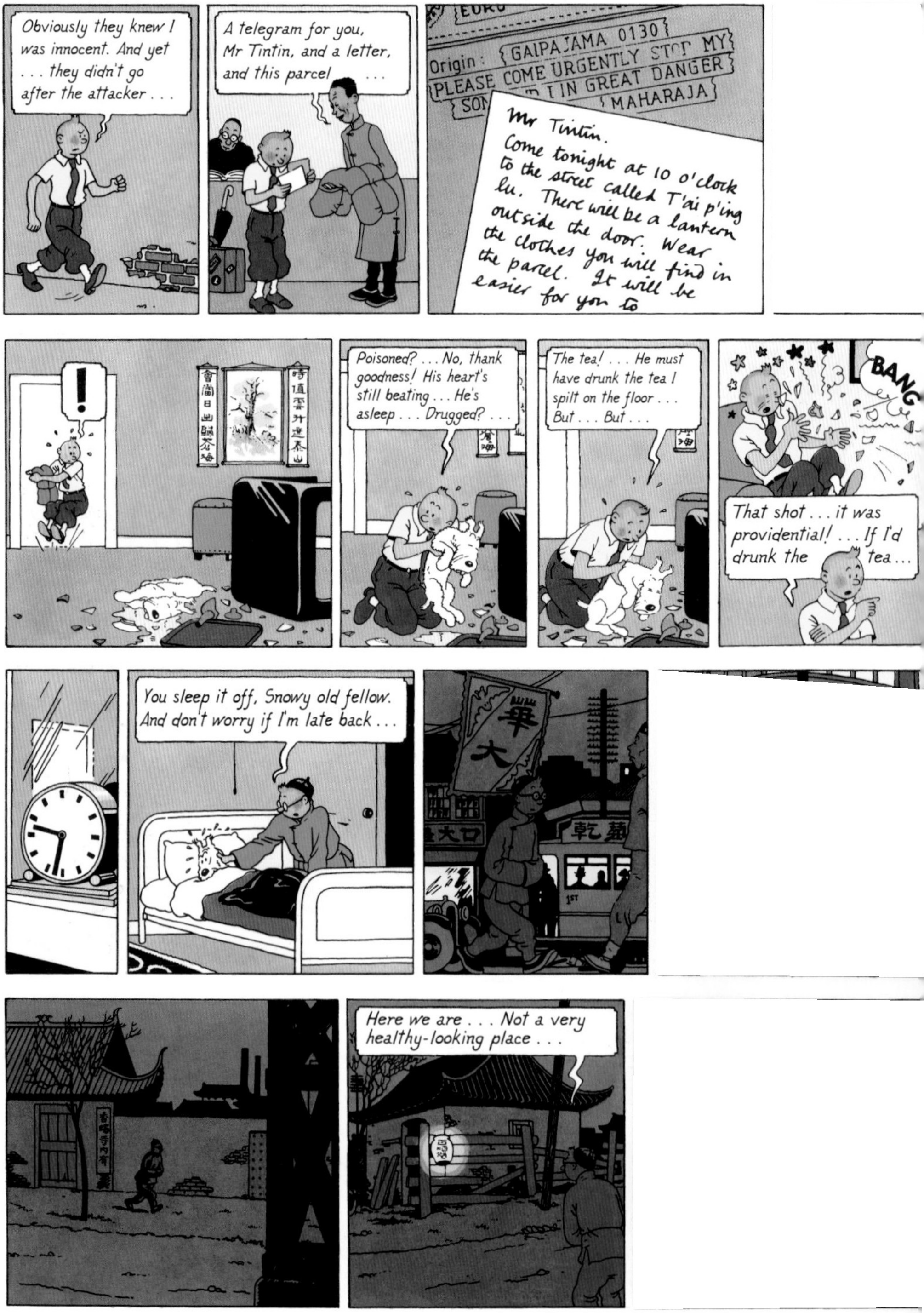
Obviously they knew I was innocent. And yet . . . they didn't go after the attacker . . .
A telegram for you, Mr Tintin, and a letter, and this parcel . . .
Origin : GAIPAJAMA 0130
PLEASE COME URGENTLY STOP MY
IN GREAT DANGER
MAHARAJA
Mr Tintin.
Come tonight at 10 o'clock to the street called T'ai p'ing lu. There will be a lantern outside the door. Wear the clothes you will find in the parcel. It will be easier for you to
!
Poisoned? . . . No, thank goodness! His heart's still beating . . . He's asleep . . . Drugged? . . .
The tea! . . . He must have drunk the tea I spilt on the floor . . . But . . . But . . .
BANG
That shot . . . it was providential! . . . If I'd drunk the tea . . .
You sleep it off, Snowy old fellow. And don't worry if I'm late back . . .
Here we are . . . Not a very healthy-looking place . . .

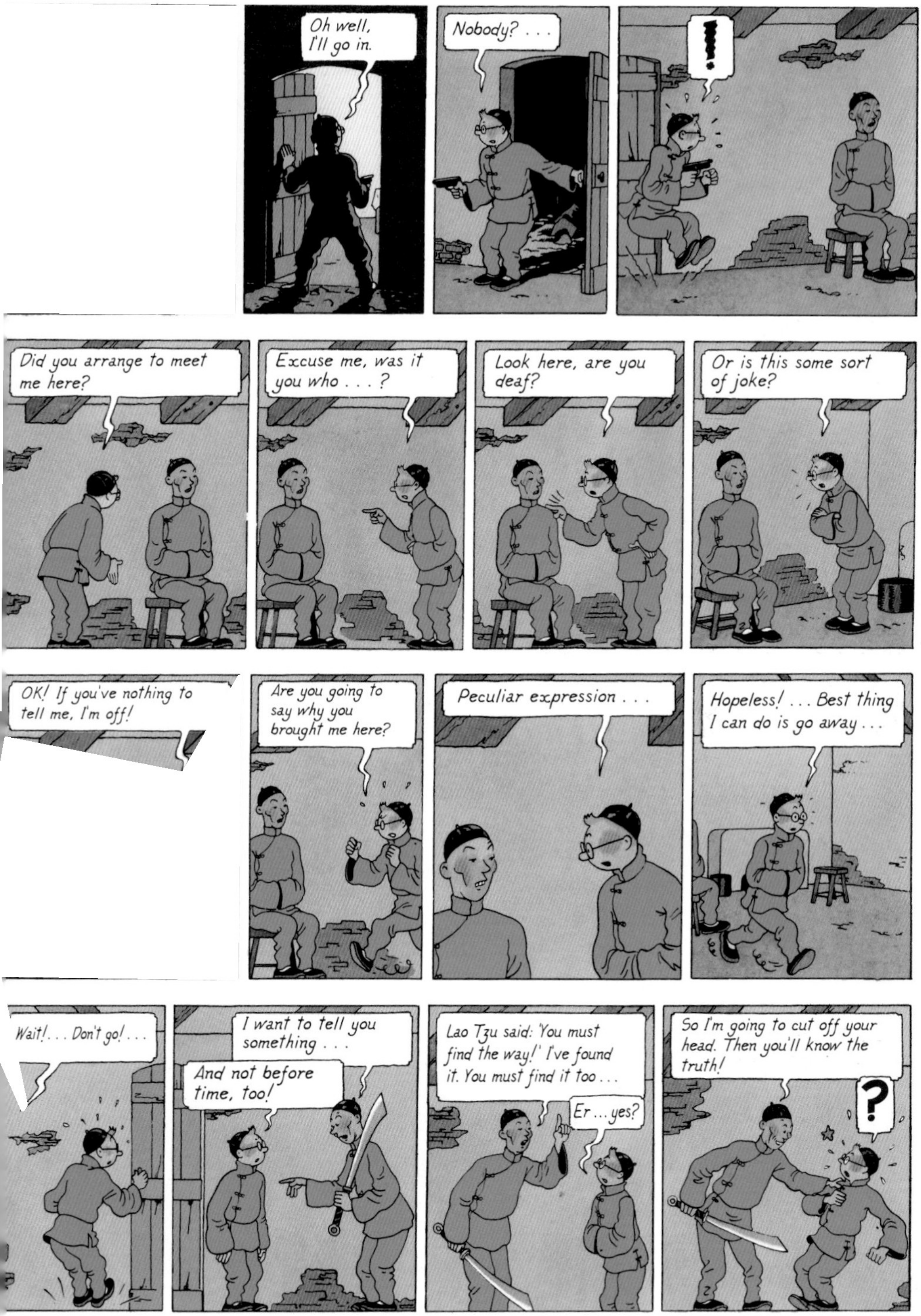
Oh well, I'll go in.
Nobody? . . .
Did you arrange to meet me here?
Excuse me, was it you who . . . ?
Look here, are you deaf?
Or is this some sort of joke?
OK! If you've nothing to tell me, I'm off!
Are you going to say why you brought me here?
Peculiar expression . . .
Hopeless! . . . Best thing I can do is go away . . .
Wait! . . . Don't go! . . .
I want to tell you something . . .
And not before time, too!
Lao Tzu said: 'You must find the way!' I've found it. You must find it too . . .
Er . . . yes?
So I'm going to cut off your head. Then you'll know the truth!
?

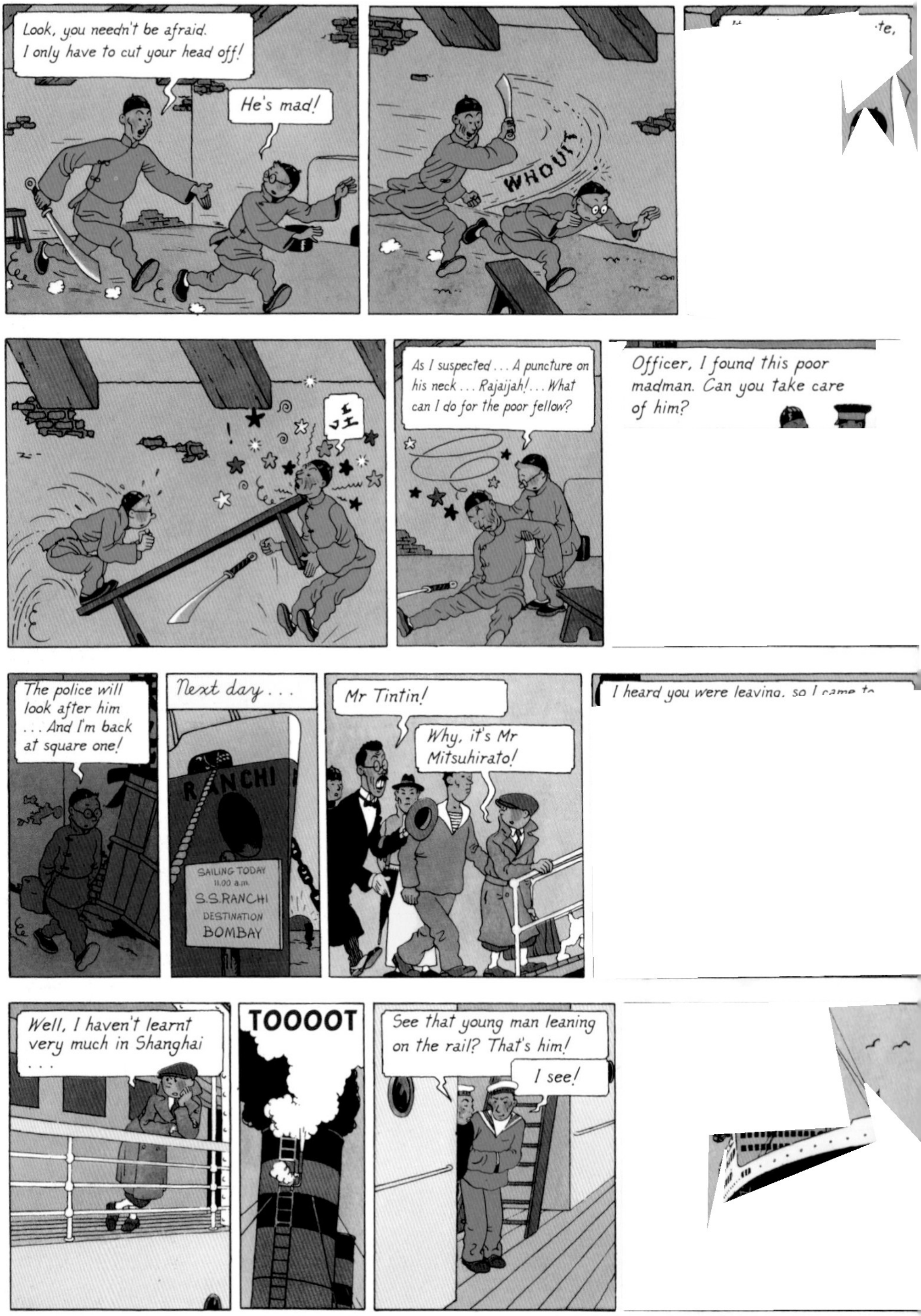
Look, you needn't be afraid. I only have to cut your head off!
He's mad!
WHOUIT
As I suspected . . . A puncture on his neck . . . Rajaijah! . . . What can I do for the poor fellow?
Officer, I found this poor madman. Can you take care of him?
The police will look after him . . . And I'm back at square one!
Next day . . .
RANCHI
SAILING TODAY 11.00 a.m. S.S.RANCHI DESTINATION BOMBAY
Mr Tintin!
Why, it's Mr Mitsuhirato!
Well, I haven't learnt very much in Shanghai . . .
TOOOOT
See that young man leaning on the rail? That's him!
I see!

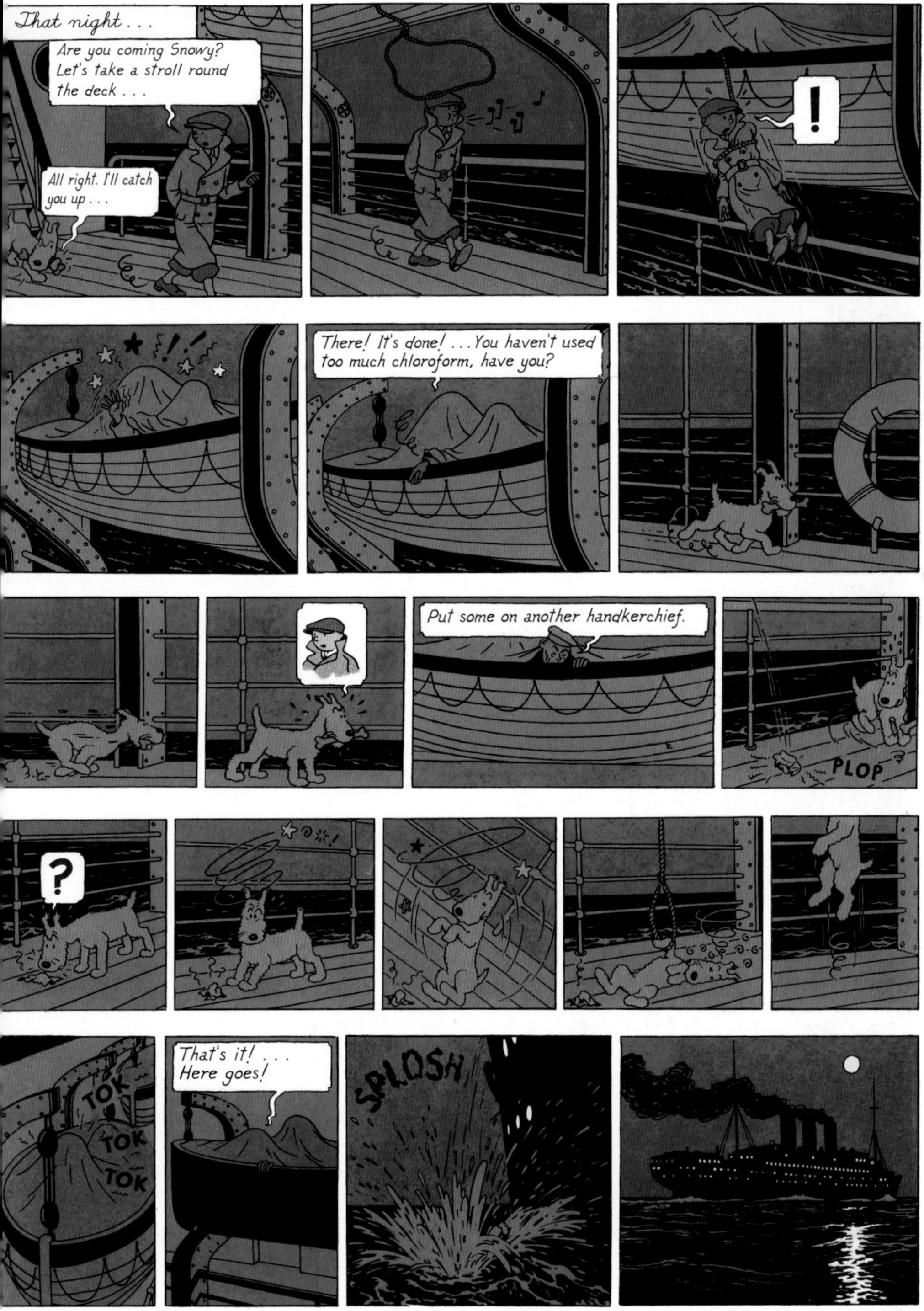

That night . . .
Are you coming Snowy? Let's take a stroll round the deck . . .
All right. I'll catch you up . . .
!
There! It's done! . . . You haven't used too much chloroform, have you?
?
Put some on another handkerchief.
PLOP
?
TOK
TOK
TOK
That's it! . . . Here goes!
SPLOSH

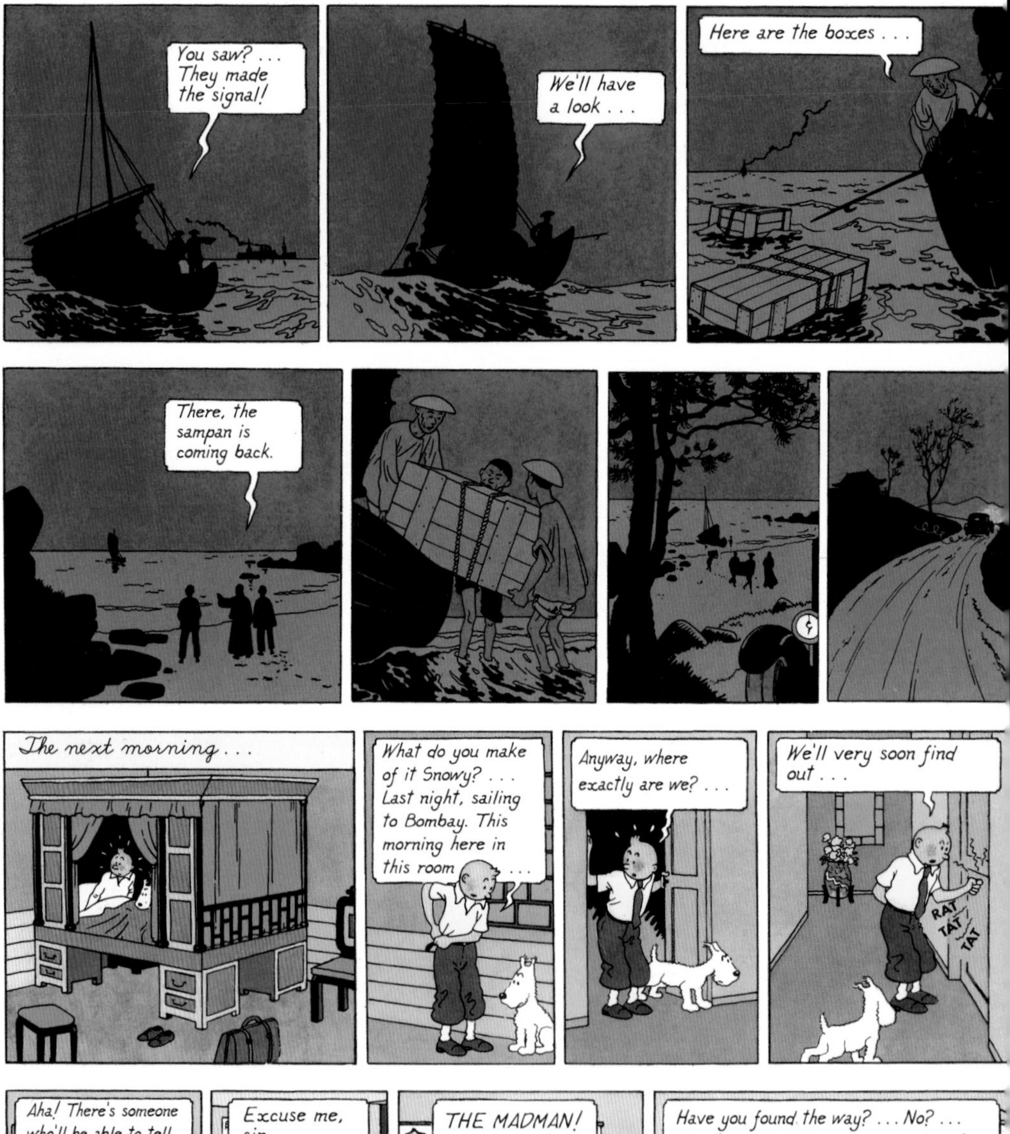
You saw? ... They made the signal!
We'll have a look ...
Here are the boxes ...
There, the sampan is coming back.
The next morning ...
What do you make of it Snowy? ... Last night, sailing to Bombay. This morning here in this room ...
Anyway, where exactly are we? ...
We'll very soon find out ...
RAT TAT TAT
Aha! There's someone who'll be able to tell us ...
Excuse me, sir ...
THE MADMAN! SHANGHAI! ...
Have you found the way? ... No? ... Good! ... Then I'll cut off your head! ...
Again! ...

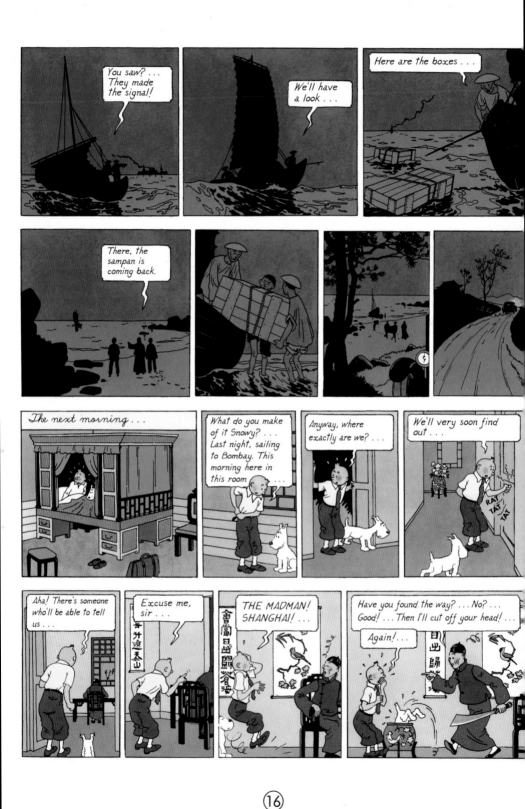

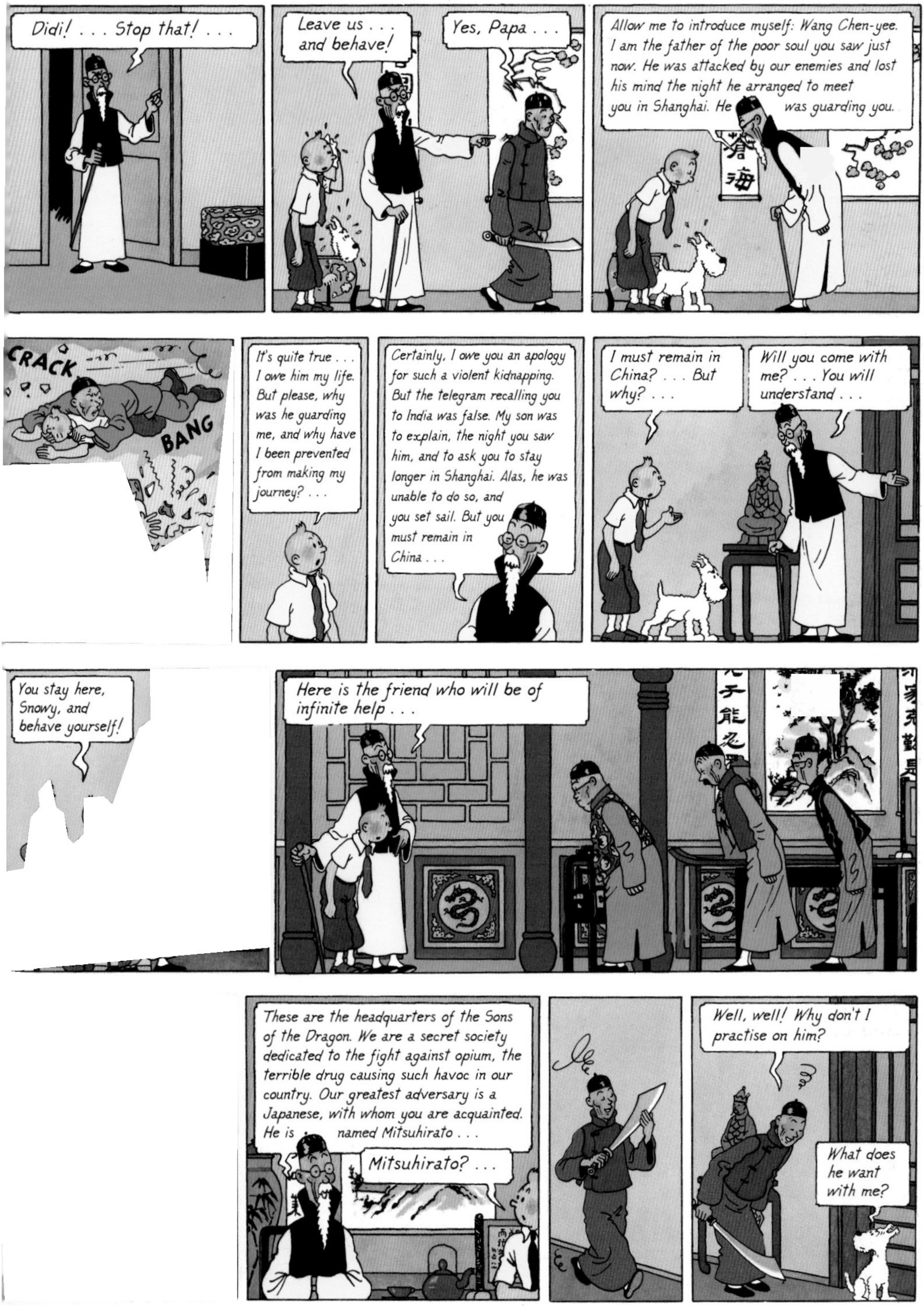

Didi! . . . Stop that! . . .
Leave us . . . and behave!
Yes, Papa . . .
Allow me to introduce myself: Wang Chen-yee. I am the father of the poor soul you saw just now. He was attacked by our enemies and lost his mind the night he arranged to meet you in Shanghai. He was guarding you.
CRACK
BANG
It's quite true . . . I owe him my life. But please, why was he guarding me, and why have I been prevented from making my journey? . . .
Certainly, I owe you an apology for such a violent kidnapping. But the telegram recalling you to India was false. My son was to explain, the night you saw him, and to ask you to stay longer in Shanghai. Alas, he was unable to do so, and you set sail. But you must remain in China . . .
I must remain in China? . . . But why? . . .
Will you come with me? . . . You will understand . . .
You stay here, Snowy, and behave yourself!
Here is the friend who will be of infinite help . . .
These are the headquarters of the Sons of the Dragon. We are a secret society dedicated to the fight against opium, the terrible drug causing such havoc in our country. Our greatest adversary is a Japanese, with whom you are acquainted. He is named Mitsuhirato . . .
Mitsuhirato? . . .
Well, well! Why don't I practise on him?
What does he want with me?

Yes, Mitsuhirato. He's a Japanese secret agent in China . . . and at the same time, one of the most active and evil of men . . .

Hello, Tokyo?

SHIP	CARGO	DESTINATION
MARICOLD	OPIUM	MARSEILLE!
LL ON	OPIUM	ANTWERP
	OPIUM	LE HAVRE
BLACK STAR	OPIUM	ROTTERDAM
EVEREST	OPIUM	HAMBURG
SATURN	OPIUM	LIVERPOOL

. . . Not content with spying, he has joined forces with opium smugglers . . . He helps them distribute all over the world, but mostly here in China.

Hello? . . . Hello? Tokyo here . . . Ah, it's you . . .

Yes, Excellency . . . All is well . . . Tintin? . . . On the way to India . . . recalled by telegram, sent by me, of course . . . No, not easy . . . Those meddling Sons of the Dragon tried to keep him here . . . I had to take extreme measures . . .

Perfect! . . . Now the coast is clear for . . . you know what. Succeed in that . . . and you will receive the Order of Fujiyama, first class!

I'm certain to succeed, Excellency, provided your propaganda is well organised . . . It will be? . . . That is good! . . . Goodbye then, Excellency . . .

We hoped you would be willing to help us, so we sent a messenger to India . . . But Mitsuhirato's spy network is excellent. They attacked the messenger and he went mad . . . Yet you still came, and . . .

WOOAH! WOOAH!

That's Snowy!

Snowy! . . . He's gone!

I'm going to help you to find the way. Don't worry, there's nothing to it . . . It just means cutting off your head . . .

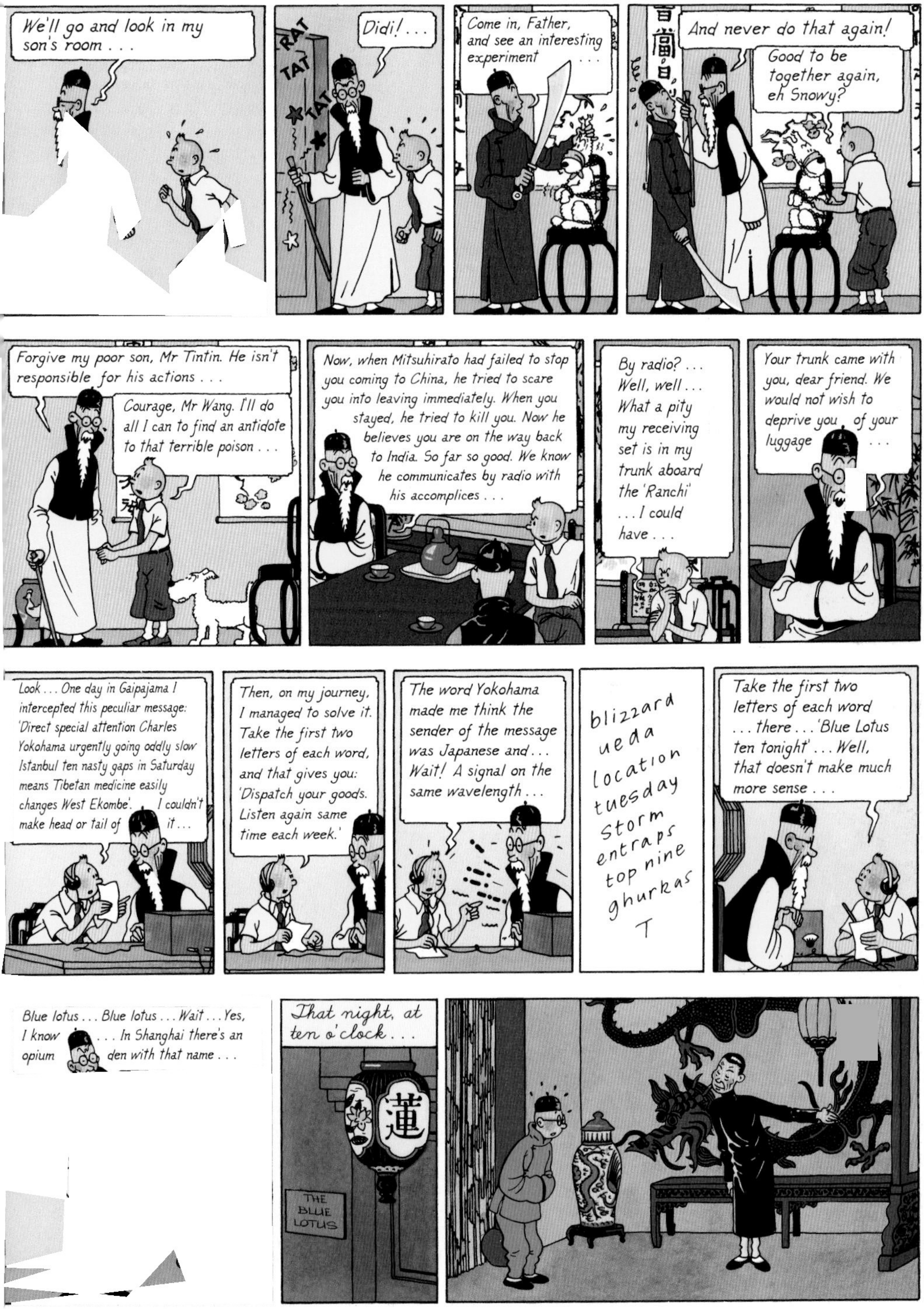
We'll go and look in my son's room . . .
RAT TAT TAT
Didi! . . .
Come in, Father, and see an interesting experiment . . .
And never do that again!
Good to be together again, eh Snowy?
Forgive my poor son, Mr Tintin. He isn't responsible for his actions . . .
Courage, Mr Wang. I'll do all I can to find an antidote to that terrible poison . . .
Now, when Mitsuhirato had failed to stop you coming to China, he tried to scare you into leaving immediately. When you stayed, he tried to kill you. Now he believes you are on the way back to India. So far so good. We know he communicates by radio with his accomplices . . .
By radio? . . . Well, well . . . What a pity my receiving set is in my trunk aboard the 'Ranchi' . . . I could have . . .
Your trunk came with you, dear friend. We would not wish to deprive you of your luggage . . .
Look . . . One day in Gaipajama I intercepted this peculiar message: 'Direct special attention Charles Yokohama urgently going oddly slow Istanbul ten nasty gaps in Saturday means Tibetan medicine easily changes West Ekombe'. I couldn't make head or tail of it . . .
Then, on my journey, I managed to solve it. Take the first two letters of each word, and that gives you: 'Dispatch your goods. Listen again same time each week.'
The word Yokohama made me think the sender of the message was Japanese and . . . Wait! A signal on the same wavelength . . .
blizzard
ueda
location
tuesday
storm
entraps
top nine
ghurkas
T
Take the first two letters of each word . . . there . . . 'Blue Lotus ten tonight' . . . Well, that doesn't make much more sense . . .
Blue lotus . . . Blue lotus . . . Wait . . . Yes, I know . . . In Shanghai there's an opium den with that name . . .
That night, at ten o'clock . . .
THE BLUE LOTUS

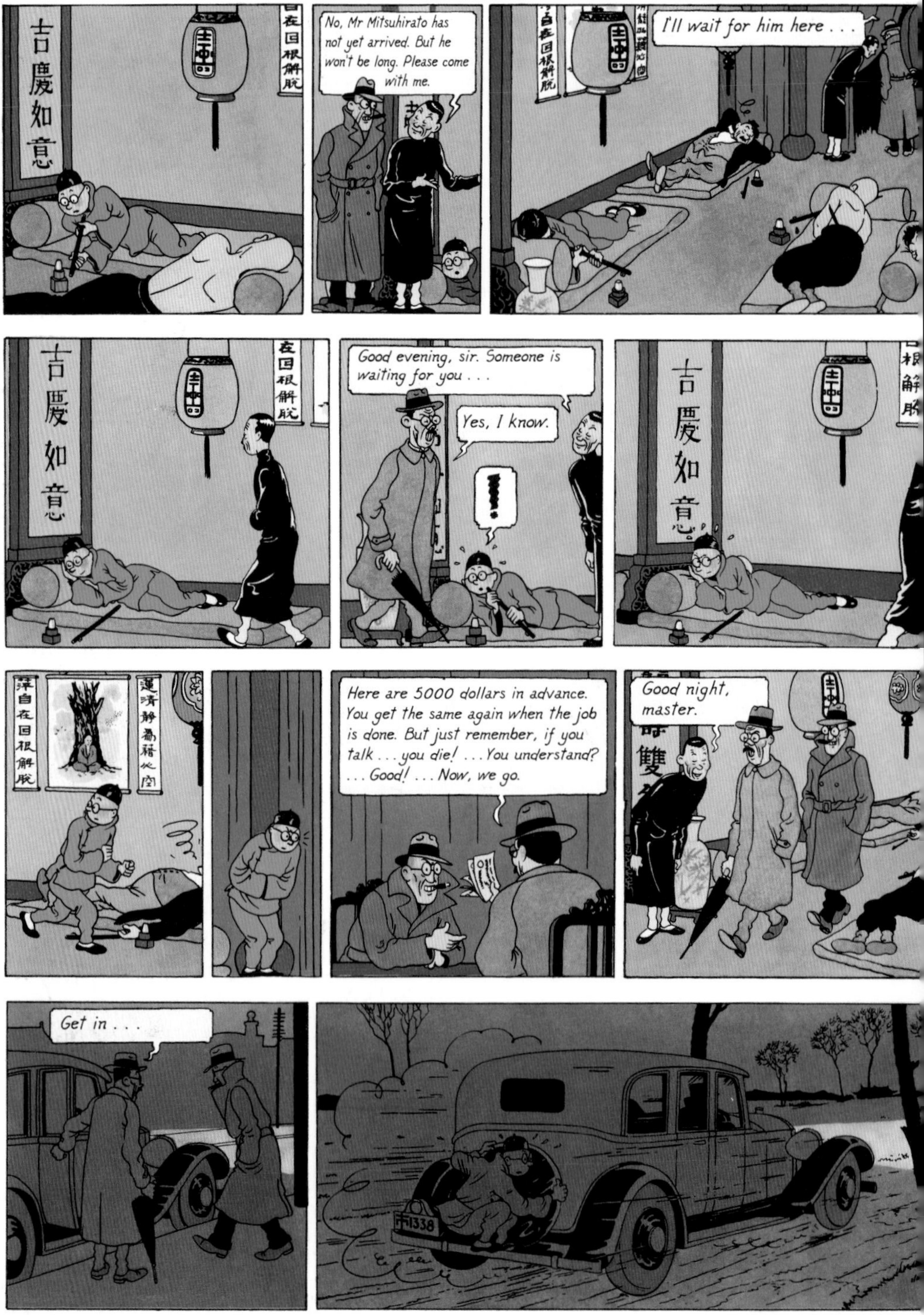
No, Mr Mitsuhirato has not yet arrived. But he won't be long. Please come with me.
I'll wait for him here . . .
Good evening, sir. Someone is waiting for you . . .
Yes, I know.
Here are 5000 dollars in advance. You get the same again when the job is done. But just remember, if you talk . . . you die! . . . You understand? . . . Good! . . . Now, we go.
Good night, master.
Get in . . .

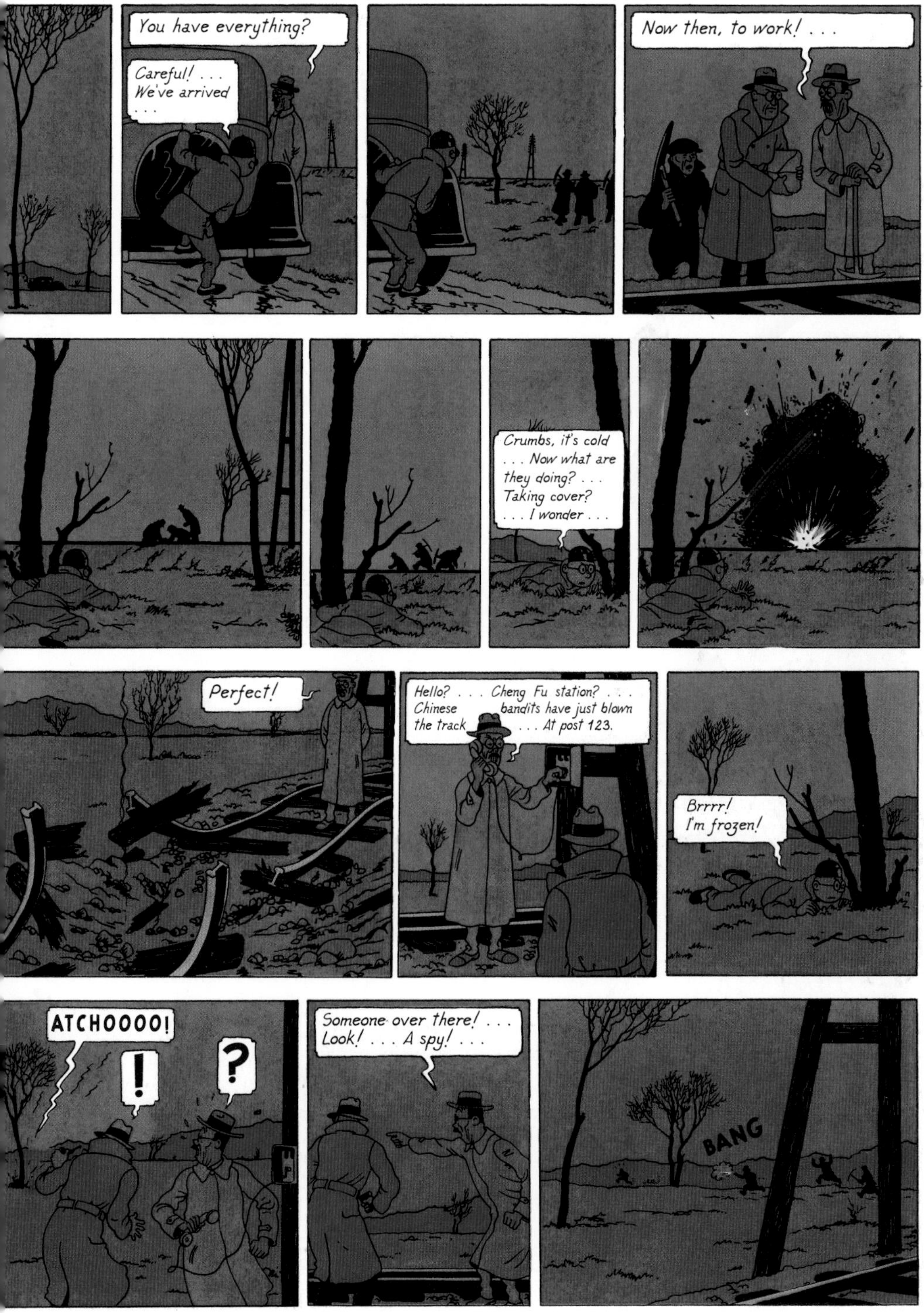
You have everything?
Careful! . . . We've arrived . . .
Now then, to work! . . .
Crumbs, it's cold . . . Now what are they doing? . . . Taking cover? . . . I wonder . . .
Perfect!
Hello? . . . Cheng Fu station? . . . Chinese bandits have just blown the track . . . At post 123.
Brrrr! I'm frozen!
ATCHOOOO!
!
?
Someone over there! . . . Look! . . . A spy! . . .
BANG

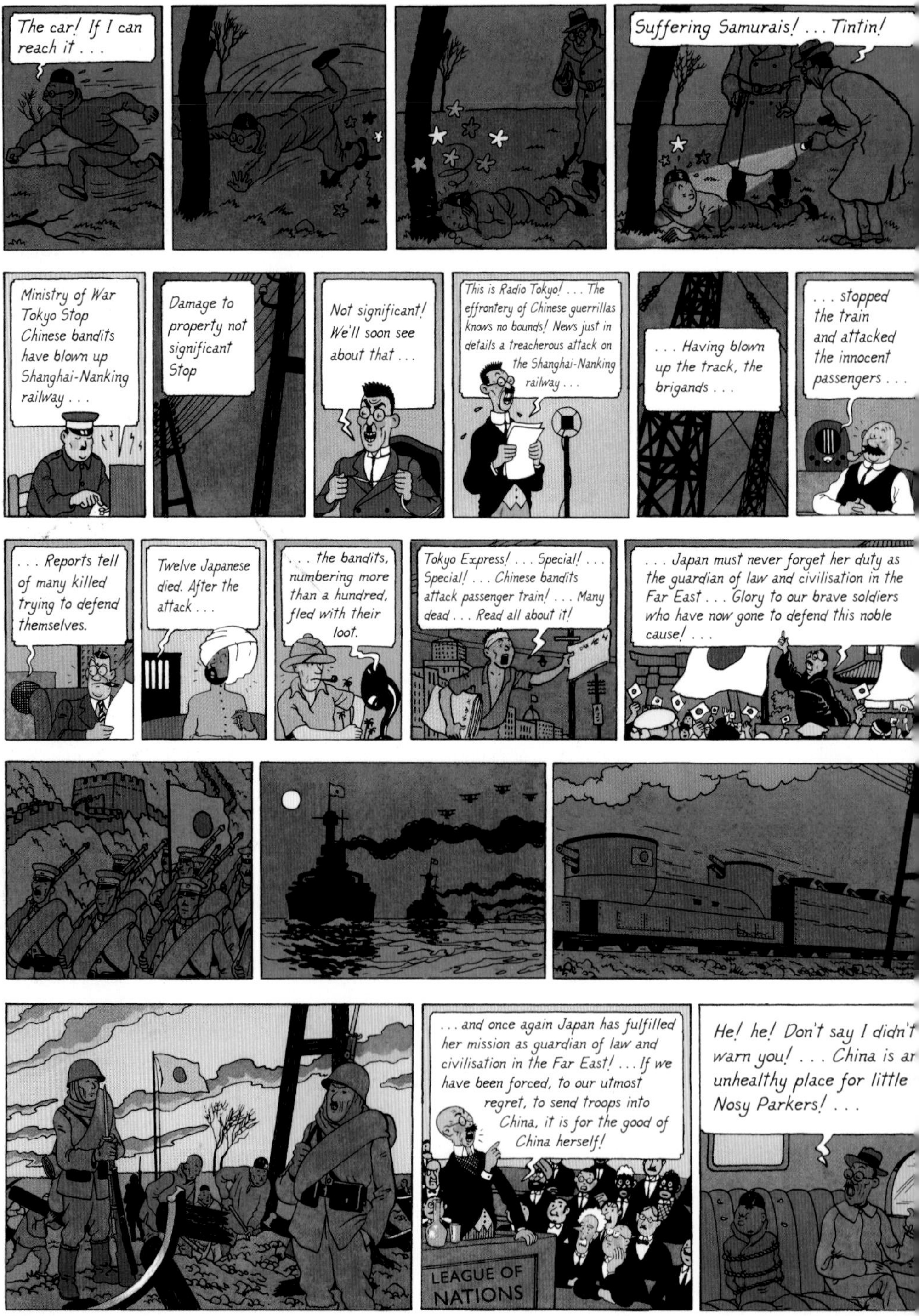
The car! If I can reach it . . .
Suffering Samurais! . . . Tintin!
Ministry of War Tokyo Stop Chinese bandits have blown up Shanghai-Nanking railway . . .
Damage to property not significant Stop
Not significant! We'll soon see about that . . .
This is Radio Tokyo! . . . The effrontery of Chinese guerrillas knows no bounds! News just in details a treacherous attack on the Shanghai-Nanking railway . . .
. . . Having blown up the track, the brigands . . .
. . . stopped the train and attacked the innocent passengers . . .
. . . Reports tell of many killed trying to defend themselves.
Twelve Japanese died. After the attack . . .
. . . the bandits, numbering more than a hundred, fled with their loot.
Tokyo Express! . . . Special! . . . Special! . . . Chinese bandits attack passenger train! . . . Many dead . . . Read all about it!
. . . Japan must never forget her duty as the guardian of law and civilisation in the Far East . . . Glory to our brave soldiers who have now gone to defend this noble cause! . . .
. . . and once again Japan has fulfilled her mission as guardian of law and civilisation in the Far East! . . . If we have been forced, to our utmost regret, to send troops into China, it is for the good of China herself!
LEAGUE OF NATIONS
He! he! Don't say I didn't warn you! . . . China is an unhealthy place for little Nosy Parkers! . . .

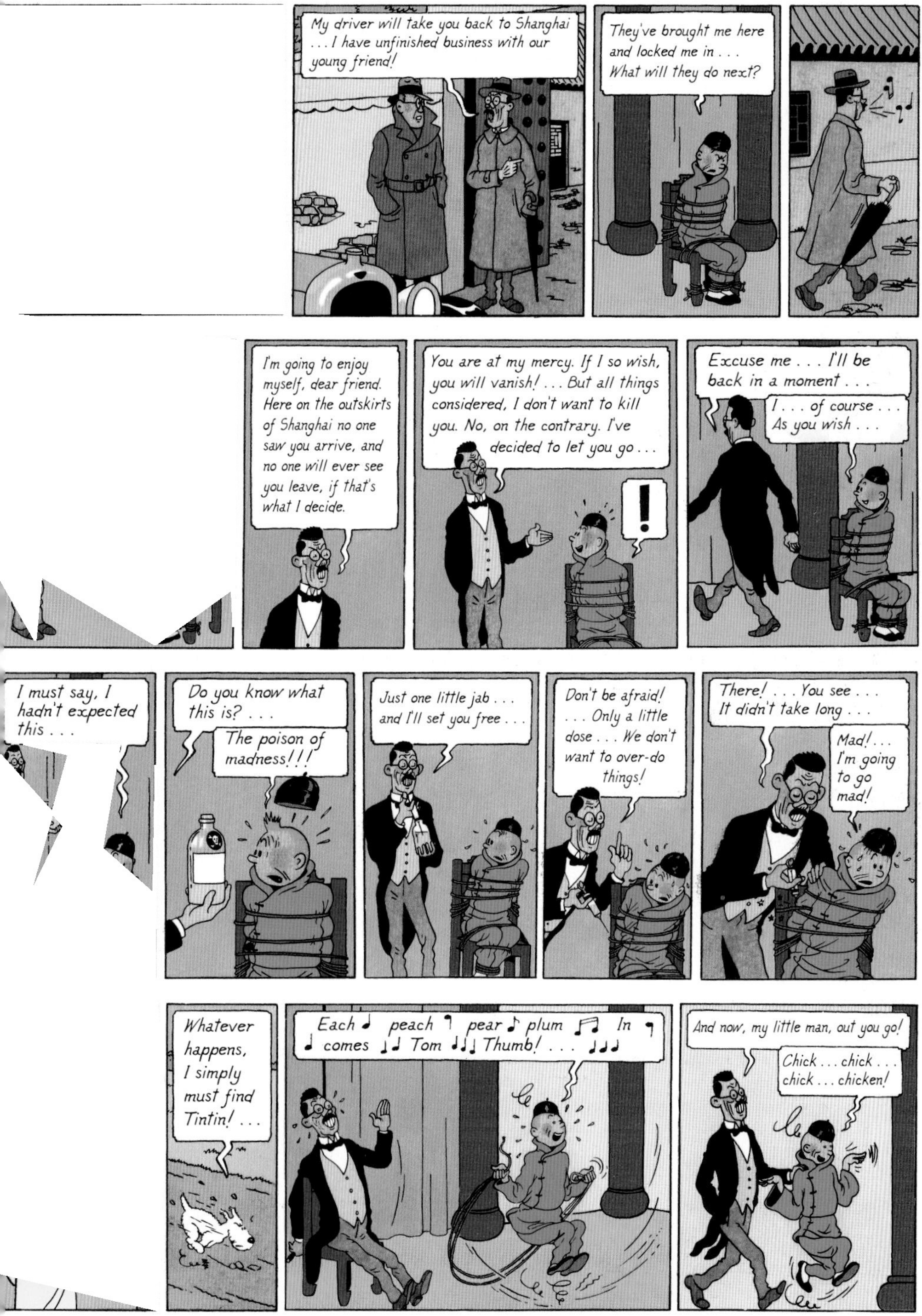
My driver will take you back to Shanghai . . . I have unfinished business with our young friend!
They've brought me here and locked me in . . . What will they do next?
I'm going to enjoy myself, dear friend. Here on the outskirts of Shanghai no one saw you arrive, and no one will ever see you leave, if that's what I decide.
You are at my mercy. If I so wish, you will vanish! . . . But all things considered, I don't want to kill you. No, on the contrary. I've decided to let you go . . .
!
Excuse me . . . I'll be back in a moment . . .
I . . . of course . . . As you wish . . .
I must say, I hadn't expected this . . .
Do you know what this is? . . .
The poison of madness!!!
Just one little jab . . . and I'll set you free . . .
Don't be afraid! . . . Only a little dose . . . We don't want to over-do things!
There! . . . You see . . . It didn't take long . . .
Mad! . . . I'm going to go mad!
Whatever happens, I simply must find Tintin! . . .
Each peach pear plum In comes Tom Thumb! . . .
And now, my little man, out you go!
Chick . . . chick . . . chick . . . chicken!

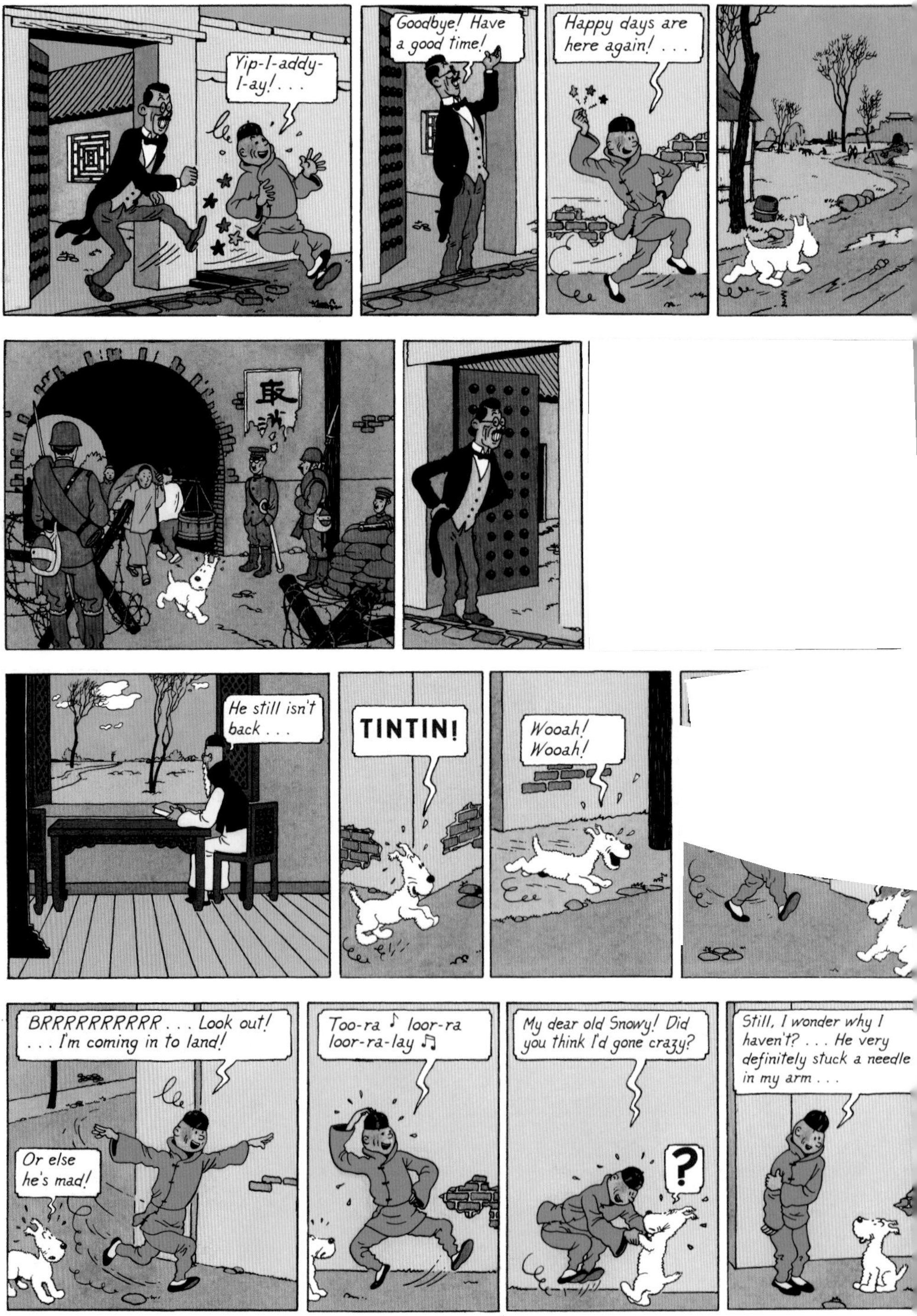
Yip-I-addy-I-ay! . . .
Goodbye! Have a good time!
Happy days are here again! . . .
He still isn't back . . .
TINTIN!
Wooah! Wooah!
BRRRRRRRRRR . . . Look out! . . . I'm coming in to land!
Or else he's mad!
Too-ra ♪ loor-ra loor-ra-lay ♫
My dear old Snowy! Did you think I'd gone crazy?
?
Still, I wonder why I haven't? . . . He very definitely stuck a needle in my arm . . .

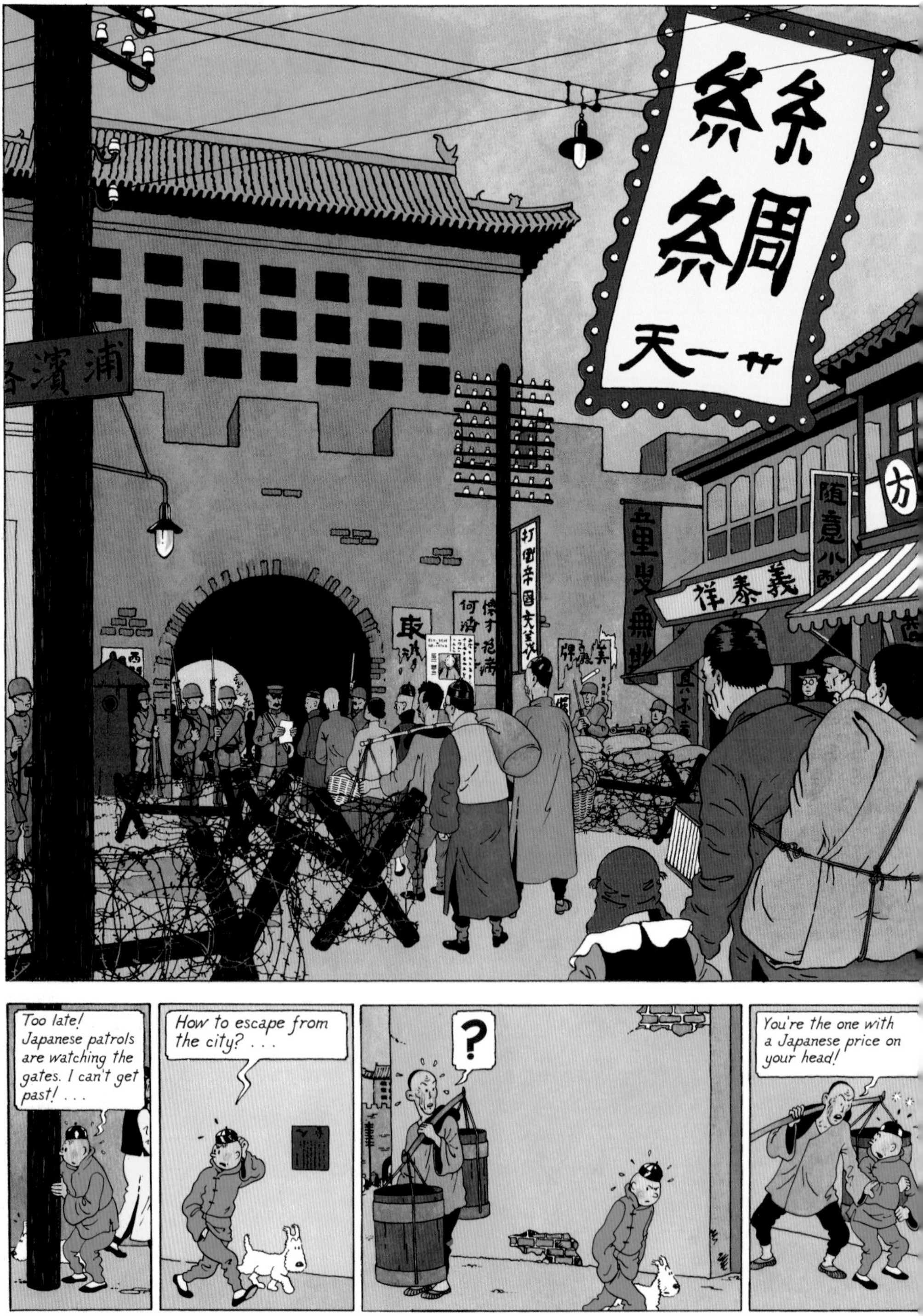
Too late! Japanese patrols are watching the gates. I can't get past! . . .
How to escape from the city? . . .
?
You're the one with a Japanese price on your head!

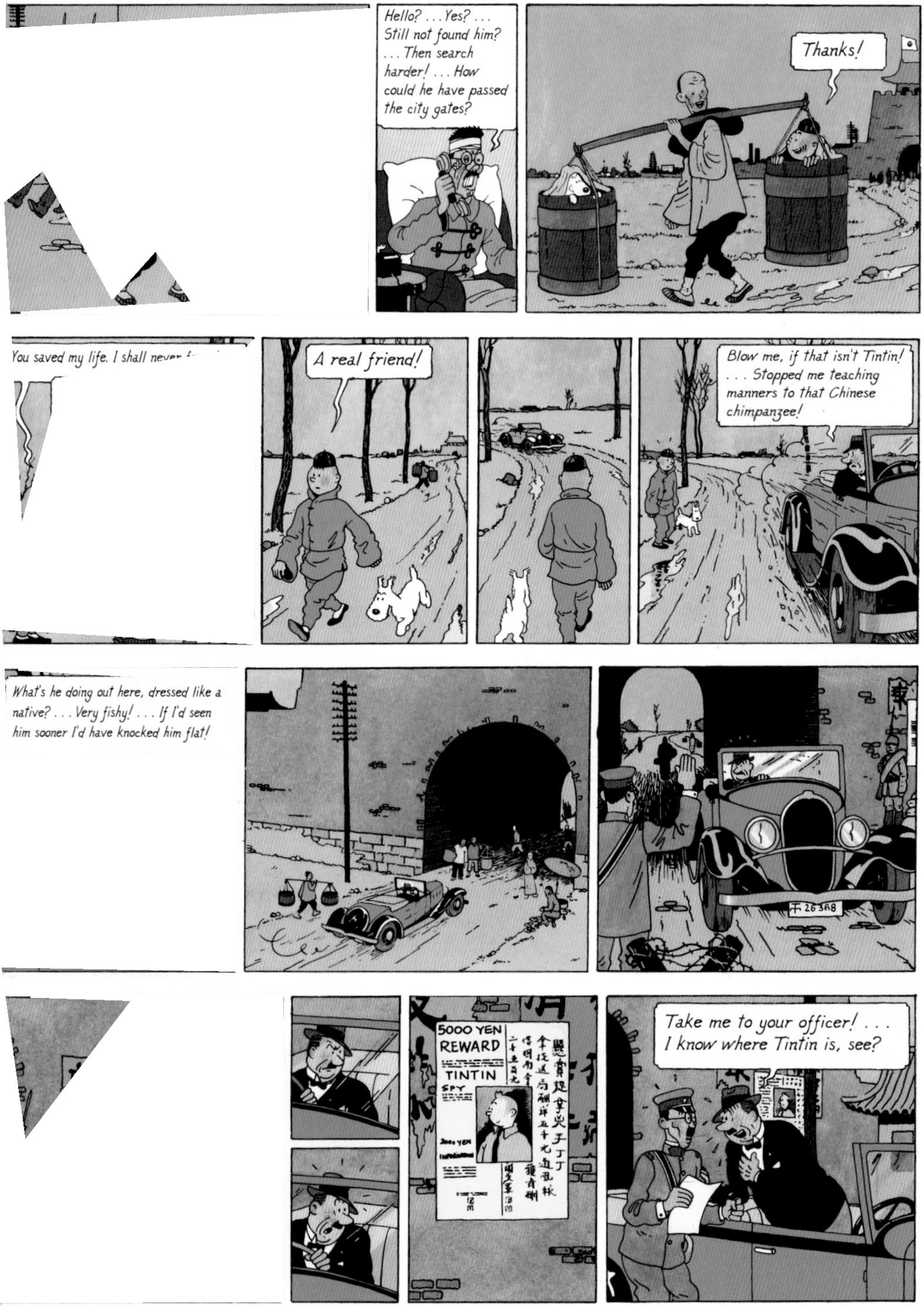

Hello? . . . Yes? . . . Still not found him? . . . Then search harder! . . . How could he have passed the city gates?
Thanks!
You saved my life. I shall never
A real friend!
Blow me, if that isn't Tintin! . . . Stopped me teaching manners to that Chinese chimpanzee!
What's he doing out here, dressed like a native? . . . Very fishy! . . . If I'd seen him sooner I'd have knocked him flat!
5000 YEN
REWARD
TINTIN
SPY
Take me to your officer! . . . I know where Tintin is, see?

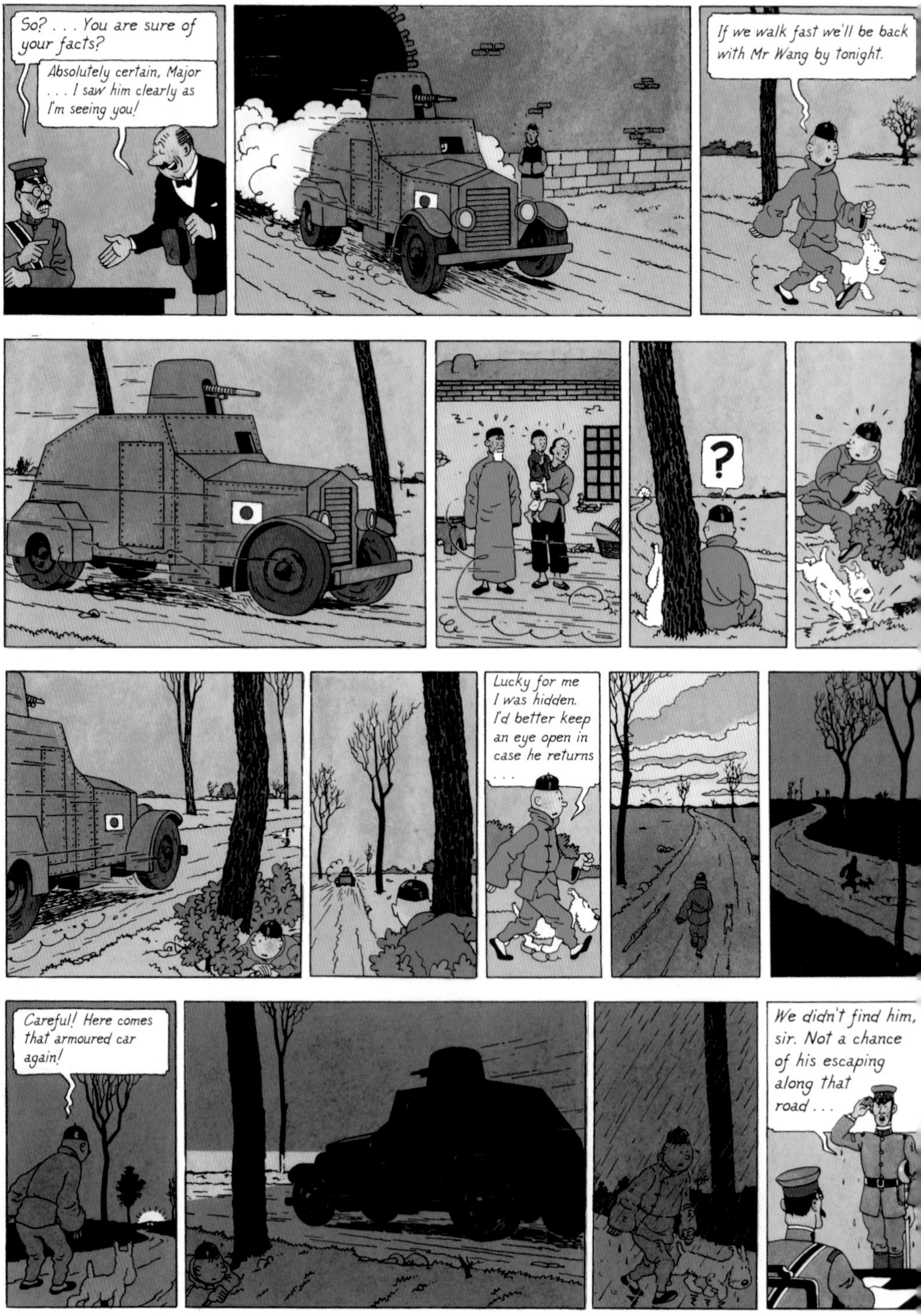
So? . . . You are sure of your facts?
Absolutely certain, Major . . . I saw him clearly as I'm seeing you!
If we walk fast we'll be back with Mr Wang by tonight.
?
Lucky for me I was hidden. I'd better keep an eye open in case he returns . . .
Careful! Here comes that armoured car again!
We didn't find him, sir. Not a chance of his escaping along that road . . .

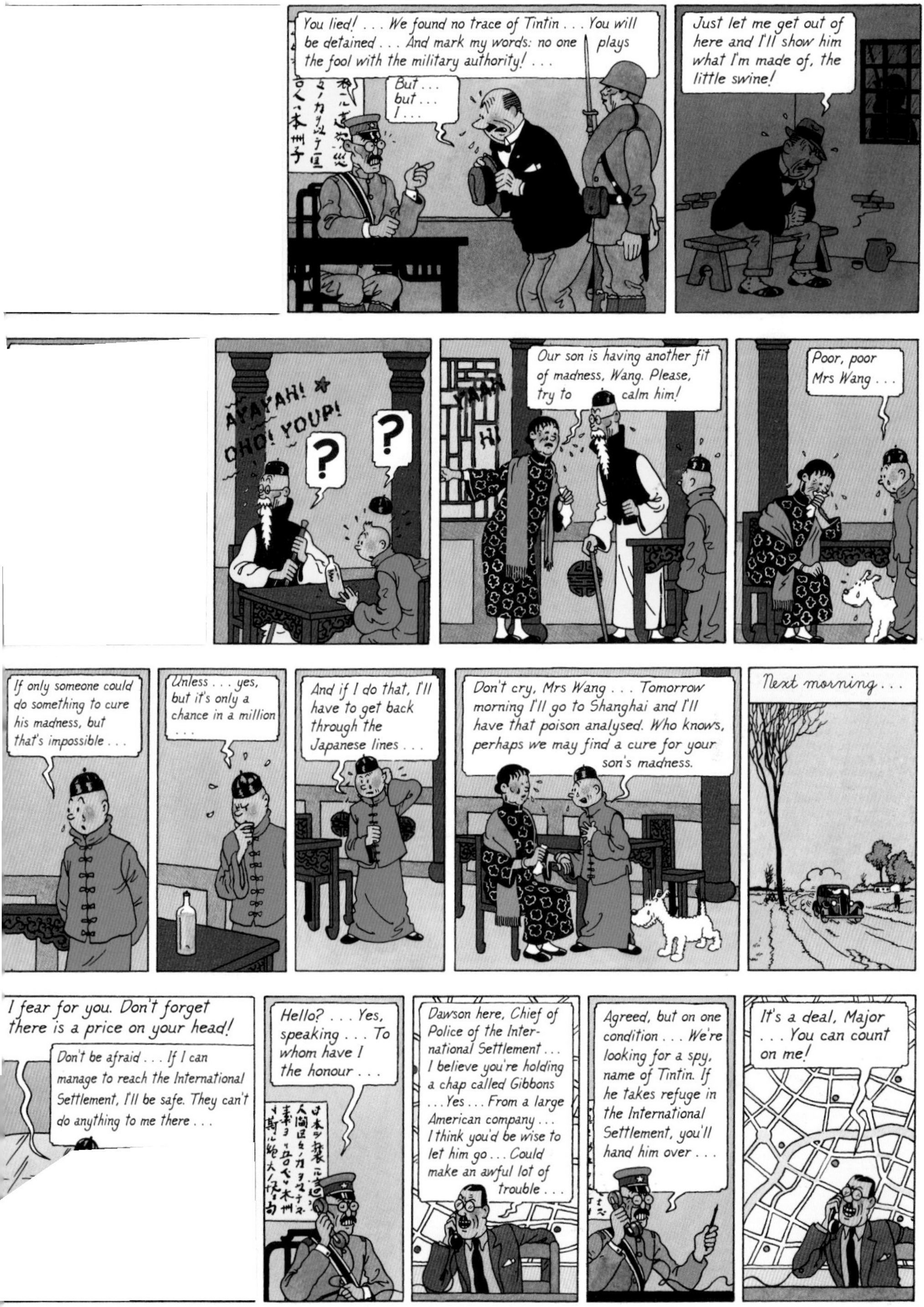
You lied! . . . We found no trace of Tintin . . . You will be detained . . . And mark my words: no one plays the fool with the military authority! . . .
But . . . but . . . I . . .
Just let me get out of here and I'll show him what I'm made of, the little swine!
AYAYAH! OHO! YOUP!
?
?
YAAH
Our son is having another fit of madness, Wang. Please, try to calm him!
Poor, poor Mrs Wang . . .
If only someone could do something to cure his madness, but that's impossible . . .
Unless . . . yes, but it's only a chance in a million . . .
And if I do that, I'll have to get back through the Japanese lines . . .
Don't cry, Mrs Wang . . . Tomorrow morning I'll go to Shanghai and I'll have that poison analysed. Who knows, perhaps we may find a cure for your son's madness.
Next morning . . .
I fear for you. Don't forget there is a price on your head!
Don't be afraid . . . If I can manage to reach the International Settlement, I'll be safe. They can't do anything to me there . . .
Hello? . . . Yes, speaking . . . To whom have I the honour . . .
Dawson here, Chief of Police of the International Settlement . . . I believe you're holding a chap called Gibbons . . . Yes . . . From a large American company . . . I think you'd be wise to let him go . . . Could make an awful lot of trouble . . .
Agreed, but on one condition . . . We're looking for a spy, name of Tintin. If he takes refuge in the International Settlement, you'll hand him over . . .
It's a deal, Major . . . You can count on me!

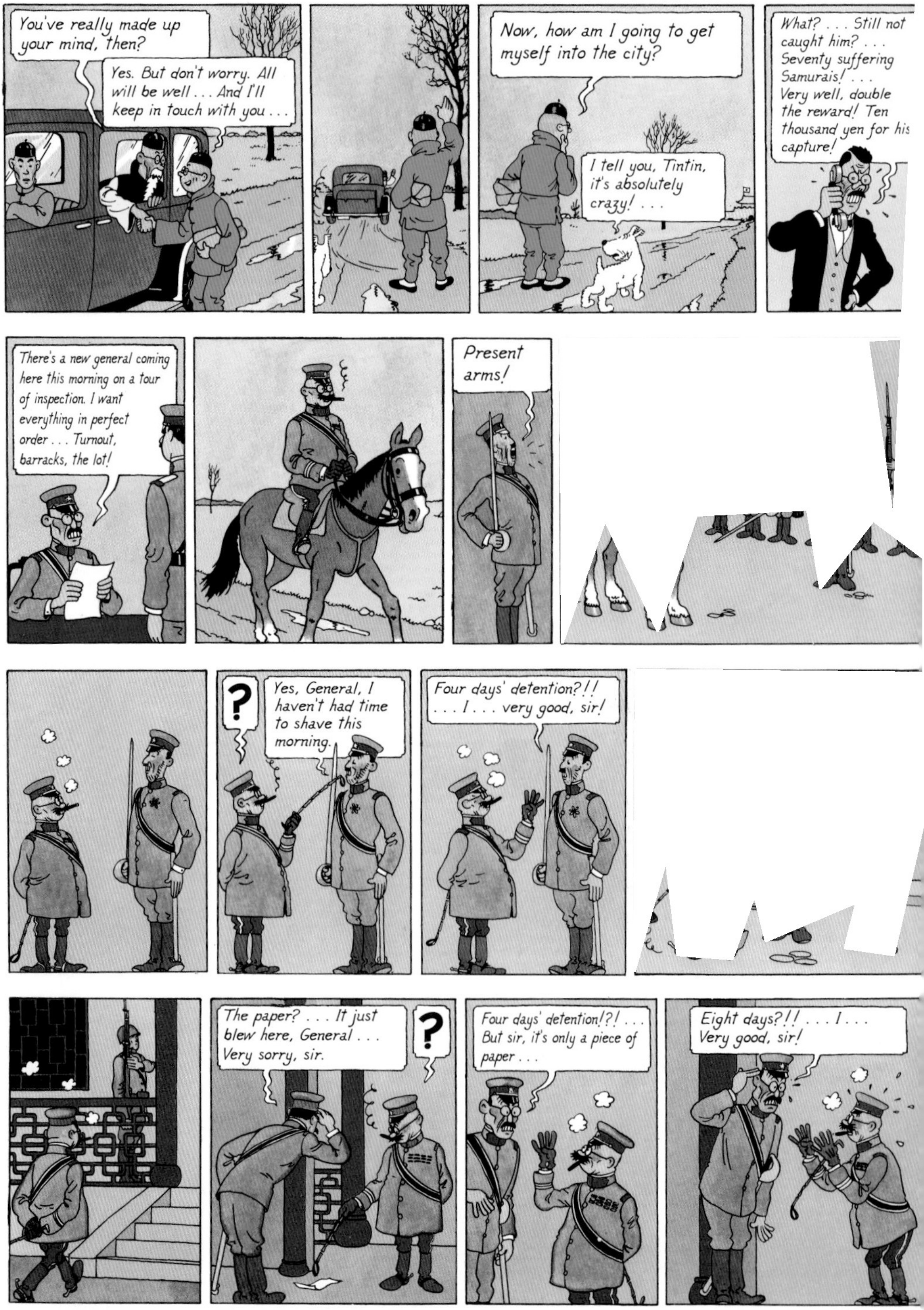
You've really made up your mind, then?
Yes. But don't worry. All will be well . . . And I'll keep in touch with you . . .
Now, how am I going to get myself into the city?
I tell you, Tintin, it's absolutely crazy! . . .
What? . . . Still not caught him? . . . Seventy suffering Samurais! . . . Very well, double the reward! Ten thousand yen for his capture!
There's a new general coming here this morning on a tour of inspection. I want everything in perfect order . . . Turnout, barracks, the lot!
Present arms!
?
Yes, General, I haven't had time to shave this morning.
Four days' detention?!! . . . I . . . very good, sir!
The paper? . . . It just blew here, General . . . Very sorry, sir.
?
Four days' detention!?! . . . But sir, it's only a piece of paper . . .
Eight days?!! . . . I . . . Very good, sir!

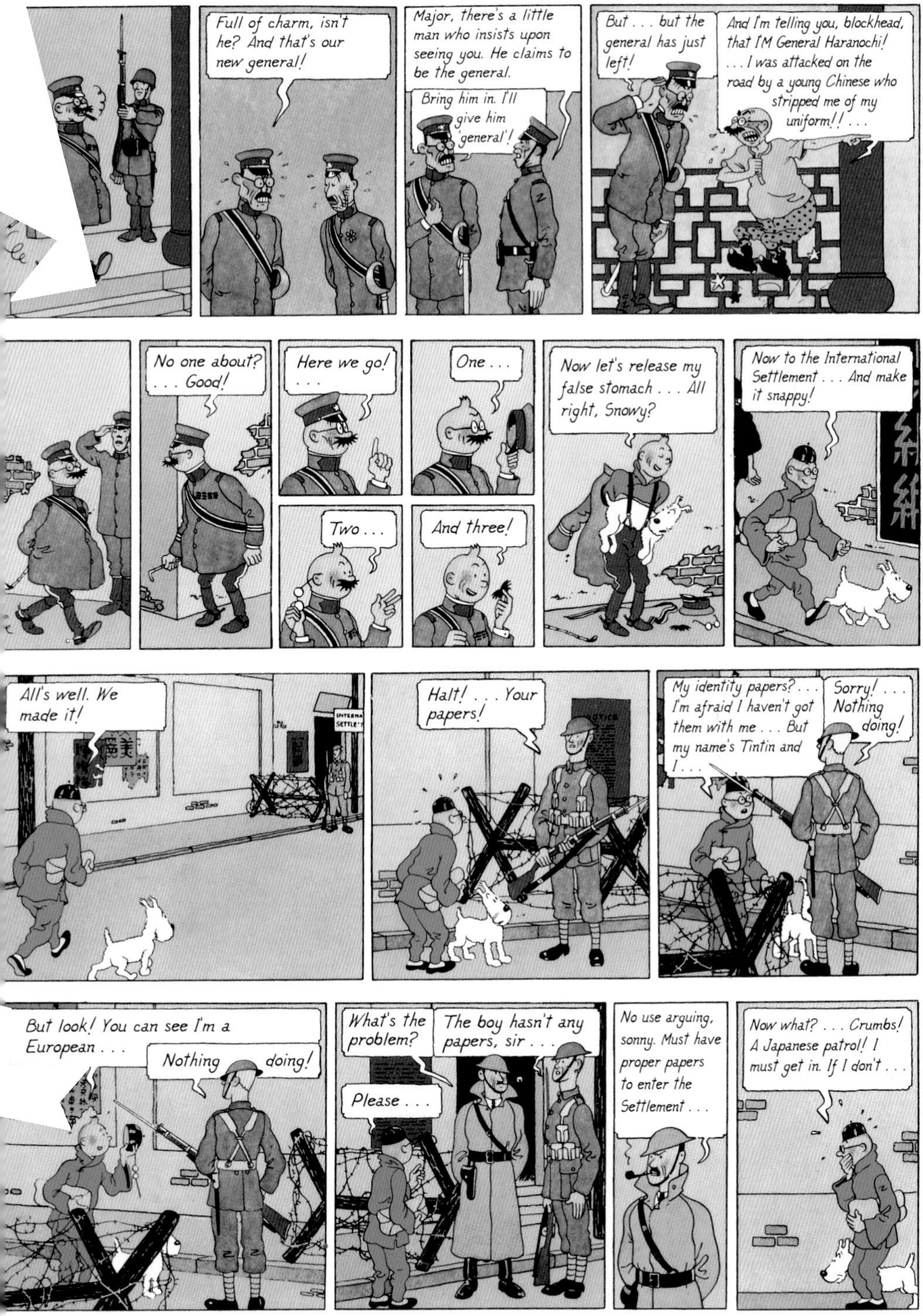

Full of charm, isn't he? And that's our new general!
Major, there's a little man who insists upon seeing you. He claims to be the general.
Bring him in. I'll give him 'general'!
But . . . but the general has just left!
And I'm telling you, blockhead, that I'M General Haranochi! . . . I was attacked on the road by a young Chinese who stripped me of my uniform!! . . .
No one about? . . . Good!
Here we go! . . .
One . . .
Two . . .
And three!
Now let's release my false stomach . . . All right, Snowy?
Now to the International Settlement . . . And make it snappy!
All's well. We made it!
Halt! . . . Your papers!
My identity papers? . . . I'm afraid I haven't got them with me . . . But my name's Tintin and I . . .
Sorry! . . . Nothing doing!
But look! You can see I'm a European . . .
Nothing doing!
What's the problem?
The boy hasn't any papers, sir . . .
Please . . .
No use arguing, sonny. Must have proper papers to enter the Settlement . . .
Now what? . . . Crumbs! A Japanese patrol! I must get in. If I don't . . .

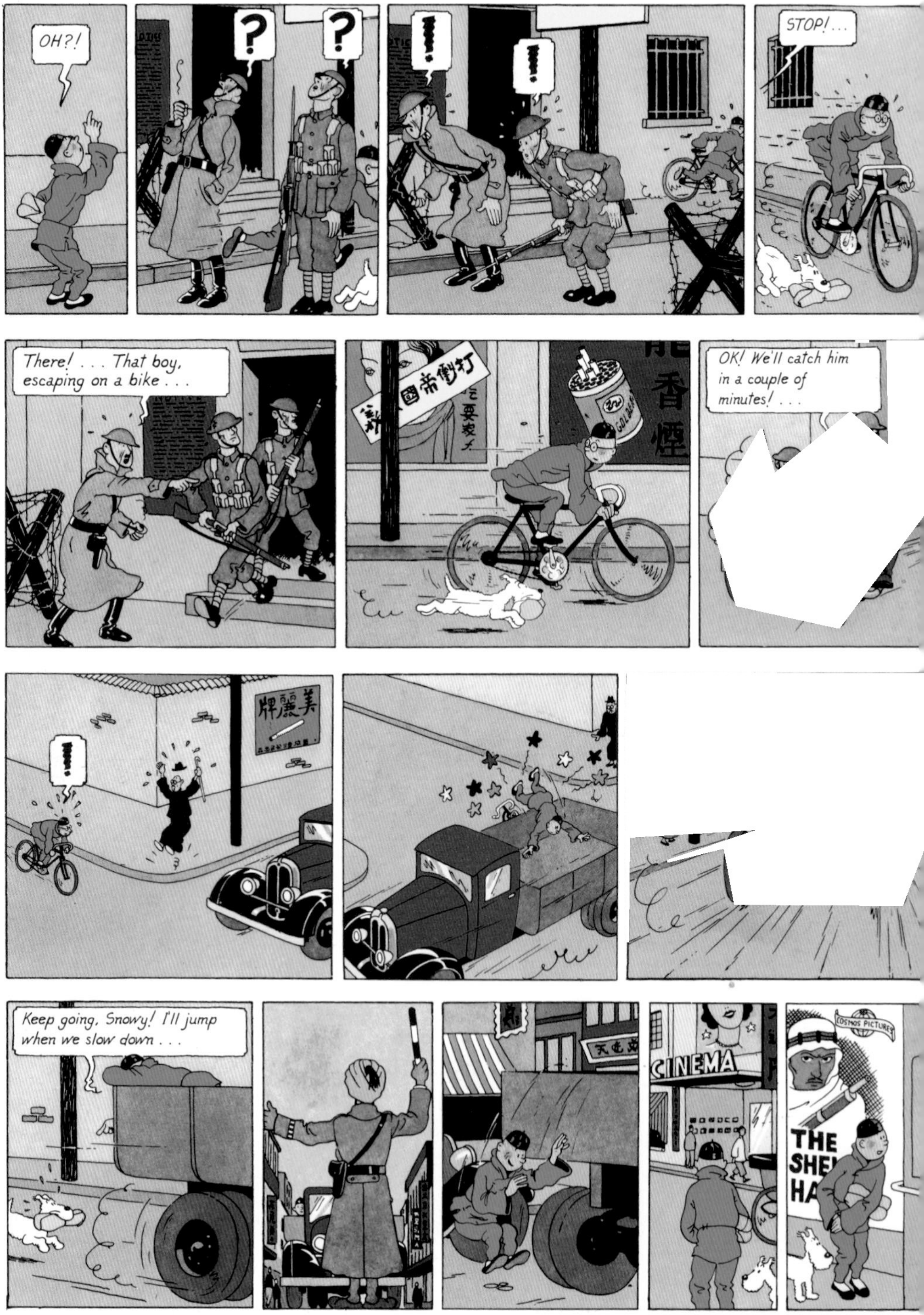
OH?!
STOP! . . .
There! . . . That boy, escaping on a bike . . .
OK! We'll catch him in a couple of minutes! . . .
Keep going, Snowy! I'll jump when we slow down . . .
CINEMA
COSMOS PICTURES
THE SHE HA

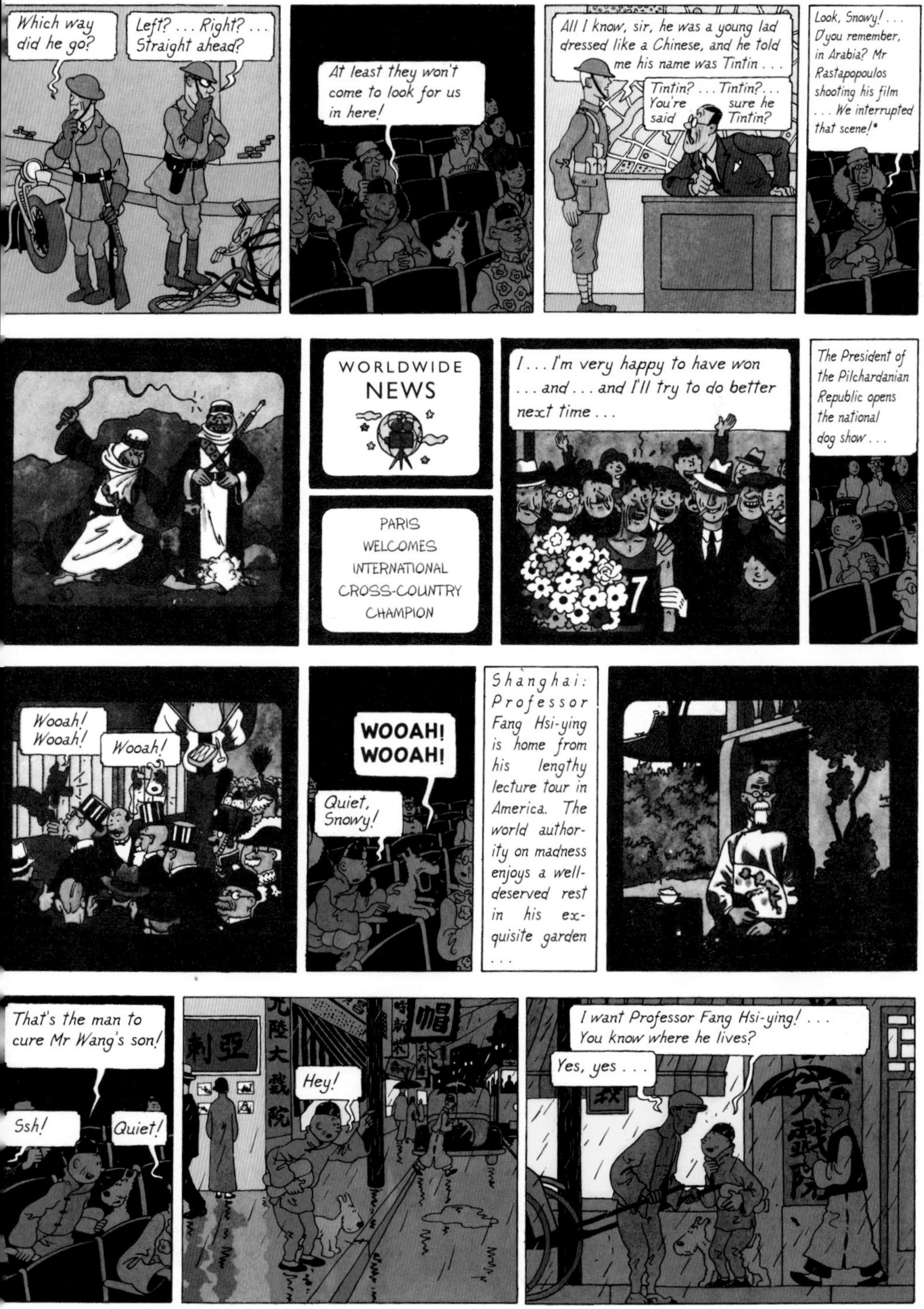
Which way did he go?
Left? ... Right? ... Straight ahead?
At least they won't come to look for us in here!
All I know, sir, he was a young lad dressed like a Chinese, and he told me his name was Tintin ...
Tintin? ... Tintin?... You're sure he said Tintin?
Look, Snowy! ... D'you remember, in Arabia? Mr Rastapopoulos shooting his film ... We interrupted that scene!*
WORLDWIDE NEWS
PARIS WELCOMES INTERNATIONAL CROSS-COUNTRY CHAMPION
I ... I'm very happy to have won ... and ... and I'll try to do better next time ...
7
The President of the Pilchardanian Republic opens the national dog show ...
Wooah! Wooah!
Wooah!
WOOAH! WOOAH!
Quiet, Snowy!
Shanghai: Professor Fang Hsi-ying is home from his lengthy lecture tour in America. The world authority on madness enjoys a well-deserved rest in his exquisite garden ...
That's the man to cure Mr Wang's son!
Ssh!
Quiet!
Hey!
I want Professor Fang Hsi-ying! ... You know where he lives?
Yes, yes ...

See Cigars of the Pharaoh

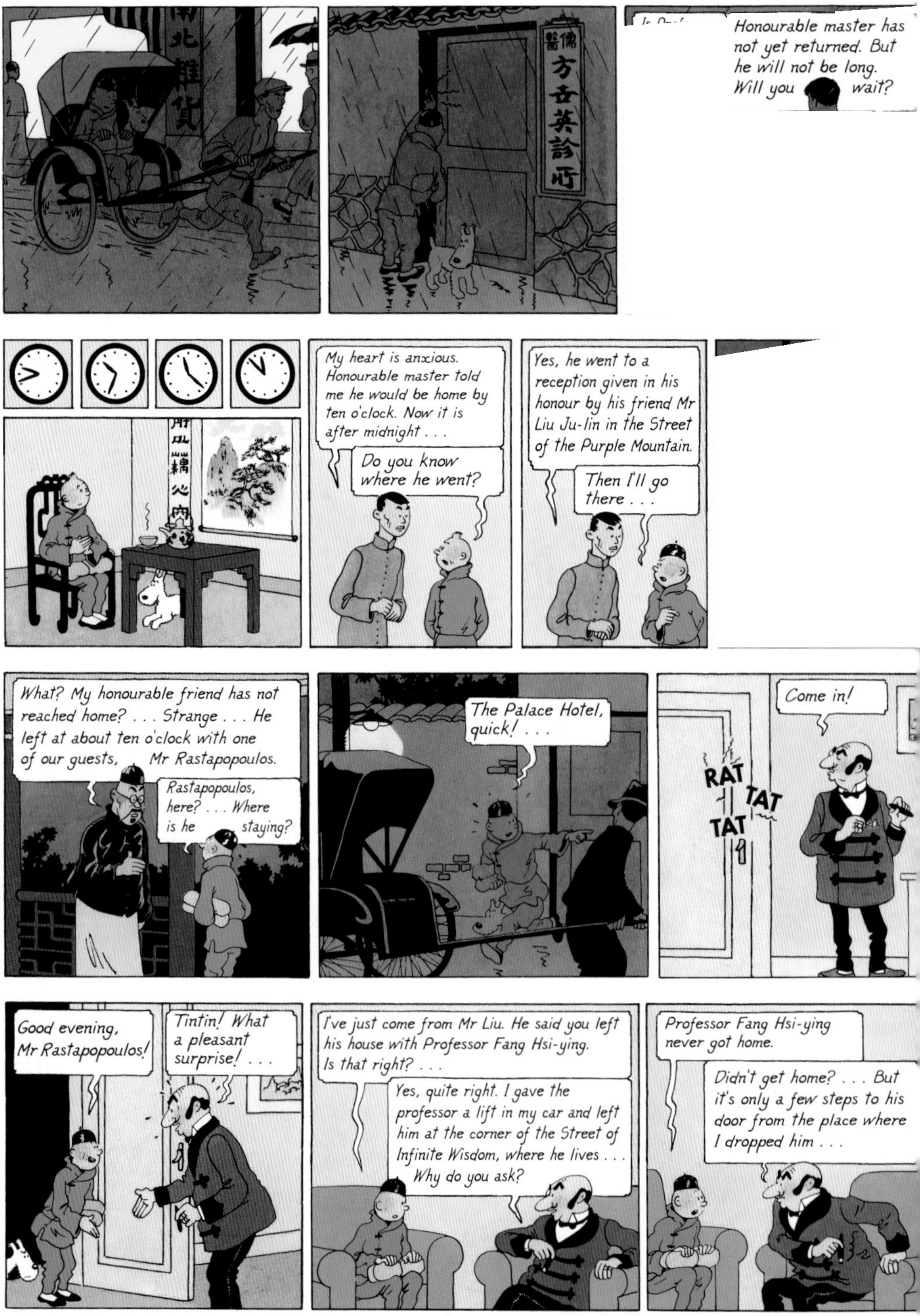

Honourable master has not yet returned. But he will not be long. Will you wait?
My heart is anxious. Honourable master told me he would be home by ten o'clock. Now it is after midnight . . .
Do you know where he went?
Yes, he went to a reception given in his honour by his friend Mr Liu Ju-lin in the Street of the Purple Mountain.
Then I'll go there . . .
What? My honourable friend has not reached home? . . . Strange . . . He left at about ten o'clock with one of our guests, Mr Rastapopoulos.
Rastapopoulos, here? . . . Where is he staying?
The Palace Hotel, quick! . . .
RAT TAT TAT
Come in!
Good evening, Mr Rastapopoulos!
Tintin! What a pleasant surprise! . . .
I've just come from Mr Liu. He said you left his house with Professor Fang Hsi-ying. Is that right? . . .
Yes, quite right. I gave the professor a lift in my car and left him at the corner of the Street of Infinite Wisdom, where he lives . . . Why do you ask?
Professor Fang Hsi-ying never got home.
Didn't get home? . . . But it's only a few steps to his door from the place where I dropped him . . .

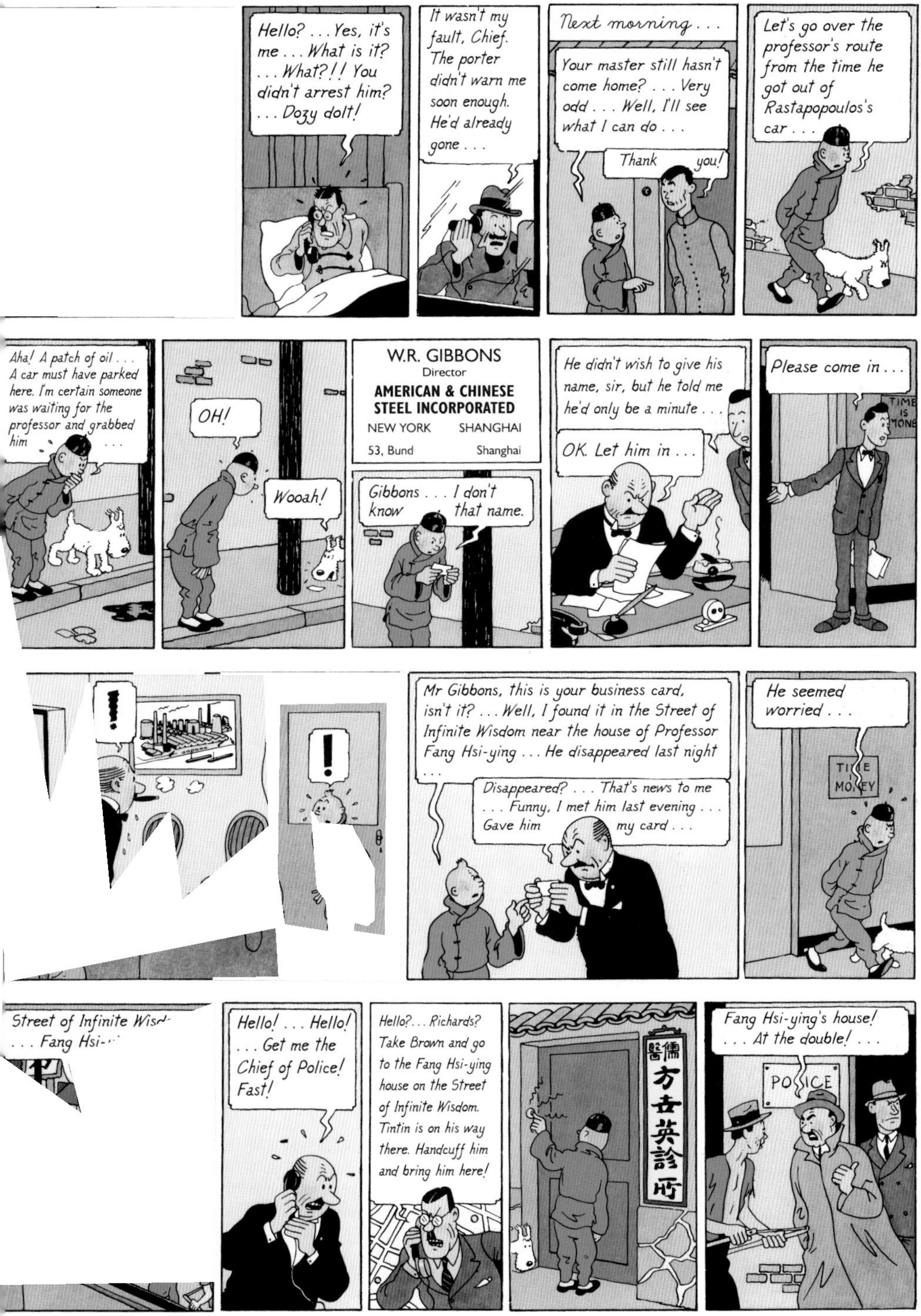
Hello? . . . Yes, it's me . . . What is it? . . . What?!! You didn't arrest him? . . . Dozy dolt!
It wasn't my fault, Chief. The porter didn't warn me soon enough. He'd already gone . . .
Next morning . . .
Your master still hasn't come home? . . . Very odd . . . Well, I'll see what I can do . . .
Thank you!
Let's go over the professor's route from the time he got out of Rastapopoulos's car . . .
Aha! A patch of oil . . . A car must have parked here. I'm certain someone was waiting for the professor and grabbed him . . .
OH!
Wooah!
W.R. GIBBONS
Director
AMERICAN & CHINESE STEEL INCORPORATED
NEW YORK SHANGHAI
53, Bund Shanghai
Gibbons . . . I don't know that name.
He didn't wish to give his name, sir, but he told me he'd only be a minute . . .
OK. Let him in . . .
Please come in . . .
TIME IS MONEY
Mr Gibbons, this is your business card, isn't it? . . . Well, I found it in the Street of Infinite Wisdom near the house of Professor Fang Hsi-ying . . . He disappeared last night . . .
Disappeared? . . . That's news to me . . . Funny, I met him last evening . . . Gave him my card . . .
He seemed worried . . .
TIME IS MONEY
Street of Infinite Wis
. . . Fang Hsi-
Hello! . . . Hello! . . . Get me the Chief of Police! Fast!
Hello? . . . Richards? Take Brown and go to the Fang Hsi-ying house on the Street of Infinite Wisdom. Tintin is on his way there. Handcuff him and bring him here!
Fang Hsi-ying's house! . . . At the double! . . .
POLICE

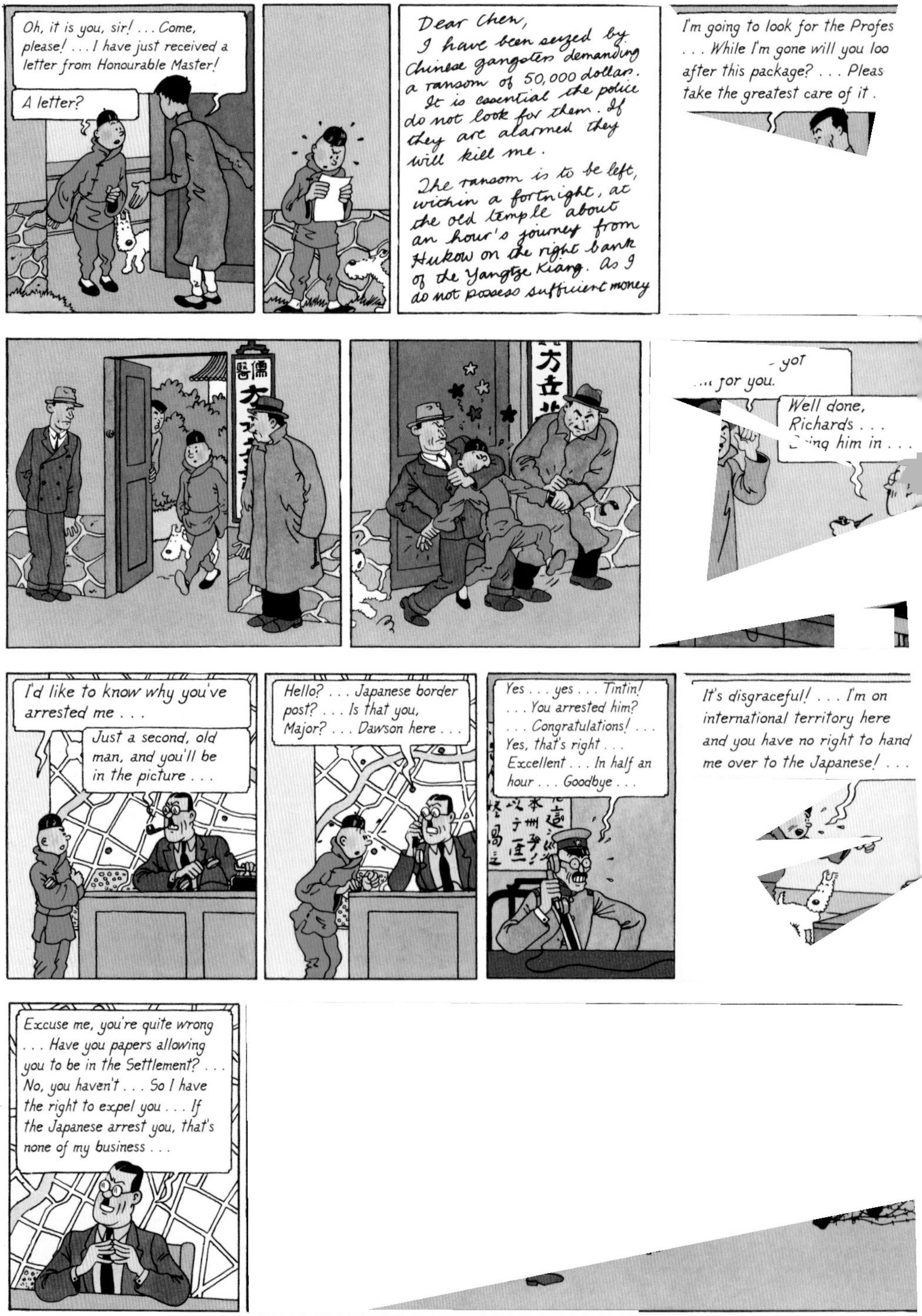

Oh, it is you, sir! . . . Come, please! . . . I have just received a letter from Honourable Master!
A letter?
Dear Chen,
I have been seized by Chinese gangsters demanding a ransom of 50,000 dollars.
It is essential the police do not look for them. If they are alarmed they will kill me.
The ransom is to be left, within a fortnight, at the old temple about an hour's journey from Hukow on the right bank of the Yangtze Kiang. As I do not possess sufficient money
I'm going to look for the Profes . . . While I'm gone will you loo after this package? . . . Pleas take the greatest care of it .
for you.
Well done, Richards . . . ing him in . . .
I'd like to know why you've arrested me . . .
Just a second, old man, and you'll be in the picture . . .
Hello? . . . Japanese border post? . . . Is that you, Major? . . . Dawson here . . .
Yes . . . yes . . . Tintin! . . . You arrested him? . . . Congratulations! . . . Yes, that's right . . . Excellent . . . In half an hour . . . Goodbye . . .
It's disgraceful! . . . I'm on international territory here and you have no right to hand me over to the Japanese! . . .
Excuse me, you're quite wrong . . . Have you papers allowing you to be in the Settlement? . . . No, you haven't . . . So I have the right to expel you . . . If the Japanese arrest you, that's none of my business . . .

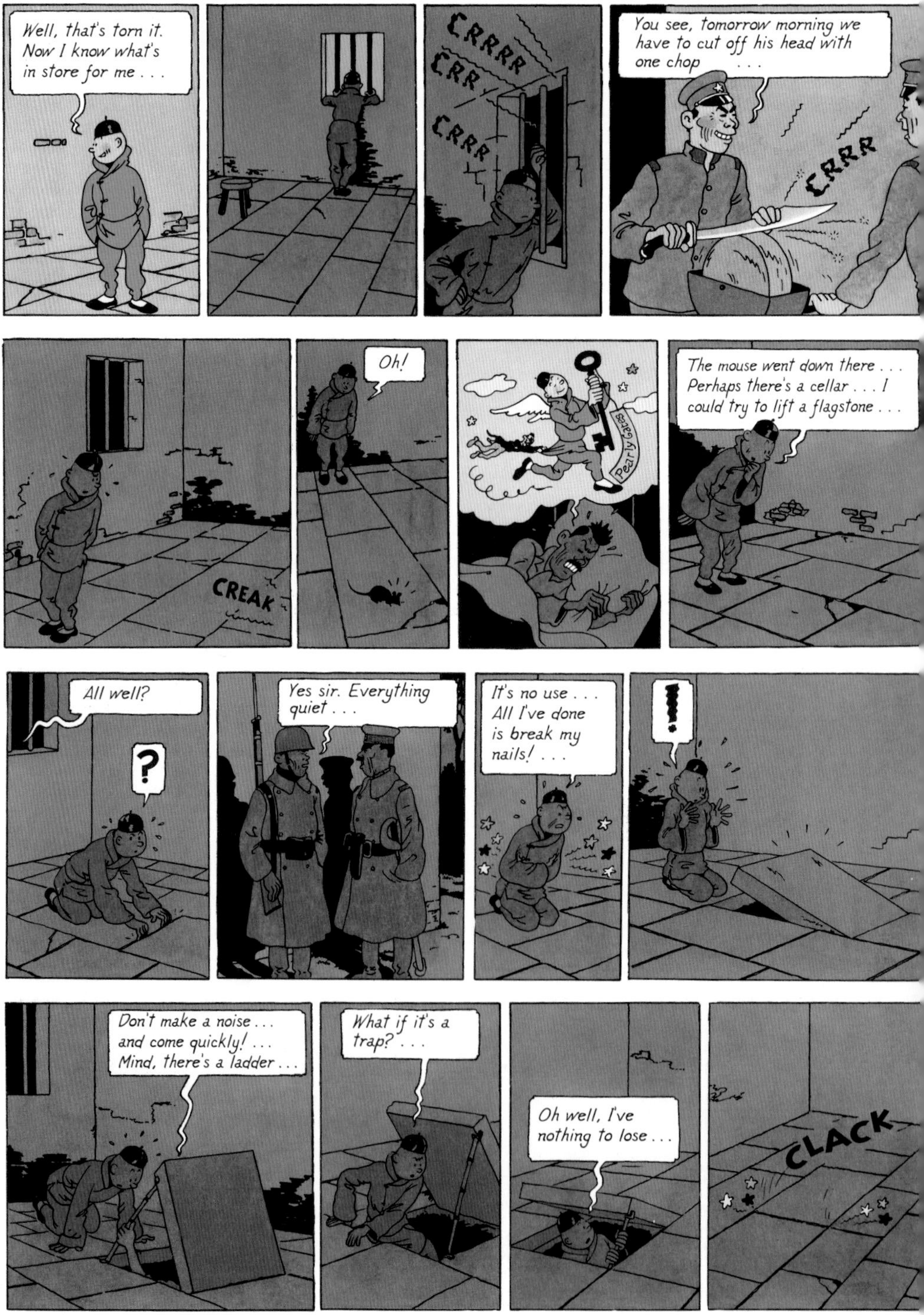
Well, that's torn it. Now I know what's in store for me . . .
CRRRR
CRR
CRRR
You see, tomorrow morning we have to cut off his head with one chop . . .
CRRR
CREAK
Oh!
Pearly Gates
The mouse went down there . . . Perhaps there's a cellar . . . I could try to lift a flagstone . . .
All well?
?
Yes sir. Everything quiet . . .
It's no use . . . All I've done is break my nails! . . .
!
Don't make a noise . . . and come quickly! . . . Mind, there's a ladder . . .
What if it's a trap? . . .
Oh well, I've nothing to lose . . .
CLACK

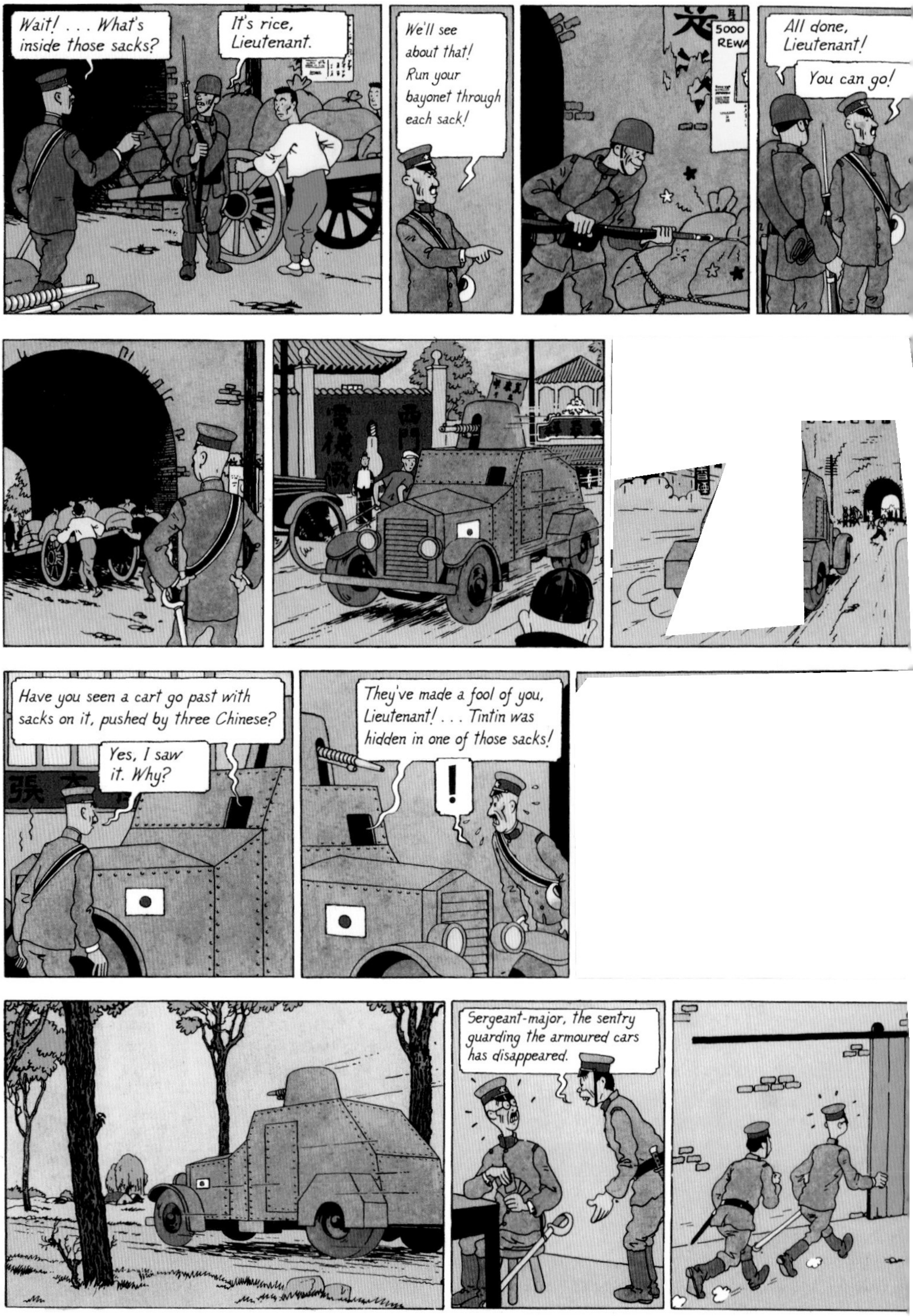
Wait! . . . What's inside those sacks?
It's rice, Lieutenant.
We'll see about that! Run your bayonet through each sack!
All done, Lieutenant!
You can go!
Have you seen a cart go past with sacks on it, pushed by three Chinese?
Yes, I saw it. Why?
They've made a fool of you, Lieutenant! . . . Tintin was hidden in one of those sacks!
!
Sergeant-major, the sentry guarding the armoured cars has disappeared.

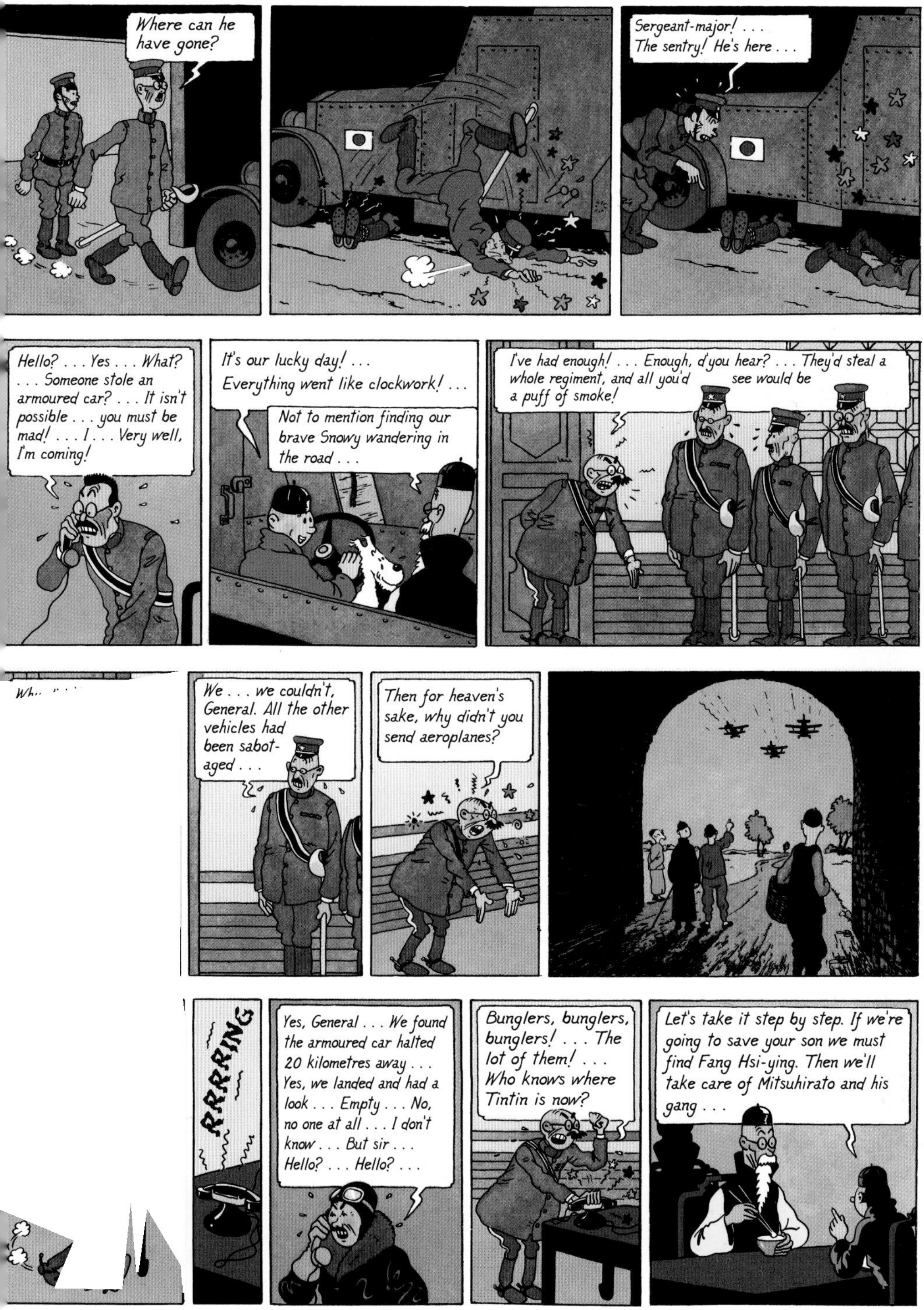

Where can he have gone?
Sergeant-major! . . . The sentry! He's here . . .
Hello? . . . Yes . . . What? . . . Someone stole an armoured car? . . . It isn't possible . . . you must be mad! . . . I . . . Very well, I'm coming!
It's our lucky day! . . . Everything went like clockwork! . . .
Not to mention finding our brave Snowy wandering in the road . . .
I've had enough! . . . Enough, d'you hear? . . . They'd steal a whole regiment, and all you'd see would be a puff of smoke!
We . . . we couldn't, General. All the other vehicles had been sabot-aged . . .
Then for heaven's sake, why didn't you send aeroplanes?
RRRRING
Yes, General . . . We found the armoured car halted 20 kilometres away . . . Yes, we landed and had a look . . . Empty . . . No, no one at all . . . I don't know . . . But sir . . . Hello? . . . Hello? . . .
Bunglers, bunglers, bunglers! . . . The lot of them! . . . Who knows where Tintin is now?
Let's take it step by step. If we're going to save your son we must find Fang Hsi-ying. Then we'll take care of Mitsuhirato and his gang . . .

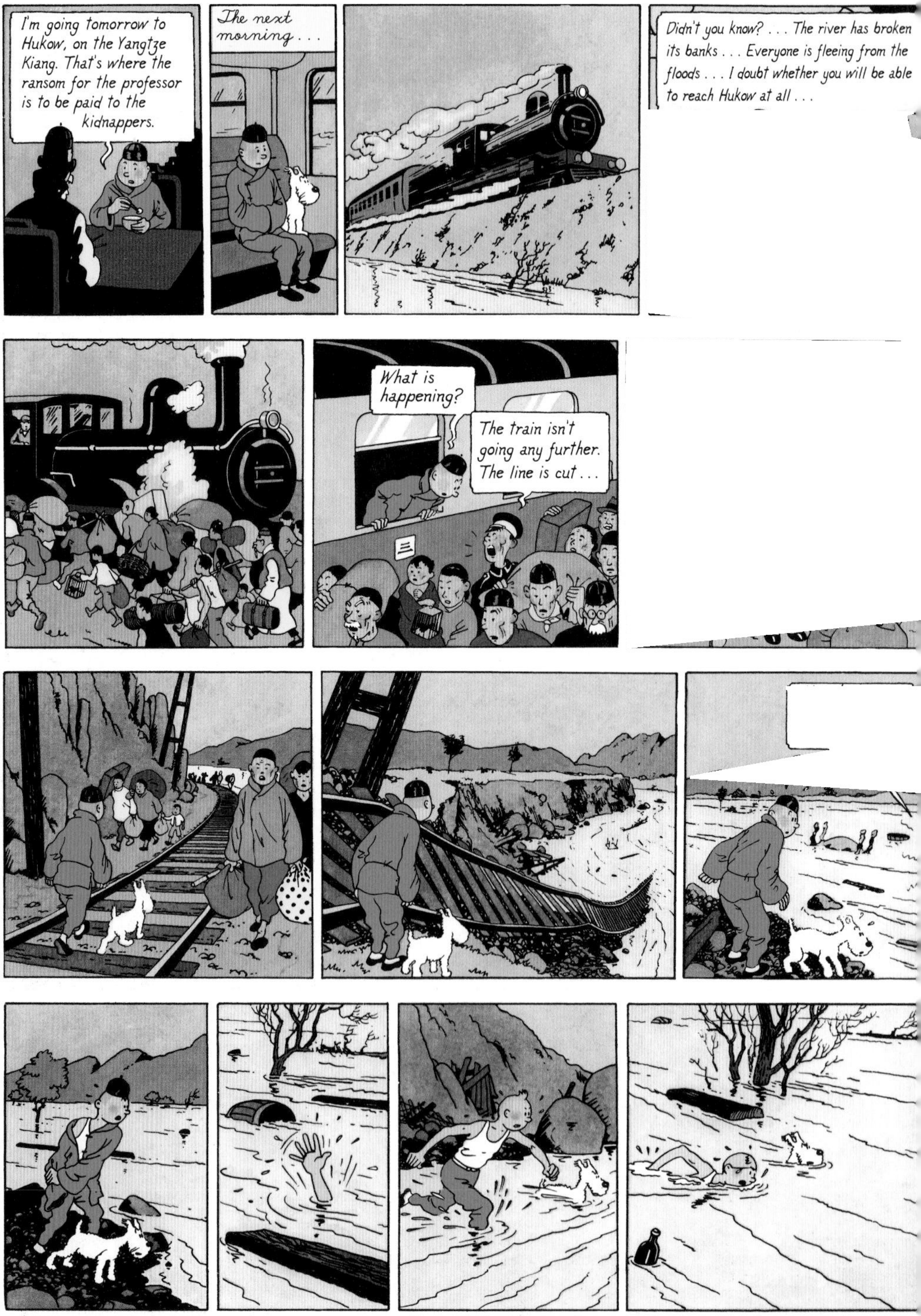
I'm going tomorrow to Hukow, on the Yangtze Kiang. That's where the ransom for the professor is to be paid to the kidnappers.
The next morning . . .
Didn't you know? . . . The river has broken its banks . . . Everyone is fleeing from the floods . . . I doubt whether you will be able to reach Hukow at all . . .
What is happening?
The train isn't going any further. The line is cut . . .

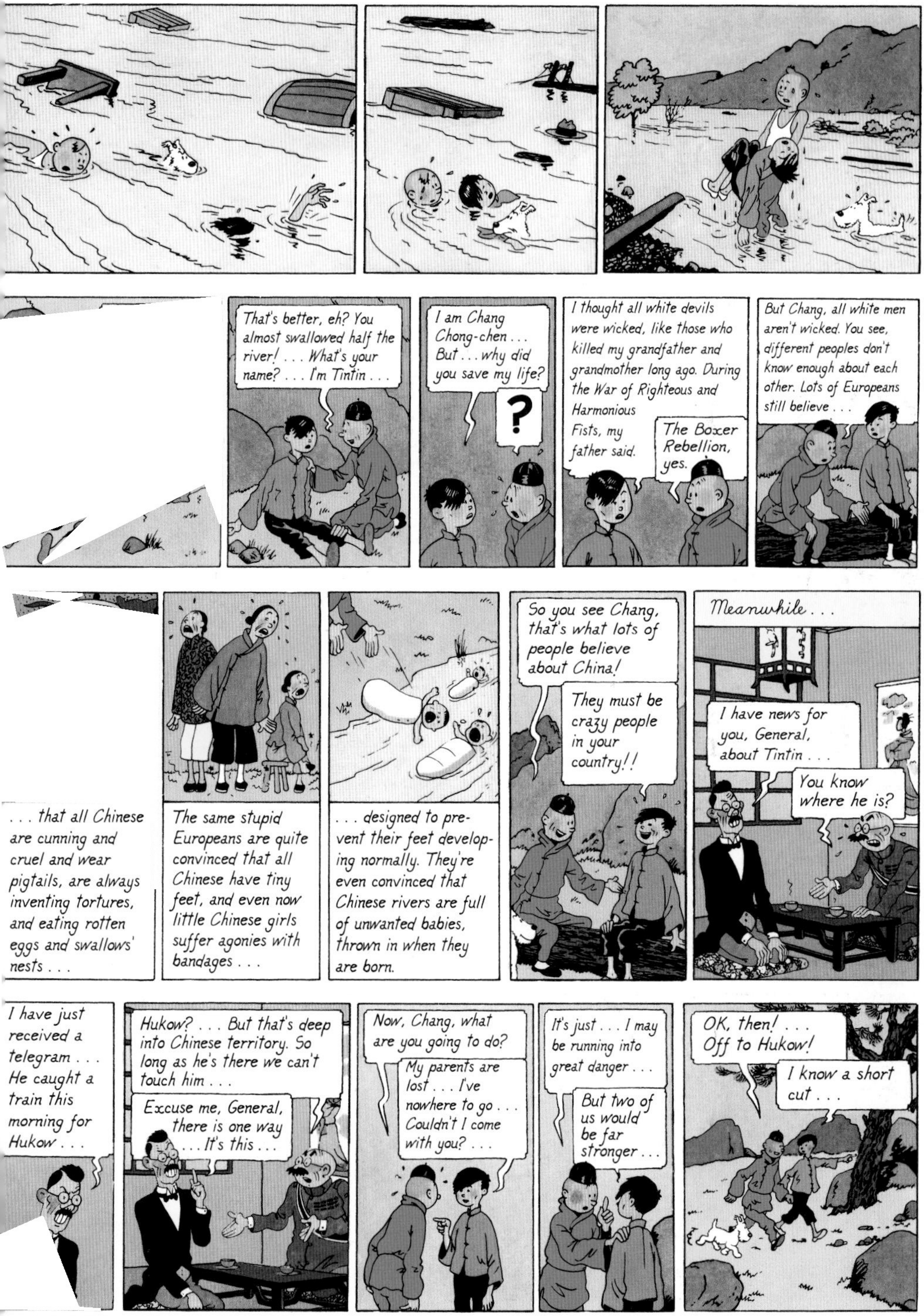
That's better, eh? You almost swallowed half the river! . . . What's your name? . . . I'm Tintin . . .
I am Chang Chong-chen . . . But . . . why did you save my life?
?
I thought all white devils were wicked, like those who killed my grandfather and grandmother long ago. During the War of Righteous and Harmonious Fists, my father said.
The Boxer Rebellion, yes.
But Chang, all white men aren't wicked. You see, different peoples don't know enough about each other. Lots of Europeans still believe . . .
. . . that all Chinese are cunning and cruel and wear pigtails, are always inventing tortures, and eating rotten eggs and swallows' nests . . .
The same stupid Europeans are quite convinced that all Chinese have tiny feet, and even now little Chinese girls suffer agonies with bandages . . .
. . . designed to prevent their feet developing normally. They're even convinced that Chinese rivers are full of unwanted babies, thrown in when they are born.
So you see Chang, that's what lots of people believe about China!
They must be crazy people in your country!!
Meanwhile . . .
I have news for you, General, about Tintin . . .
You know where he is?
I have just received a telegram . . . He caught a train this morning for Hukow . . .
Hukow? . . . But that's deep into Chinese territory. So long as he's there we can't touch him . . .
Excuse me, General, there is one way . . . It's this . . .
Now, Chang, what are you going to do?
My parents are lost . . . I've nowhere to go . . . Couldn't I come with you? . . .
It's just . . . I may be running into great danger . . .
But two of us would be far stronger . . .
OK, then! . . . Off to Hukow!
I know a short cut . . .

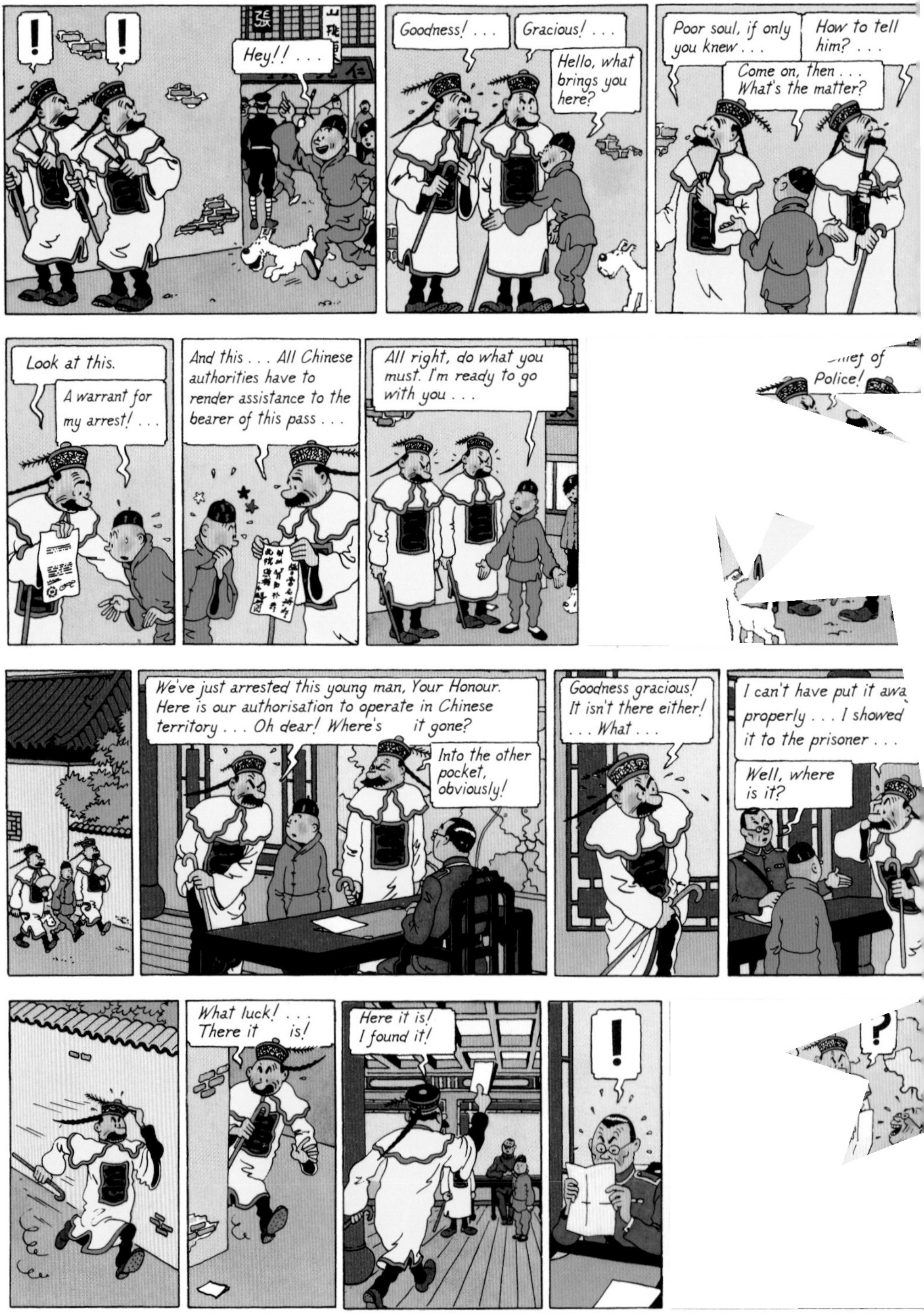
!
!
Hey!! . . .
Goodness! . . .
Gracious! . . .
Hello, what brings you here?
Poor soul, if only you knew . . .
How to tell him? . . .
Come on, then . . . What's the matter?
Look at this.
A warrant for my arrest! . . .
And this . . . All Chinese authorities have to render assistance to the bearer of this pass . . .
All right, do what you must. I'm ready to go with you . . .
Police!
We've just arrested this young man, Your Honour. Here is our authorisation to operate in Chinese territory . . . Oh dear! Where's it gone?
Into the other pocket, obviously!
Goodness gracious! It isn't there either! . . . What . . .
I can't have put it away properly . . . I showed it to the prisoner . . .
Well, where is it?
What luck! . . . There it is!
Here it is! I found it!
!
?

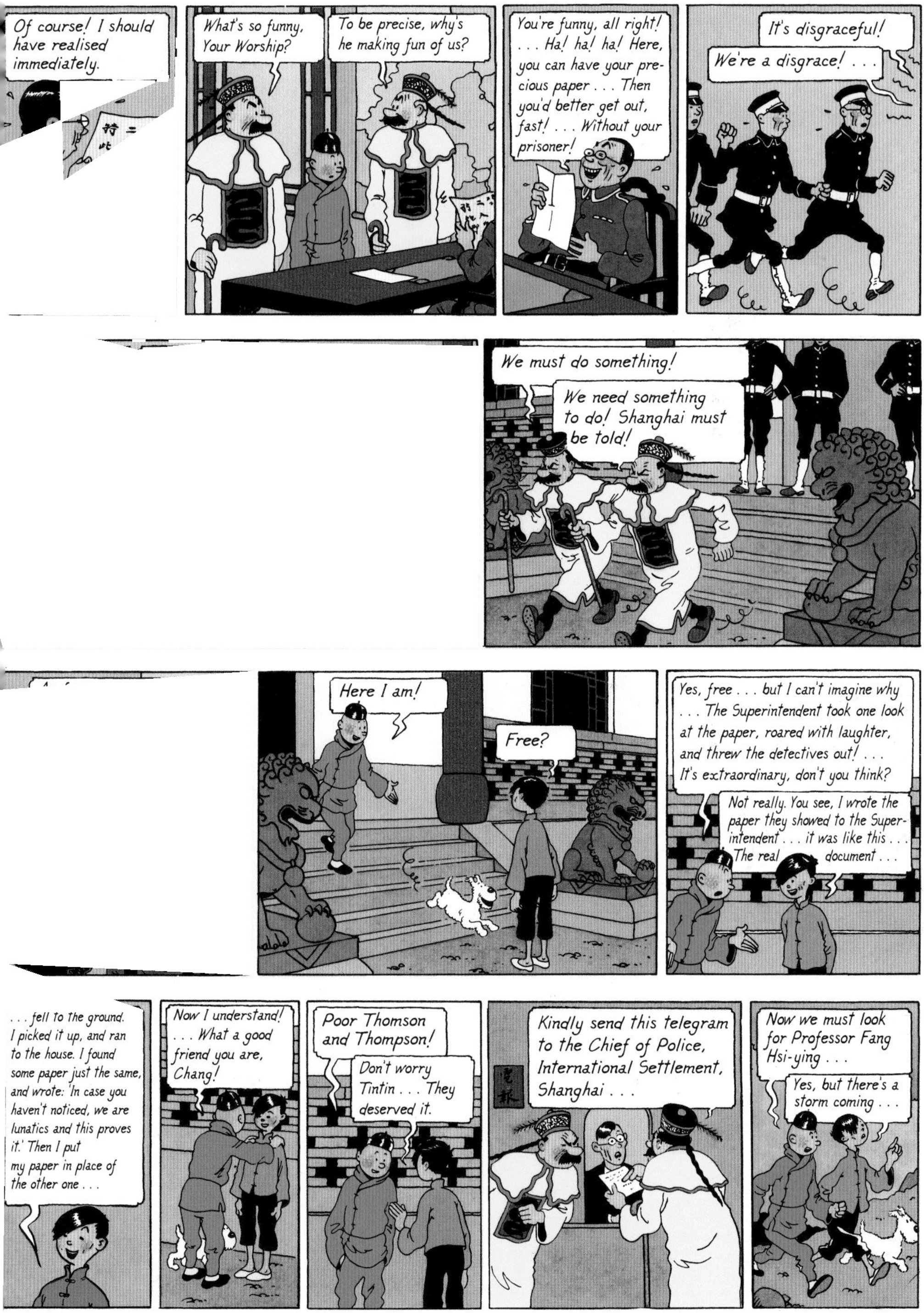

Of course! I should have realised immediately.
What's so funny, Your Worship?
To be precise, why's he making fun of us?
You're funny, all right! . . . Ha! ha! ha! Here, you can have your precious paper . . . Then you'd better get out, fast! . . . Without your prisoner!
It's disgraceful!
We're a disgrace! . . .
We must do something!
We need something to do! Shanghai must be told!
Here I am!
Free?
Yes, free . . . but I can't imagine why . . . The Superintendent took one look at the paper, roared with laughter, and threw the detectives out! . . . It's extraordinary, don't you think?
Not really. You see, I wrote the paper they showed to the Superintendent . . . it was like this . . . The real document . . .
. . . fell to the ground. I picked it up, and ran to the house. I found some paper just the same, and wrote: 'In case you haven't noticed, we are lunatics and this proves it.' Then I put my paper in place of the other one . . .
Now I understand! . . . What a good friend you are, Chang!
Poor Thomson and Thompson!
Don't worry Tintin . . . They deserved it.
Kindly send this telegram to the Chief of Police, International Settlement, Shanghai . . .
Now we must look for Professor Fang Hsi-ying . . .
Yes, but there's a storm coming . . .

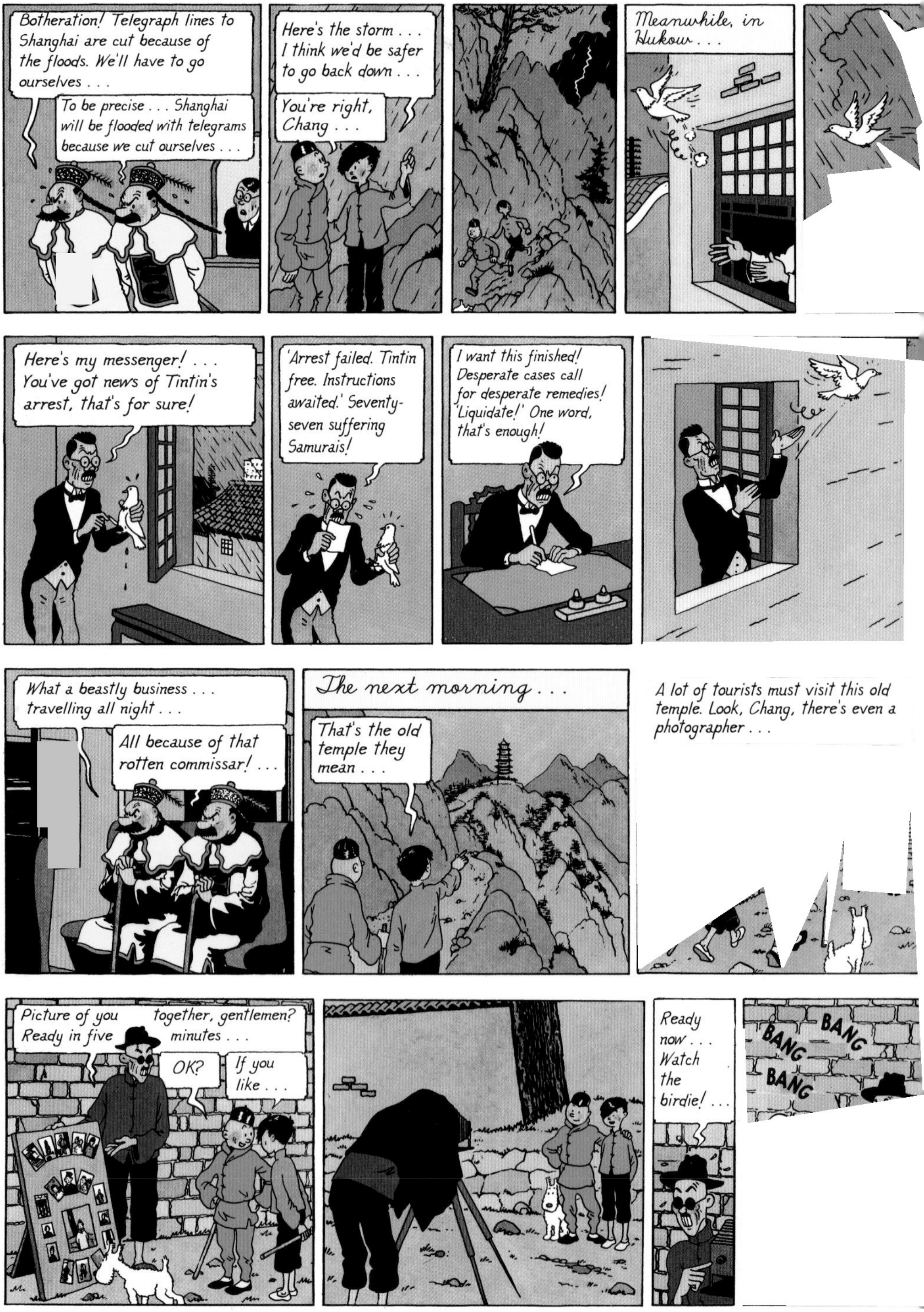
Botheration! Telegraph lines to Shanghai are cut because of the floods. We'll have to go ourselves . . .
To be precise . . . Shanghai will be flooded with telegrams because we cut ourselves . . .
Here's the storm . . . I think we'd be safer to go back down . . .
You're right, Chang . . .
Meanwhile, in Hukow . . .
Here's my messenger! . . . You've got news of Tintin's arrest, that's for sure!
'Arrest failed. Tintin free. Instructions awaited.' Seventy-seven suffering Samurais!
I want this finished! Desperate cases call for desperate remedies! 'Liquidate!' One word, that's enough!
What a beastly business . . . travelling all night . . .
All because of that rotten commissar! . . .
The next morning . . .
That's the old temple they mean . . .
A lot of tourists must visit this old temple. Look, Chang, there's even a photographer . . .
Picture of you together, gentlemen? Ready in five minutes . . .
OK?
If you like . . .
Ready now . . . Watch the birdie! . . .
BANG
BANG
BANG

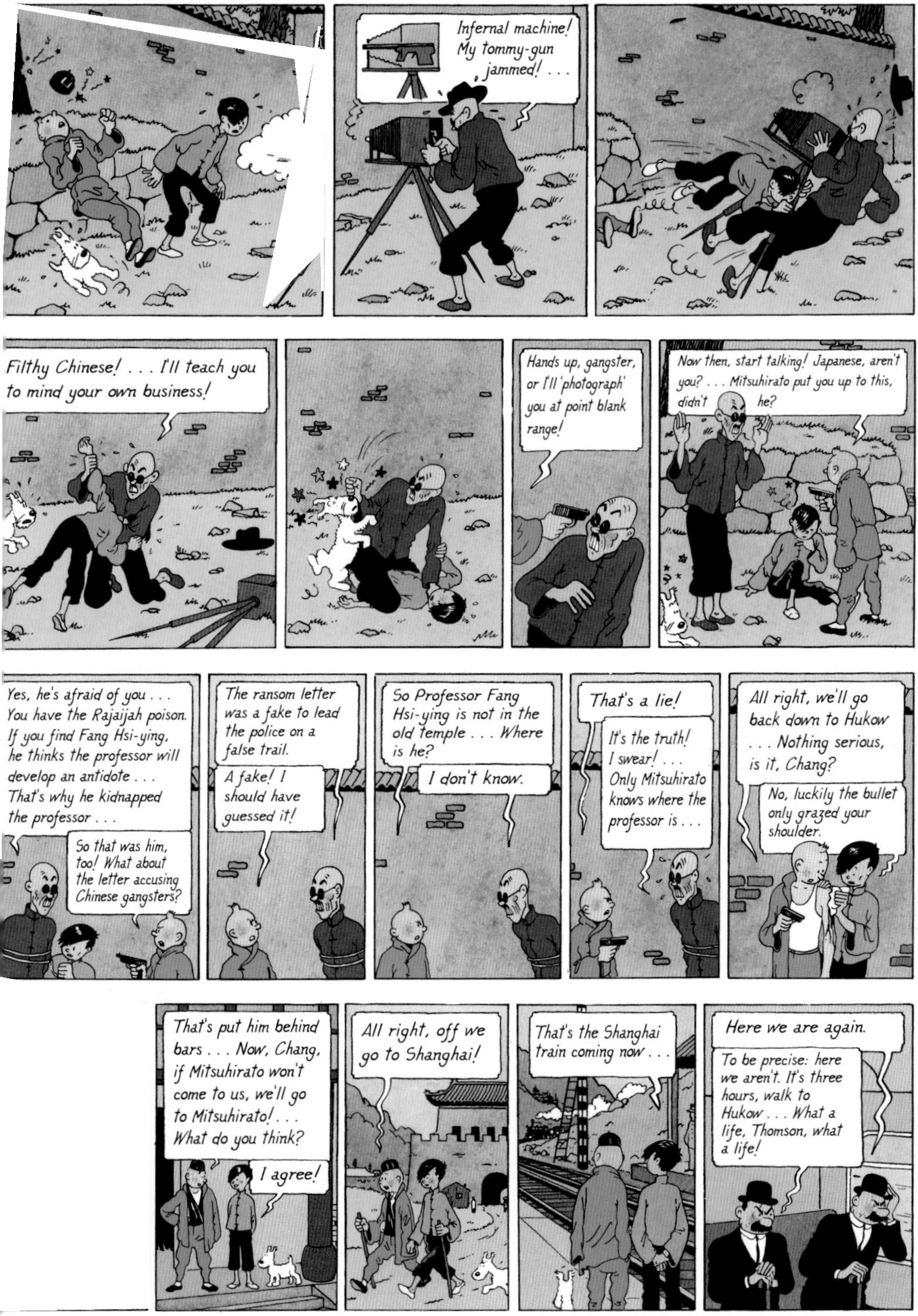

Infernal machine! My tommy-gun jammed! . . .
Filthy Chinese! . . . I'll teach you to mind your own business!
Hands up, gangster, or I'll 'photograph' you at point blank range!
Now then, start talking! Japanese, aren't you? . . . Mitsuhirato put you up to this, didn't he?
Yes, he's afraid of you . . . You have the Rajaijah poison. If you find Fang Hsi-ying, he thinks the professor will develop an antidote . . . That's why he kidnapped the professor . . .
So that was him, too! What about the letter accusing Chinese gangsters?
The ransom letter was a fake to lead the police on a false trail.
A fake! I should have guessed it!
So Professor Fang Hsi-ying is not in the old temple . . . Where is he?
I don't know.
That's a lie!
It's the truth! I swear! . . . Only Mitsuhirato knows where the professor is . . .
All right, we'll go back down to Hukow . . . Nothing serious, is it, Chang?
No, luckily the bullet only grazed your shoulder.
That's put him behind bars . . . Now, Chang, if Mitsuhirato won't come to us, we'll go to Mitsuhirato! . . . What do you think?
I agree!
All right, off we go to Shanghai!
That's the Shanghai train coming now . . .
Here we are again.
To be precise: here we aren't. It's three hours, walk to Hukow . . . What a life, Thomson, what a life!

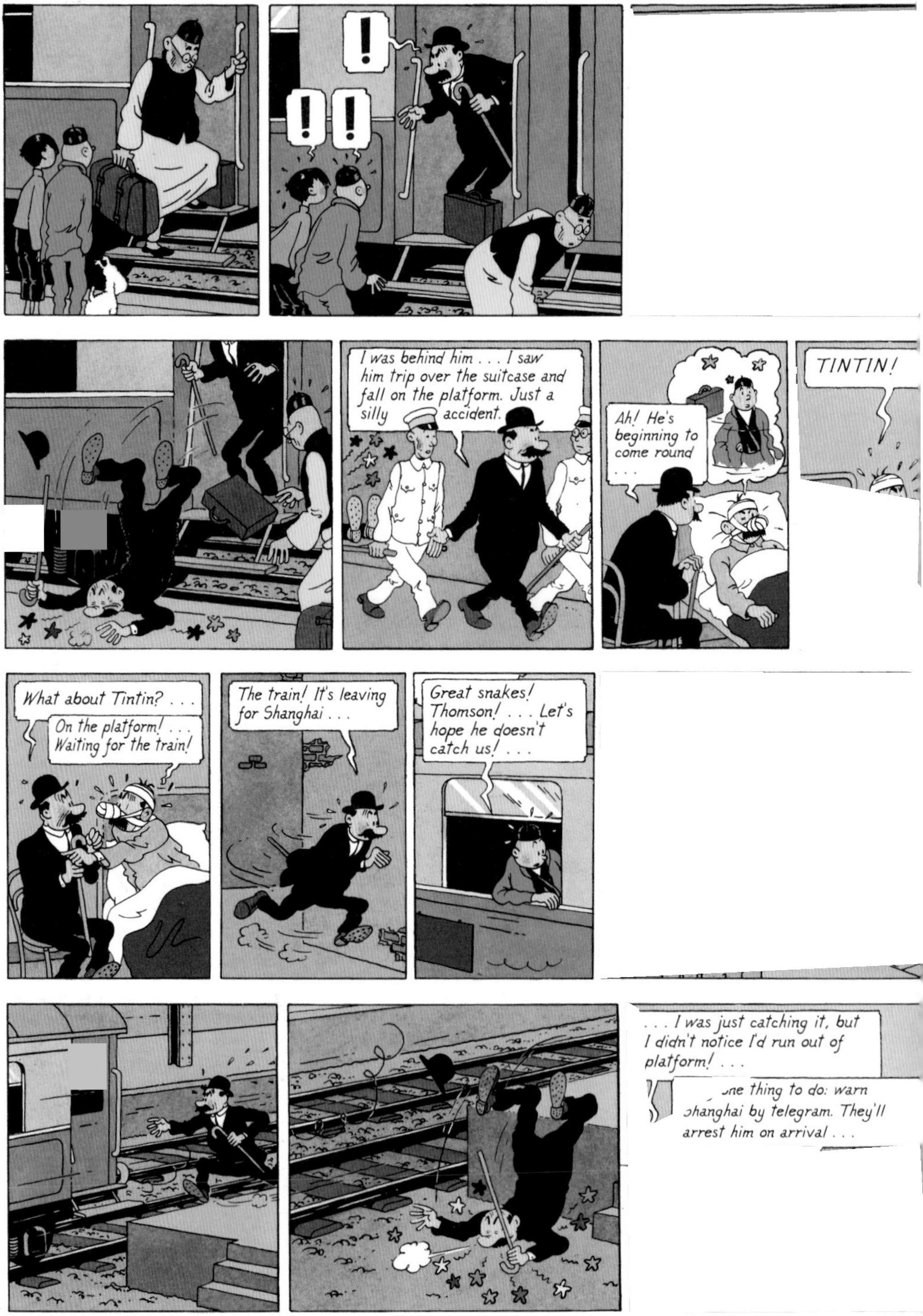
!
!!
I was behind him . . . I saw him trip over the suitcase and fall on the platform. Just a silly accident.
Ah! He's beginning to come round . . .
TINTIN!
What about Tintin? . . .
On the platform! . . . Waiting for the train!
The train! It's leaving for Shanghai . . .
Great snakes! Thomson! . . . Let's hope he doesn't catch us! . . .
. . . I was just catching it, but I didn't notice I'd run out of platform! . . .
ne thing to do: warn
hanghai by telegram. They'll
arrest him on arrival . . .

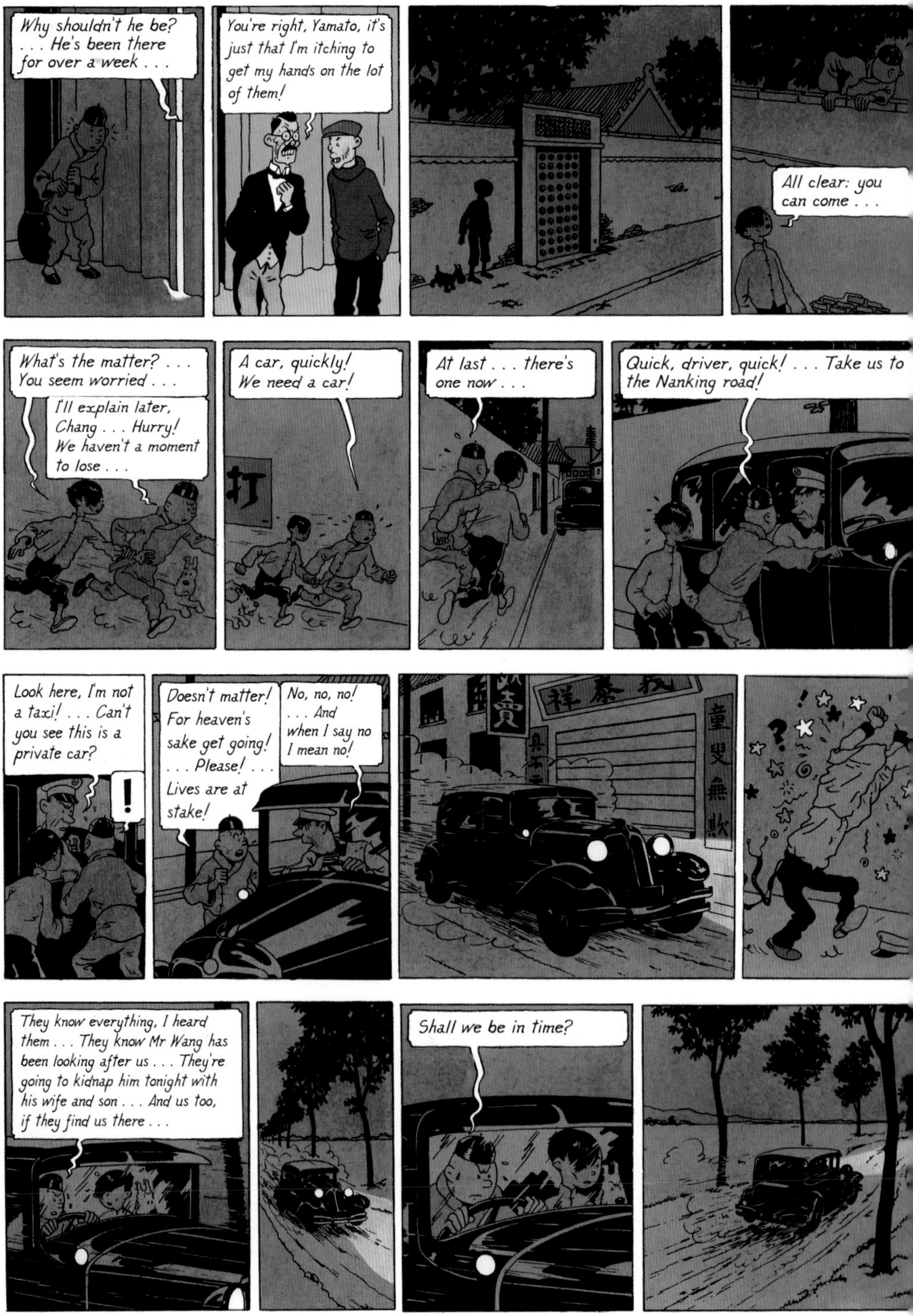
Why shouldn't he be? . . . He's been there for over a week . . .
You're right, Yamato, it's just that I'm itching to get my hands on the lot of them!
All clear: you can come . . .
What's the matter? . . . You seem worried . . .
I'll explain later, Chang . . . Hurry! We haven't a moment to lose . . .
A car, quickly! We need a car!
At last . . . there's one now . . .
Quick, driver, quick! . . . Take us to the Nanking road!
Look here, I'm not a taxi! . . . Can't you see this is a private car?
!
Doesn't matter! For heaven's sake get going! . . . Please! . . . Lives are at stake!
No, no, no! . . . And when I say no I mean no!
They know everything, I heard them . . . They know Mr Wang has been looking after us . . . They're going to kidnap him tonight with his wife and son . . . And us too, if they find us there . . .
Shall we be in time?

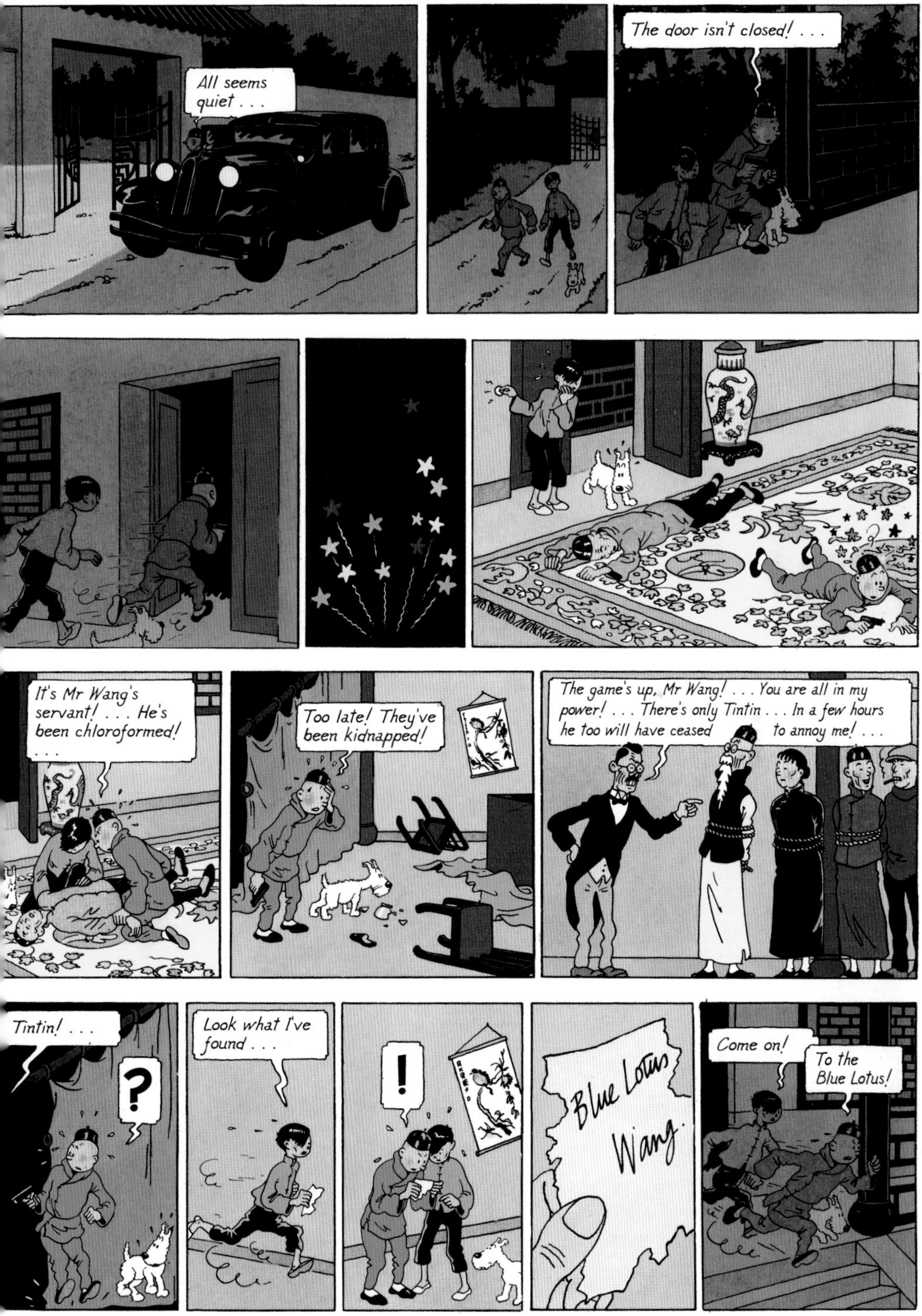
All seems quiet . . .
The door isn't closed! . . .
It's Mr Wang's servant! . . . He's been chloroformed! . . .
Too late! They've been kidnapped!
The game's up, Mr Wang! . . . You are all in my power! . . . There's only Tintin . . . In a few hours he too will have ceased to annoy me! . . .
Tintin! . . .
?
Look what I've found . . .
!
Blue Lotus
Wang
Come on!
To the Blue Lotus!

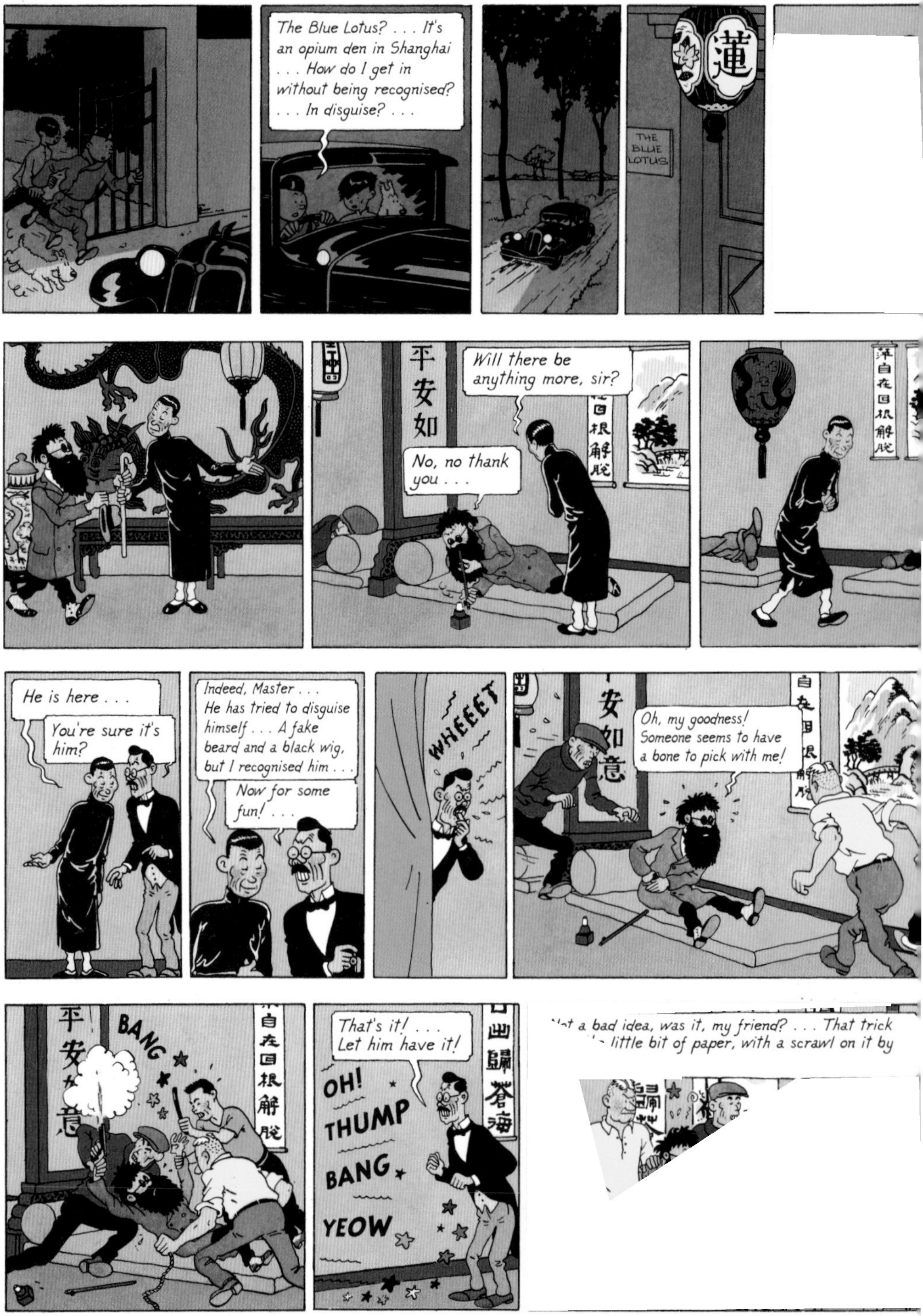

The Blue Lotus? . . . It's an opium den in Shanghai . . . How do I get in without being recognised? . . . In disguise? . . .
蓮
THE BLUE LOTUS
Will there be anything more, sir?
No, no thank you . . .
He is here . . .
You're sure it's him?
Indeed, Master . . . He has tried to disguise himself . . . A fake beard and a black wig, but I recognised him . . .
Now for some fun! . . .
WHEEET
Oh, my goodness! Someone seems to have a bone to pick with me!
BANG
That's it! . . . Let him have it!
OH!
THUMP
BANG
YEOW
a bad idea, was it, my friend? . . . That trick
little bit of paper, with a scrawl on it by

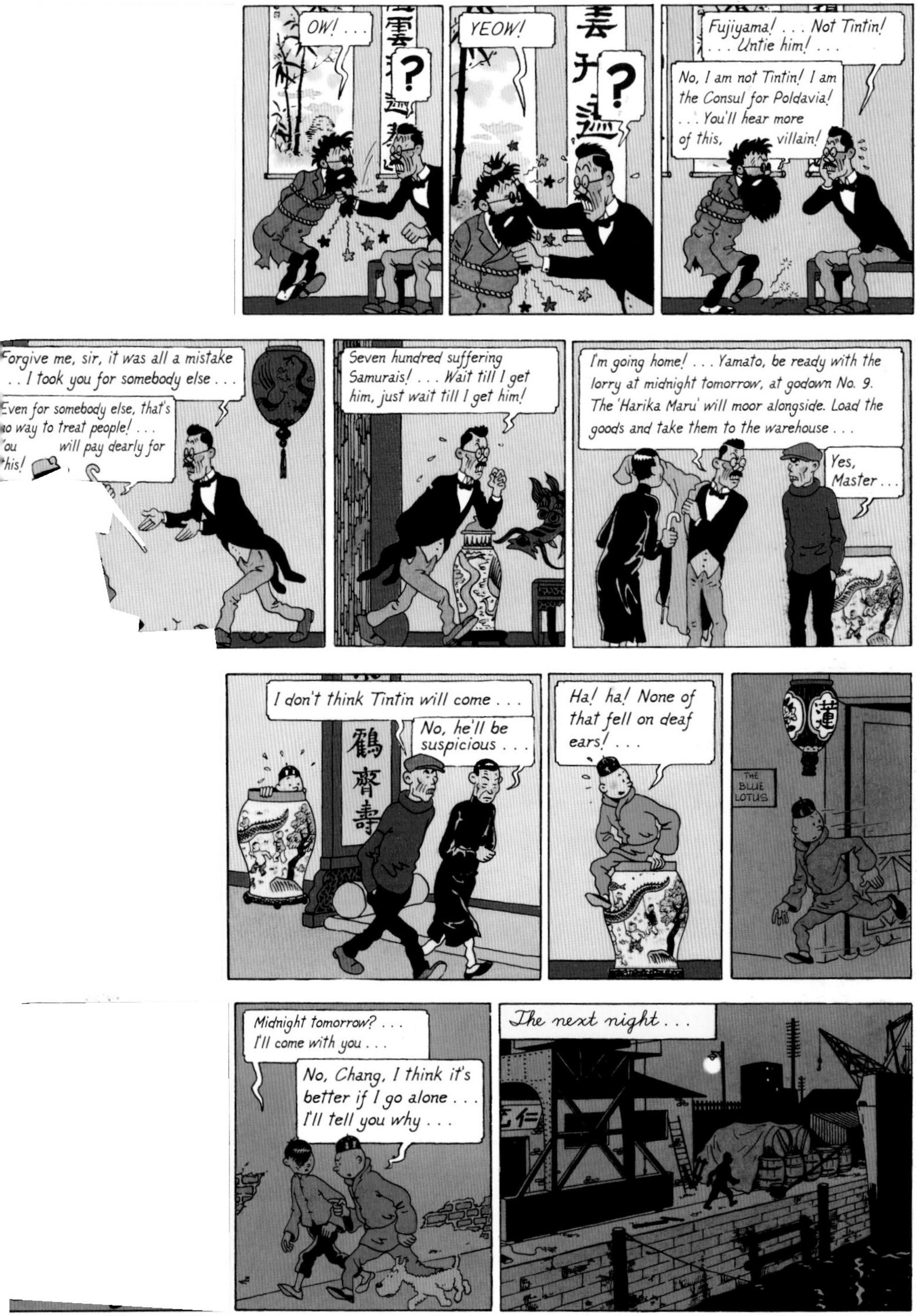

OW! . . .
?
YEOW!
?
Fujiyama! . . . Not Tintin! . . . Untie him! . . .
No, I am not Tintin! I am the Consul for Poldavia! . . . You'll hear more of this, villain!
Forgive me, sir, it was all a mistake . . . I took you for somebody else . . .
Even for somebody else, that's o way to treat people! . . . ou will pay dearly for his!
Seven hundred suffering Samurais! . . . Wait till I get him, just wait till I get him!
I'm going home! . . . Yamato, be ready with the lorry at midnight tomorrow, at godown No. 9. The 'Harika Maru' will moor alongside. Load the goods and take them to the warehouse . . .
Yes, Master . . .
I don't think Tintin will come . . .
No, he'll be suspicious . . .
Ha! ha! None of that fell on deaf ears! . . .
THE BLUE LOTUS
Midnight tomorrow? . . . I'll come with you . . .
No, Chang, I think it's better if I go alone . . . I'll tell you why . . .
The next night . . .

See Cigars of the Pharaoh

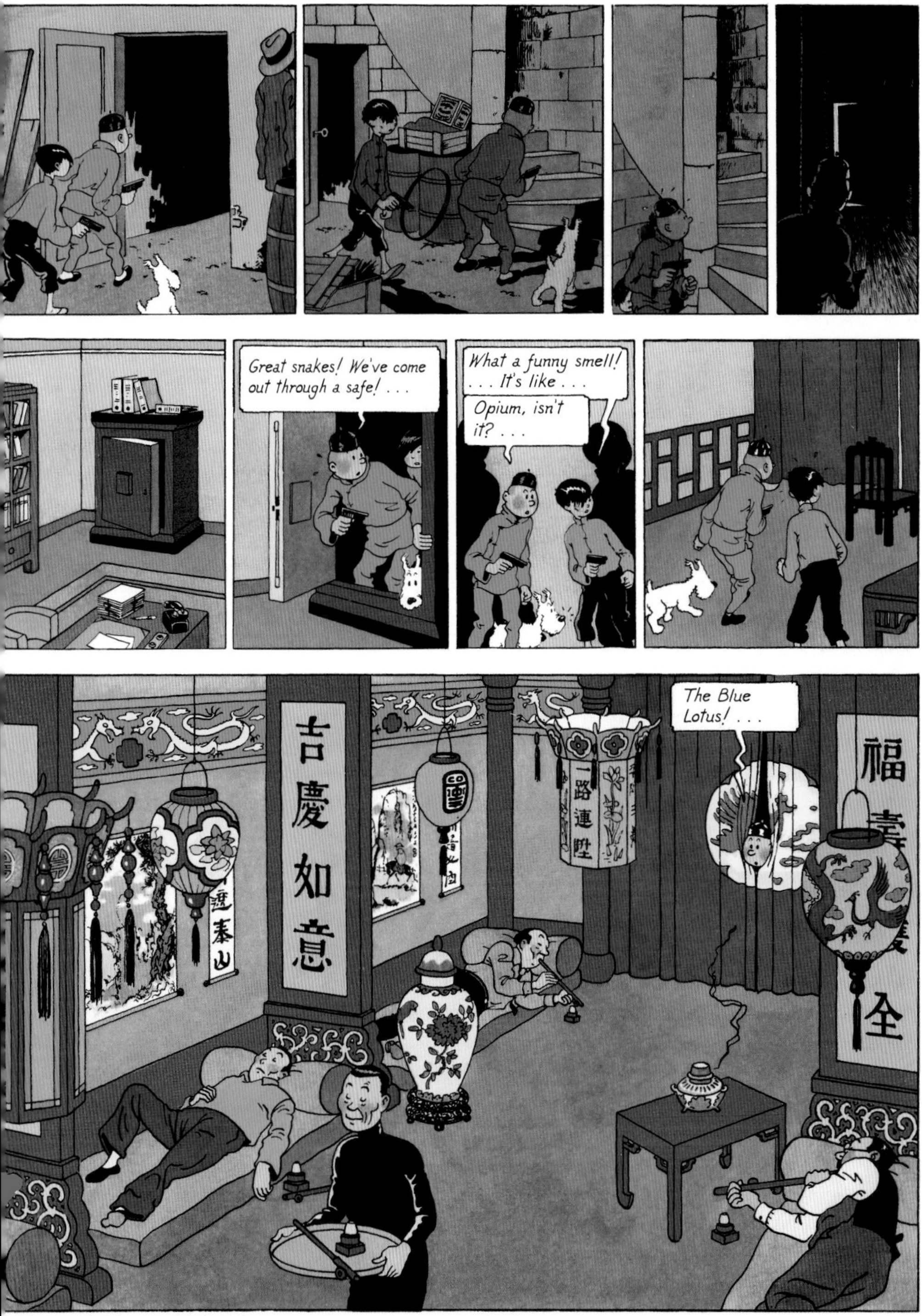
Great snakes! We've come out through a safe! . . .
What a funny smell! . . . It's like . . .
Opium, isn't it? . . .
吉慶如意
一路連陞
The Blue Lotus! . . .

SHANGHAI NEWS
上海報

FANG HSI-YING FOUND: Professor Prisoner in Opium Den

SHANGHAI, Wednesday: Professor Fang Hsi-ying has been found! The good news was flashed to us this morning.

Last week eminent scholar Fang disappeared on his way home from a party given by a friend. Police efforts to trace him were unavailing. No clues were found.

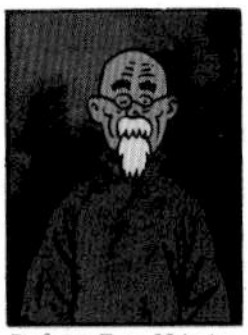
Professor Fang Hsi-ying pictured just after his release.

Young European reporter Tintin joined in the hunt for the missing man of science. Earlier we reported incidents involving Tintin and the occupying Japanese forces. Secret society Sons of the Dragon aided Tintin in the rescue. Fang Hsi-ying was kidnapped by an international gang of drug smugglers, now all safely in police custody.

A wireless transmitter was found by police at Blue Lotus opium den. The transmitter was used by the drug smugglers to communicate wth their ships on the high seas. Information radioed included sea routes, ports to be avoided, points of embarkation and uploading.

Home of Japanese subject Mitsuhirato was also searched. No comment, say police on reports of seizure of top-secret documents. Unconfirmed rumours suggest the papers concern undercover political activity by a neighbouring power. Speculation mounts that they disclose the recent Shanghai-Nanking railway incident as a pretext for extended Japanese occupation. League of Nations officials in Geneva will study the captured documents.

TINTIN'S OWN STORY

This morning, hero of the hour Mr Tintin, talked to us about his adventures.

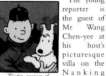

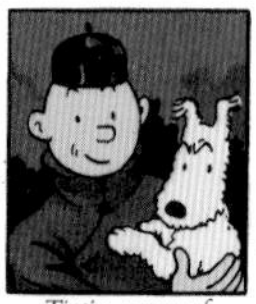
Tintin, rescuer of Professor Fang Hsi-ying, with Snowy, his faithful companion.

The young reporter is the guest of Mr Wang Chen-yee at his host's picturesque villa on the Nanking road.

When we called, our hero, young and smiling, greeted us wearing Chinese dress. Could this really be the scourge of the terrible Shanghai gangsters?

After our greetings and congratulations, we asked Mr Tintin to tell us how he succeeded in smashing the most dangerous organisation.

Mr Wang, a tall, elderly, venerable man with an impish smile said:

"You must tell the world it is entirely due to him that my wife, my son and I are alive today!"

With these words our interview was concluded, and we said farewell to the friendly reporter and his kindly host.

L.G.T.

Young people carry posters of Tintin through Shanghai streets.

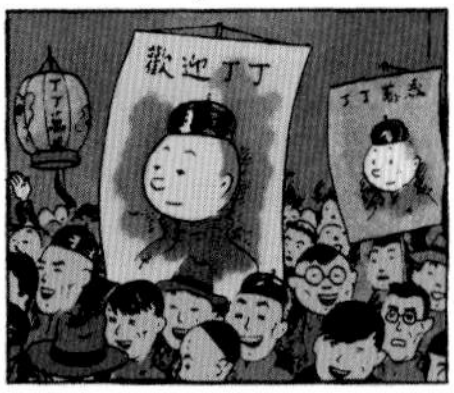

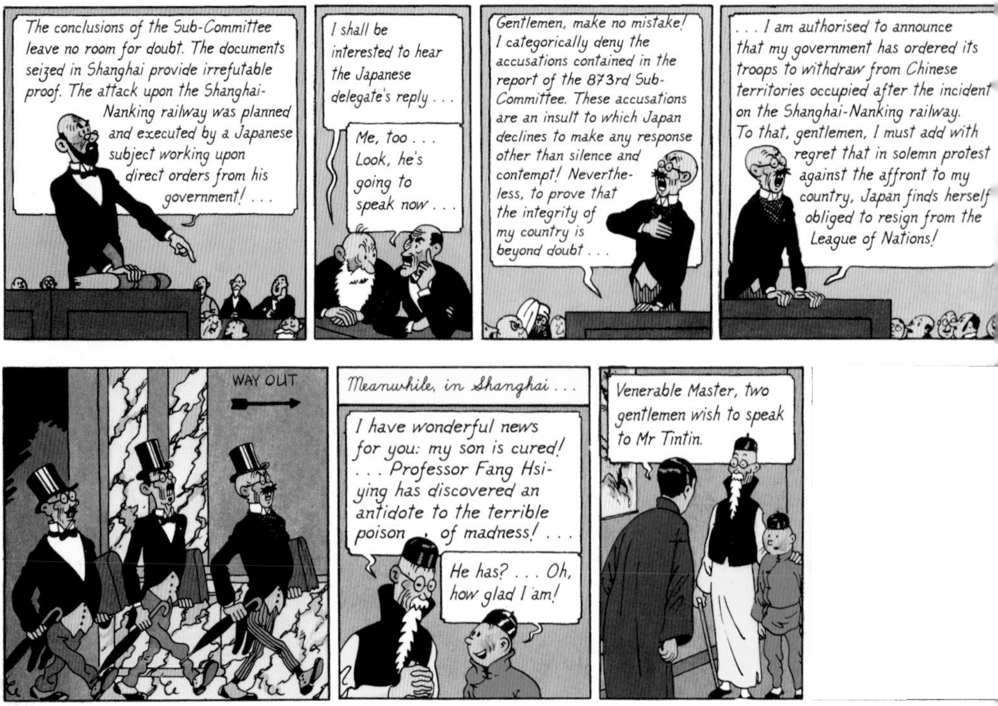
The conclusions of the Sub-Committee leave no room for doubt. The documents seized in Shanghai provide irrefutable proof. The attack upon the Shanghai-Nanking railway was planned and executed by a Japanese subject working upon direct orders from his government! . . .
I shall be interested to hear the Japanese delegate's reply . . .
Me, too . . . Look, he's going to speak now . . .
Gentlemen, make no mistake! I categorically deny the accusations contained in the report of the 873rd Sub-Committee. These accusations are an insult to which Japan declines to make any response other than silence and contempt! Nevertheless, to prove that the integrity of my country is beyond doubt . . .
. . . I am authorised to announce that my government has ordered its troops to withdraw from Chinese territories occupied after the incident on the Shanghai-Nanking railway. To that, gentlemen, I must add with regret that in solemn protest against the affront to my country, Japan finds herself obliged to resign from the League of Nations!
WAY OUT
Meanwhile, in Shanghai . . .
I have wonderful news for you: my son is cured! . . . Professor Fang Hsi-ying has discovered an antidote to the terrible poison of madness! . . .
He has? . . . Oh, how glad I am!
Venerable Master, two gentlemen wish to speak to Mr Tintin.

THE REAL-LIFE INSPIRATION
BEHIND
TINTIN'S ADVENTURES

Written by Stuart Tett
with the collaboration of Studio Moulinsart.

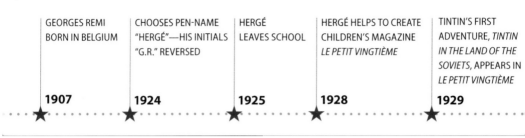

GEORGES REMI BORN IN BELGIUM

1907

CHOOSES PEN-NAME "HERGÉ"—HIS INITIALS "G.R." REVERSED

1924

HERGÉ LEAVES SCHOOL

1925

HERGÉ HELPS TO CREATE CHILDREN'S MAGAZINE *LE PETIT VINGTIÈME*

1928

TINTIN'S FIRST ADVENTURE, *TINTIN IN THE LAND OF THE SOVIETS*, APPEARS IN *LE PETIT VINGTIÈME*

1929

HERGÉ

Hergé and Chang, 1934

Discovering different cultures

When Hergé announced in the spring of 1934 that he was sending Tintin to China, he was contacted by Father Gosset, a priest in charge of the welfare of Chinese students at Leuven University in Belgium. Father Gosset was worried that Hergé would offend Chinese people if he portrayed the Chinese in stereotypical and clichéd ways. The priest put Hergé in contact with a Chinese student called Chang Chong-chen. With Chang's help, Hergé carried out extensive research on China while writing *The Blue Lotus.*

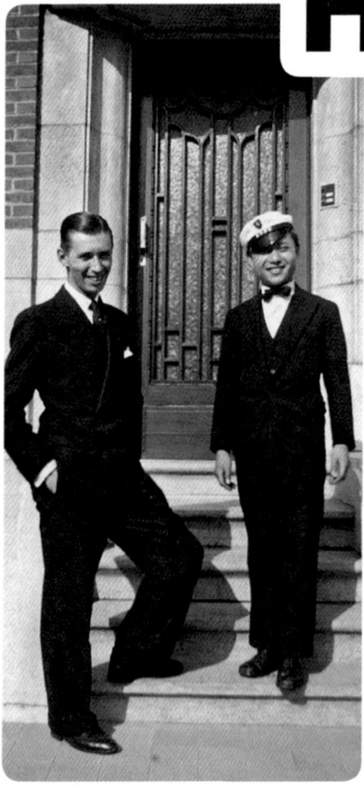

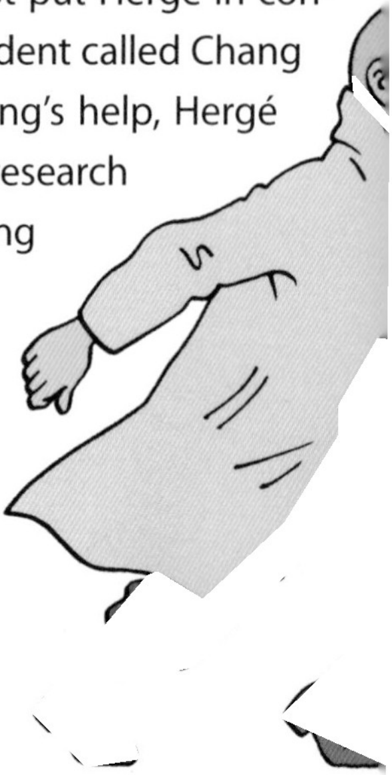

1936	1946	1971	1976	1983
PUBLICATION OF *THE BLUE LOTUS*	LAUNCH OF *TINTIN* MAGAZINE	HERGÉ VISITS AMERICA	PUBLICATION OF TINTIN'S LAST ADVENTURE, *TINTIN AND THE PICAROS*	HERGÉ DIES AGED 75

TINTIN

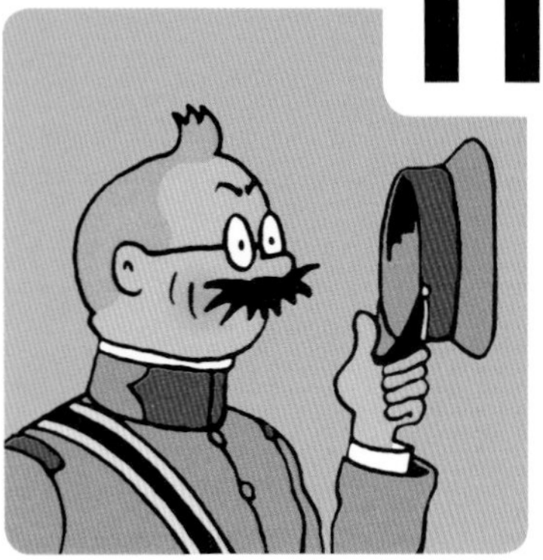

In disguise

Throughout his adventures, Tintin likes to use disguises to help him escape from villains. Below you can see Tintin wearing clothes to suit some of his different adventures. Which stories have you read?

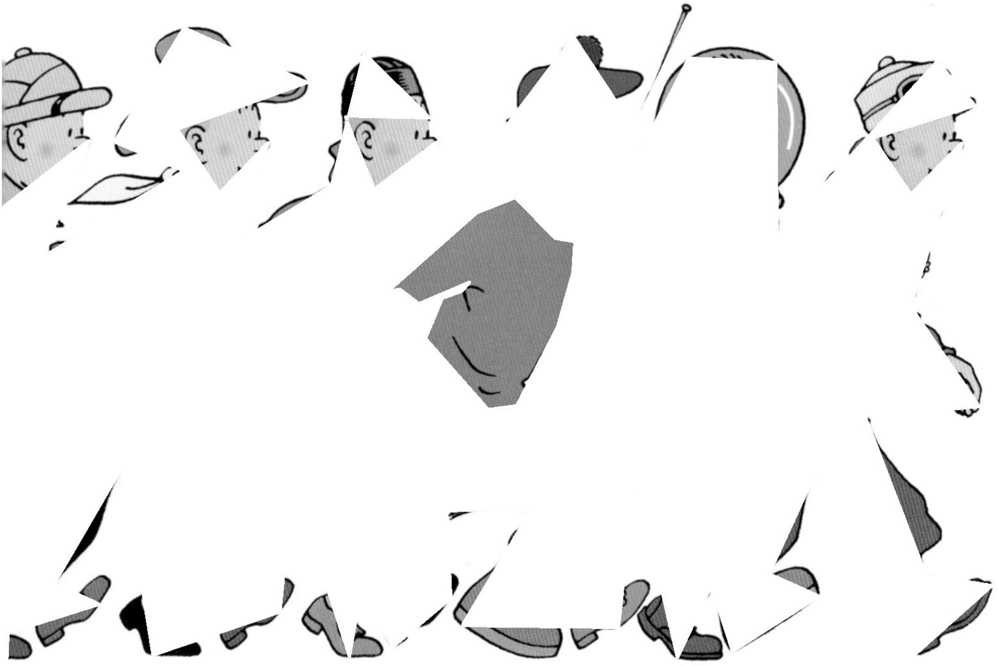

THE TRUE STORY
... behind *The Blue Lotus*

Tintin and Snowy are taking a break at the palace of the Maharaja of Gaipajama in India. They have just broken up a gang of smugglers in *Cigars of the Pharaoh*, but the leader of the gang is still at large. Tintin plays around with a short-wave radio, much to Snowy's annoyance, but what are all the dots and dashes coming out of the radio?

Once upon a time...

The symbols coming from Tintin's radio are Morse code. Each letter of the alphabet is represented by a sequence of short and long tones: dots and dashes when written out on paper. Relayed by radio, Morse code was the international standard for maritime communication from the early twentieth century until 1999.

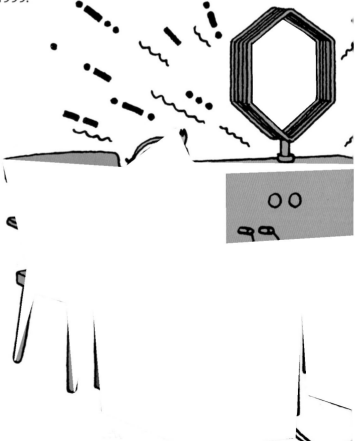

Once upon a time…

At the time when Hergé wrote *The Blue Lotus*, Tintin books were published in black-and-white. They were over 100 pages long, much longer than the 62-page color version you have just read. The picture on this page shows a map that was included in the original version of the story.

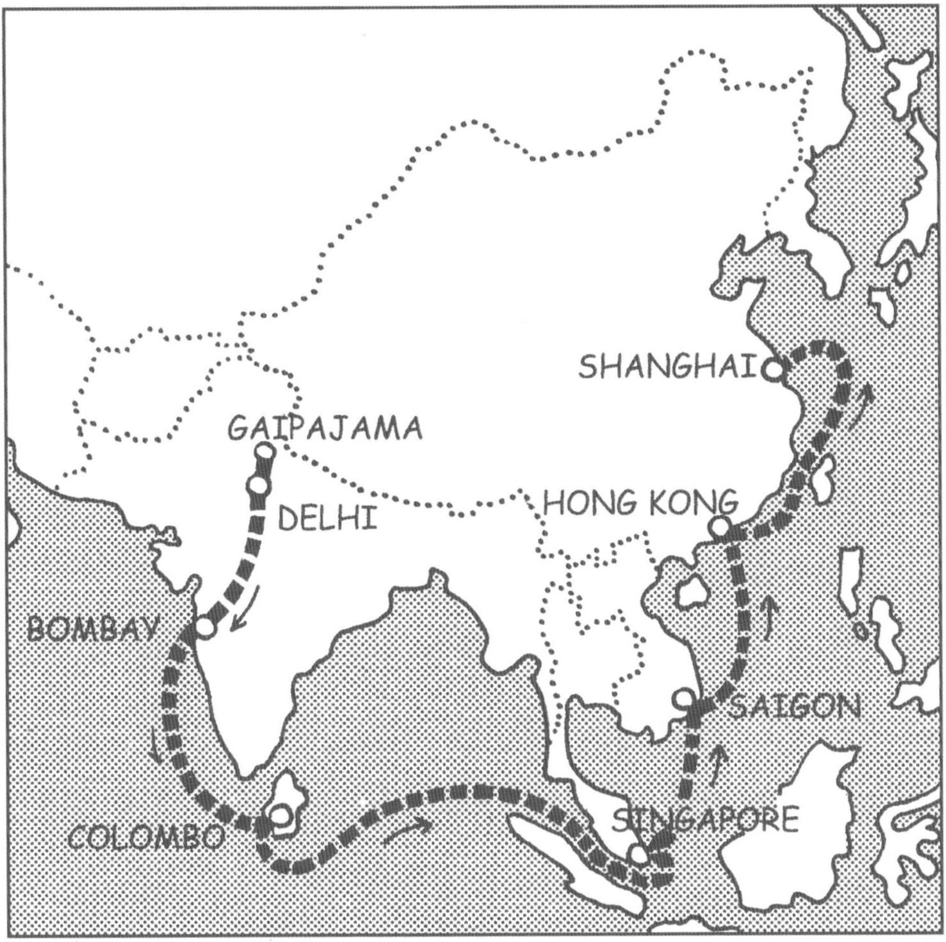

SHANGHAI
GAIPAJAMA
DELHI
HONG KONG
BOMBAY
SAIGON
SINGAPORE
COLOMBO

The map shows the route that Tintin takes from Gaipajama in India to Shanghai in China. While Gaipajama is a fictional state with a funny name (meaning bright, colorful pajamas!), Shanghai is a real place. Tintin's journey from fiction to reality reflects Hergé's determination to make *The Blue Lotus* as realistic as possible.

Once upon a time…

From the moment he arrives in Shanghai, Tintin is on the move! He has to travel to different places as he tries to get to the bottom of various mysteries. To help you to understand the story a bit better, here is a section of an old map of Shanghai in 1935. At the time Hergé wrote this story, part of Shanghai was called the International Settlement.

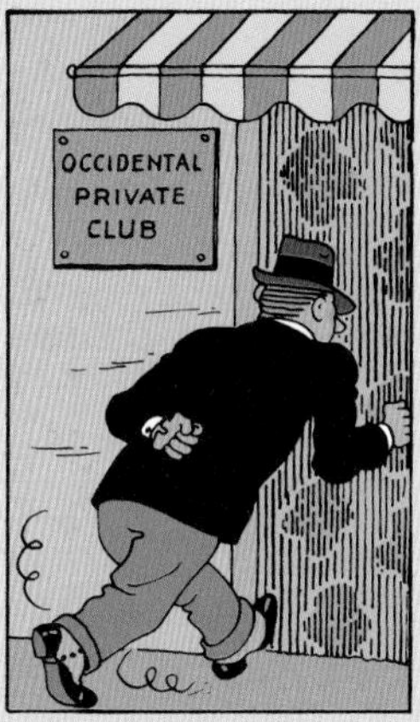

OCCIDENTAL PRIVATE CLUB

1. The Occidental Private Club is based on the real-life Shanghai Club.

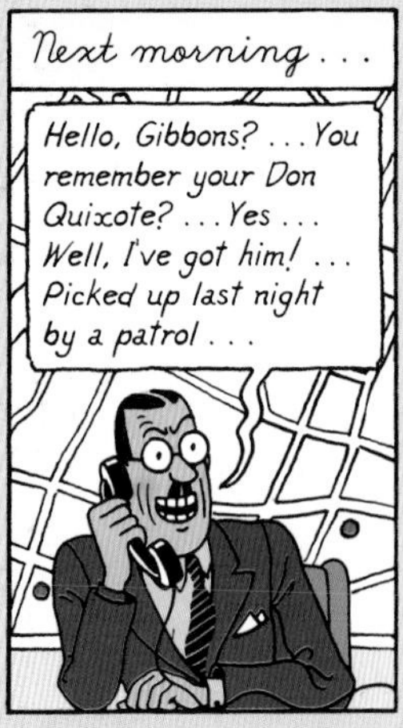

Next morning . . .
Hello, Gibbons? . . . You remember your Don Quixote? . . . Yes . . . Well, I've got him! . . . Picked up last night by a patrol . . .

2. The Chief of Police works at the Central Police Station.

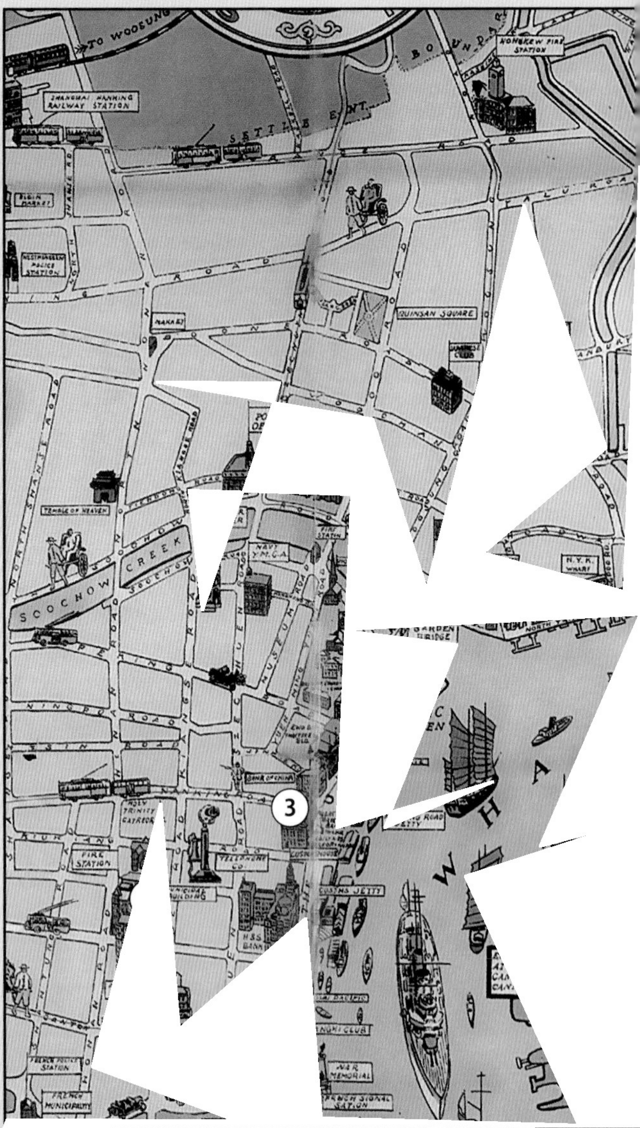

TO WOOSUNG
SHANGHAI NANKING RAILWAY STATION
QUINSAN SQUARE
TEMPLE OF HEAVEN
SOOCHOW CREEK
NAVY Y.M.C.A.
N.Y.K. WHARF
FIRE STATION
BANK OF CHINA
3
CUSTOMS JETTY
WAR MEMORIAL
FRENCH POLICE STATION
FRENCH MUNICIPALITY
FRENCH SIGNAL STATION

The International Settlement (shown in yellow) was an area run by foreign countries, including Britain, America and Japan (which controlled territory to the north and east of Soochow Creek). Treaties between China and these countries specified that foreign citizens could only be tried and punished for crimes committed in China by their own countries' authorities. But Tintin doesn't always have his identification papers and the authorities in the story are corrupt, so he had better watch out!

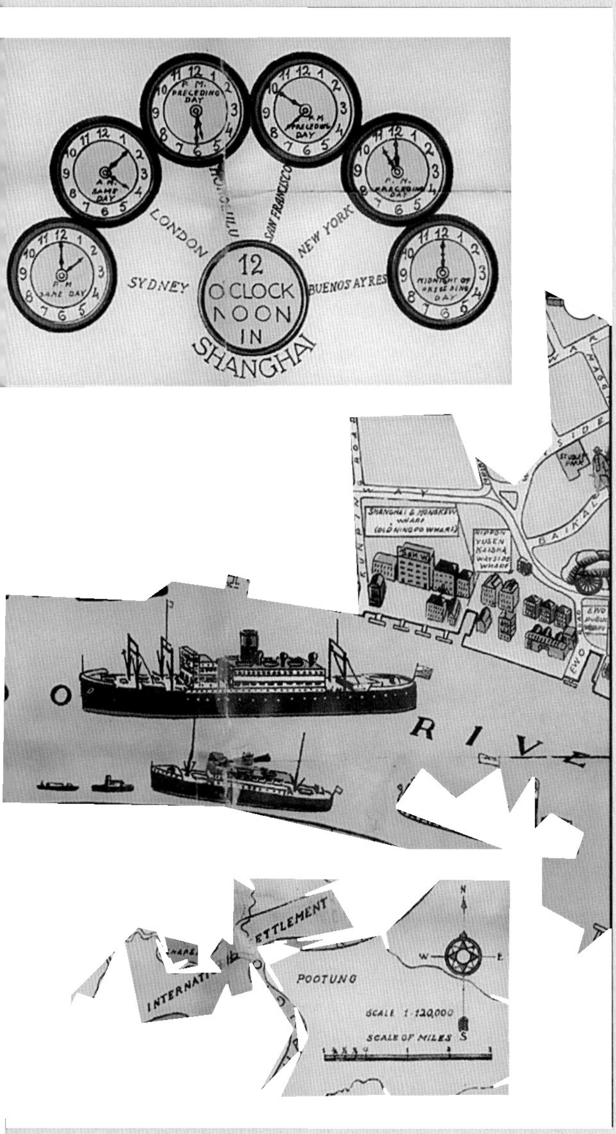
12 O'CLOCK NOON IN SHANGHAI
LONDON
SAN FRANCISCO
NEW YORK
SYDNEY
BUENOS AYRES
SHANGHAI & HONGKEW WHARF (OLD NINGPO WHARF)
NIPPON YUSEN KAISHA WAYSIDE WHARF
RIVE
SETTLEMENT
POOTUNG
SCALE 1:120,000
SCALE OF MILES

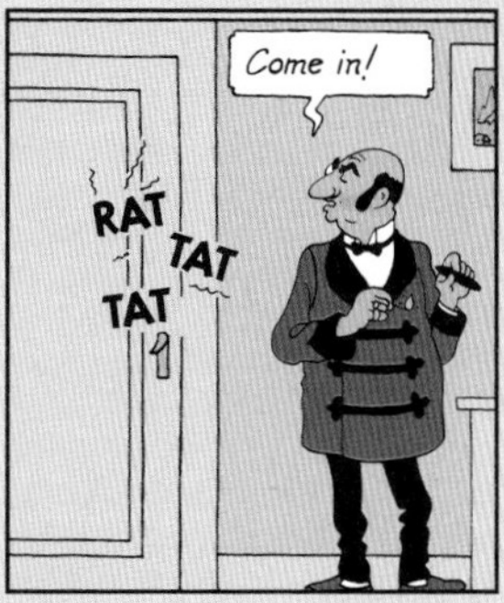
Come in!
RAT TAT TAT

3. Rastapopoulos stays at the Palace Hotel.

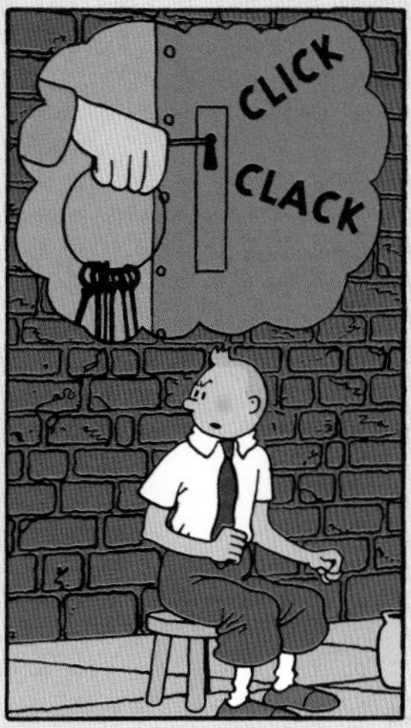
CLICK
CLACK

4. St. James Prison is based on the real-life Ward Road Jail.

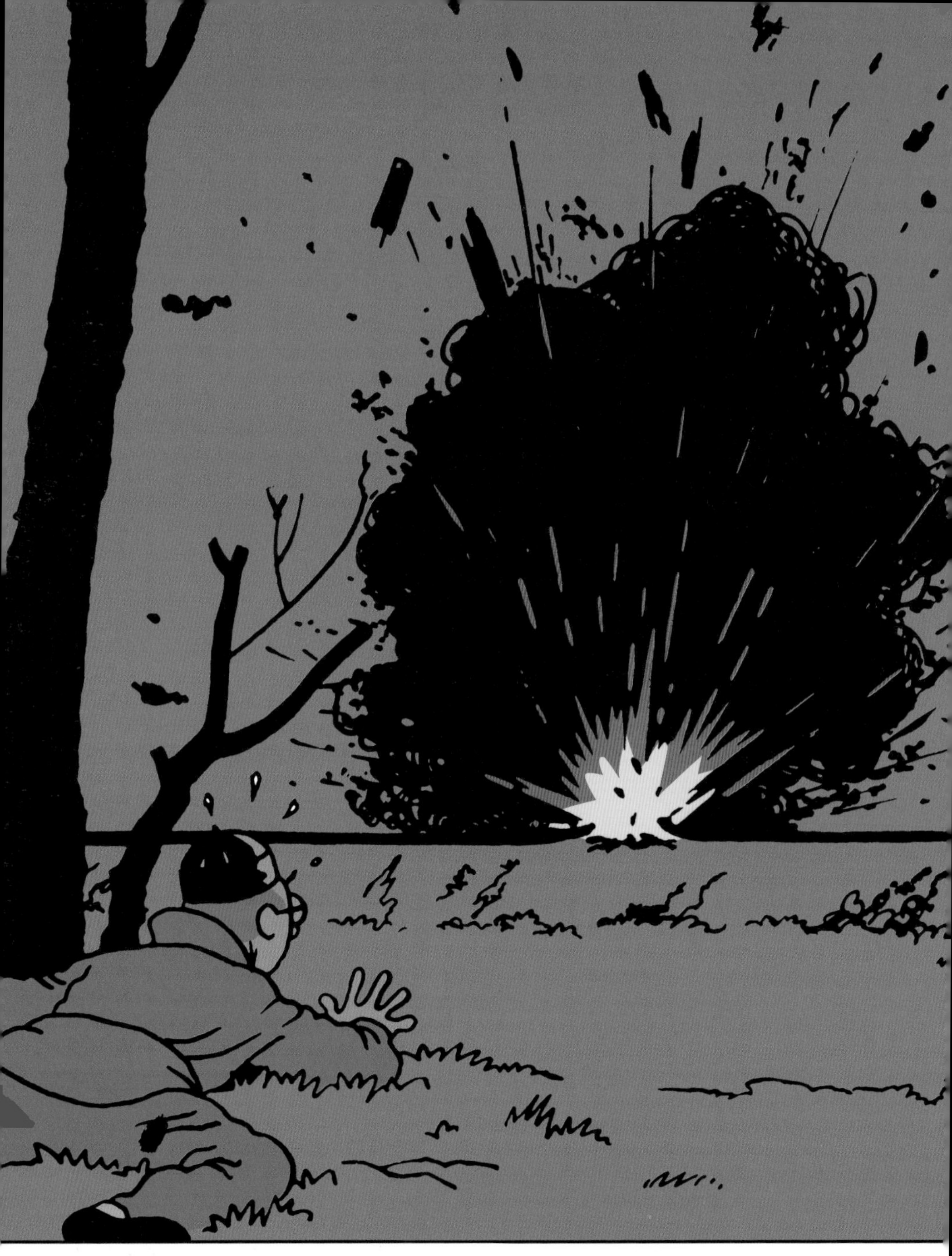

On the trail of the dangerous Japanese secret agent and smuggler Mitsuhirato, Tintin hitches a ride out of Shanghai on the back of a car. He sees three men doing something on a railway line. What are they up to? All of a sudden—BOOM!

Once upon a time…

When Hergé drew Mitsuhirato and his accomplice blowing up the Shanghai-Nanking railway line, he was inspired by a real-life event: the Mukden Incident. On September 18, 1931, Japanese troops used dynamite to sabotage a small section of a Japanese-controlled railway line in Manchuria, North China. They pretended that the Chinese had blown up their railway, and Japanese troops invaded Manchuria!

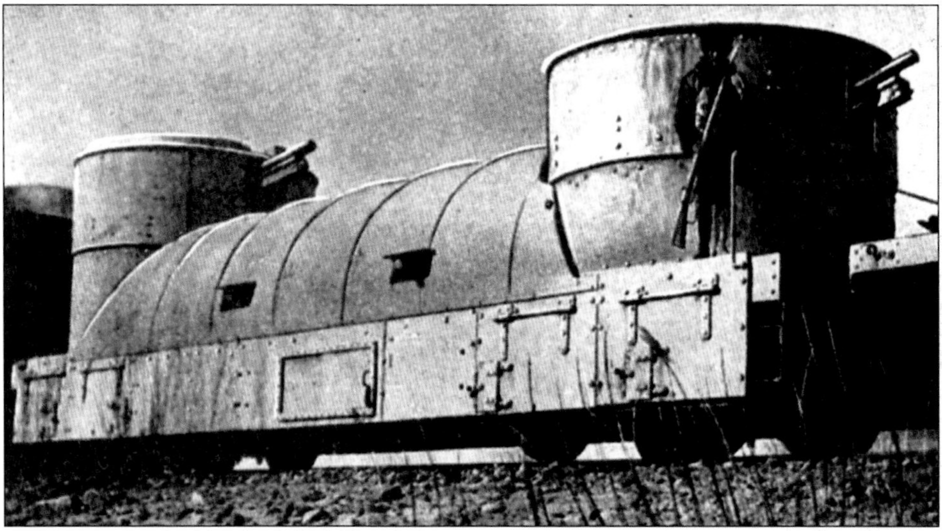

Japanese armored train near Mukden, 1931

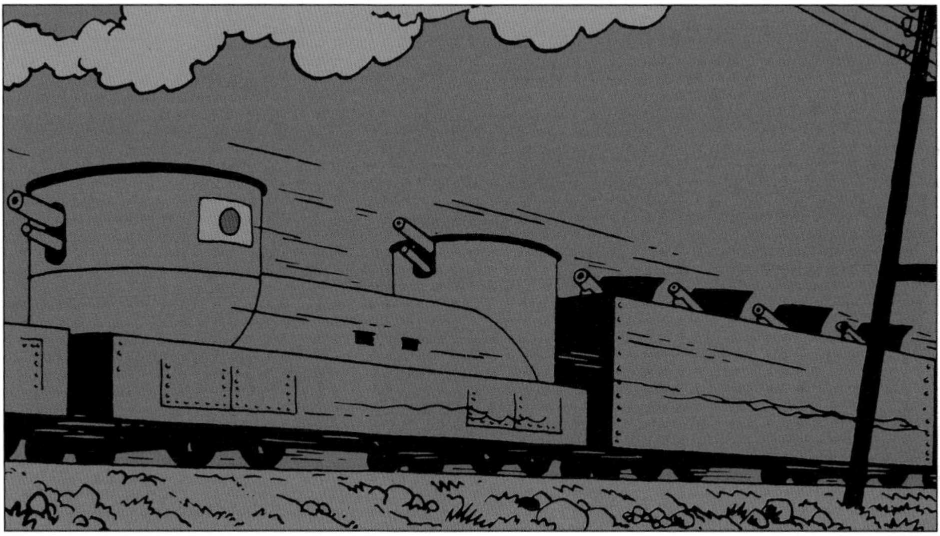

Traditional Chinese decor

Tintin spends the rest of the adventure avoiding troops and corrupt officials in the International Settlement while tracking down gangsters. He wears Chinese clothes to blend in with the scenery, and what scenery! Referring to photographs and with the help of his friend Chang, Hergé practiced drawing dragons (symbols of good fortune), furniture and… vases!

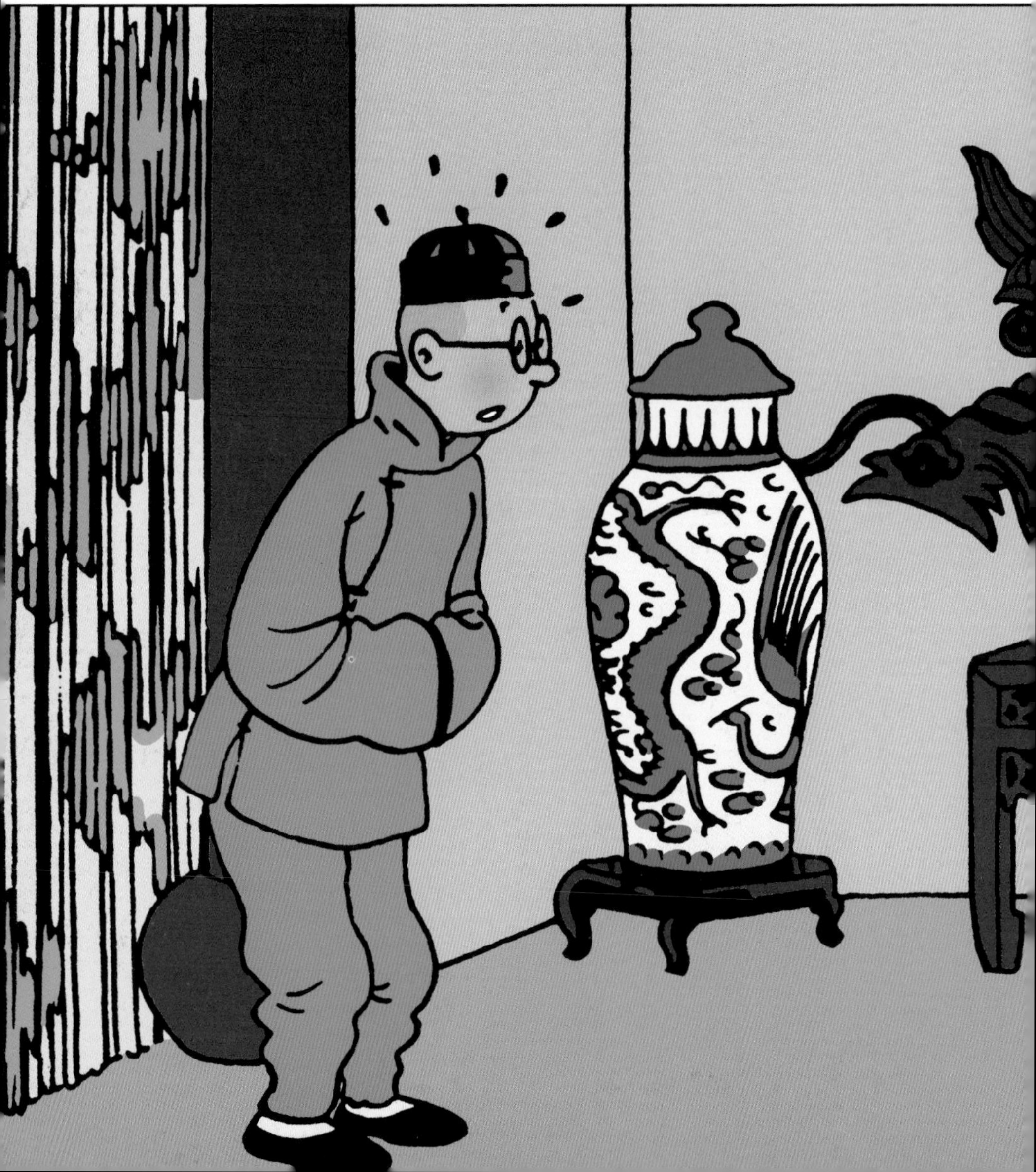

Once upon a time…

The vase behind Tintin looks like a Ming Dynasty (1368–1644) piece, created at a time when the blue color used to decorate porcelain was perfected. But it could be a copy! Chinese vases can be very valuable. In 2010 an eighteenth-century vase made for a Chinese emperor sold for $85 million. The seller had been unaware of its value: he had been using it as a bookend!

Now it's time for us to **Explore and Discover!**

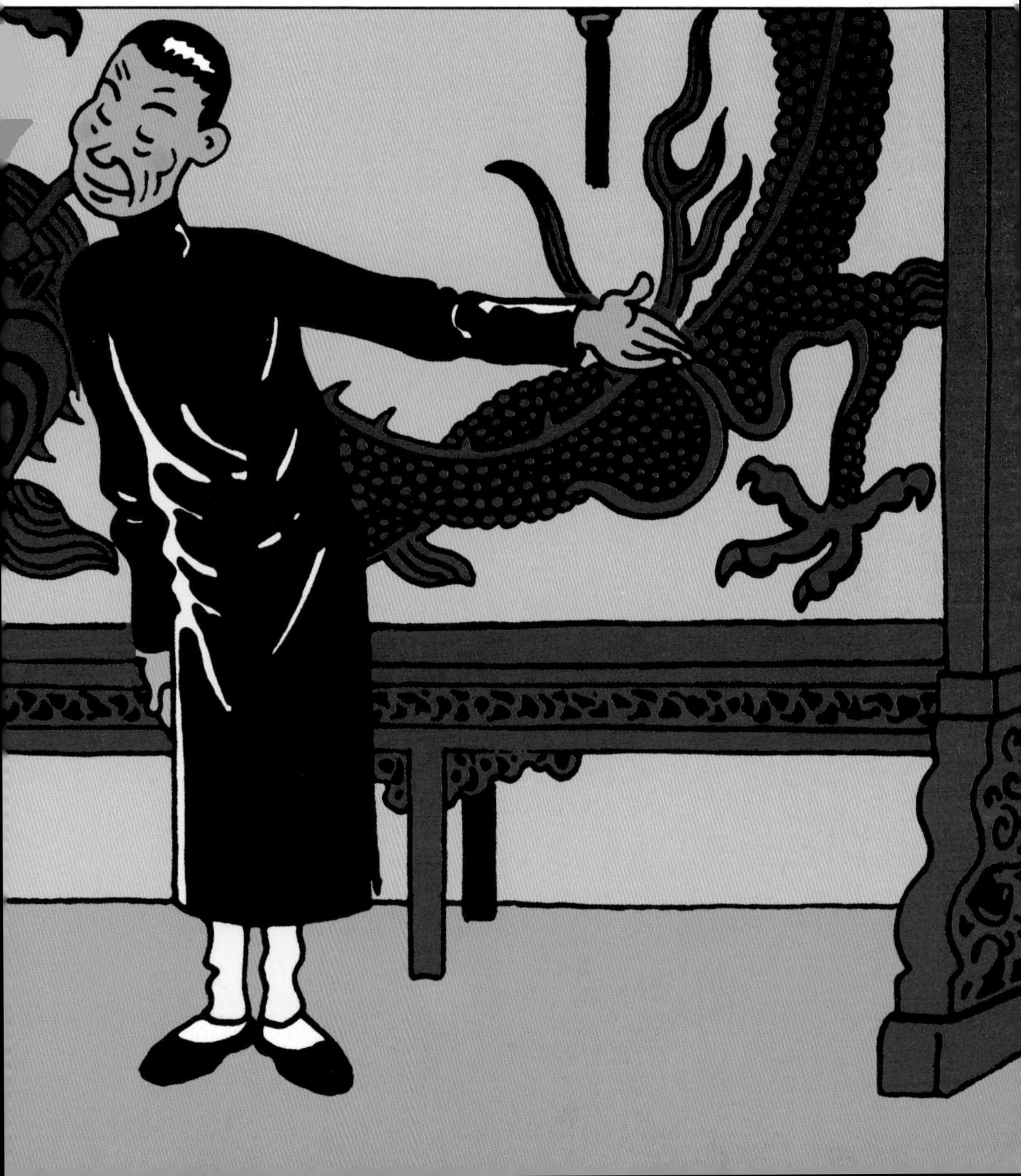

EXPLORE AND DISCOVER

Aside from providing all kinds of historical, political and cultural information about China, Hergé's new Chinese friend, Chang, helped him by adding real Chinese words to the pictures in *The Blue Lotus*. Over the next page you will find out what some of these words mean, but for the moment check out the similarities between the old photo of a Chinese street (from Hergé's archives) and the picture from the story, on the opposite page.

Realizing how important it was to be realistic, from the time of *The Blue Lotus* onwards Hergé also spent more time drawing people and places before beginning a story. Look at this sketch of the rickshaw runner. ▼

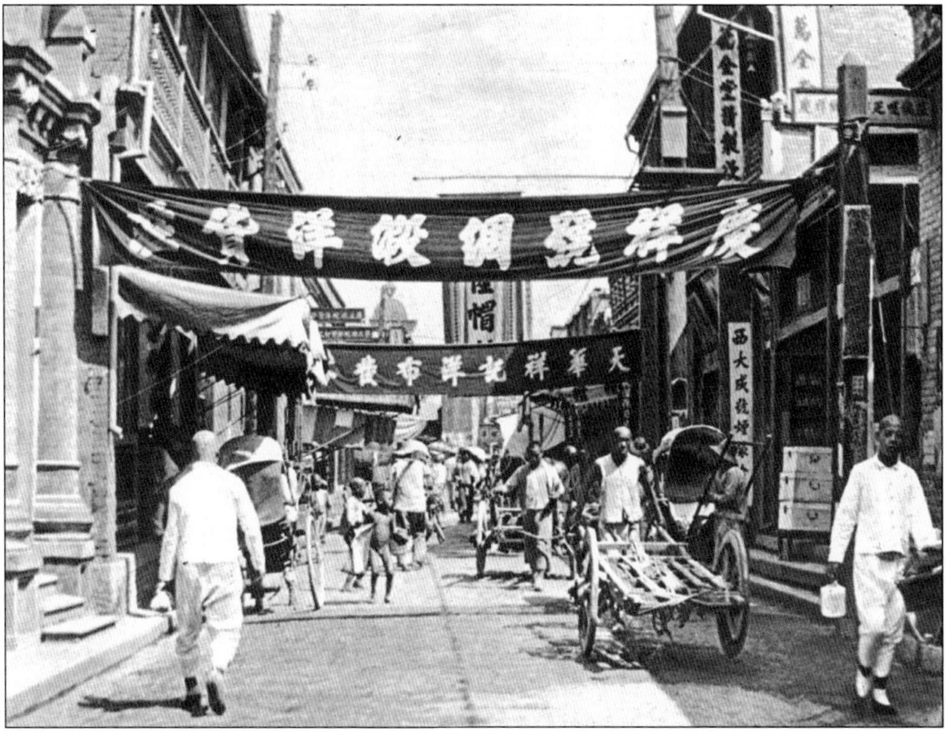

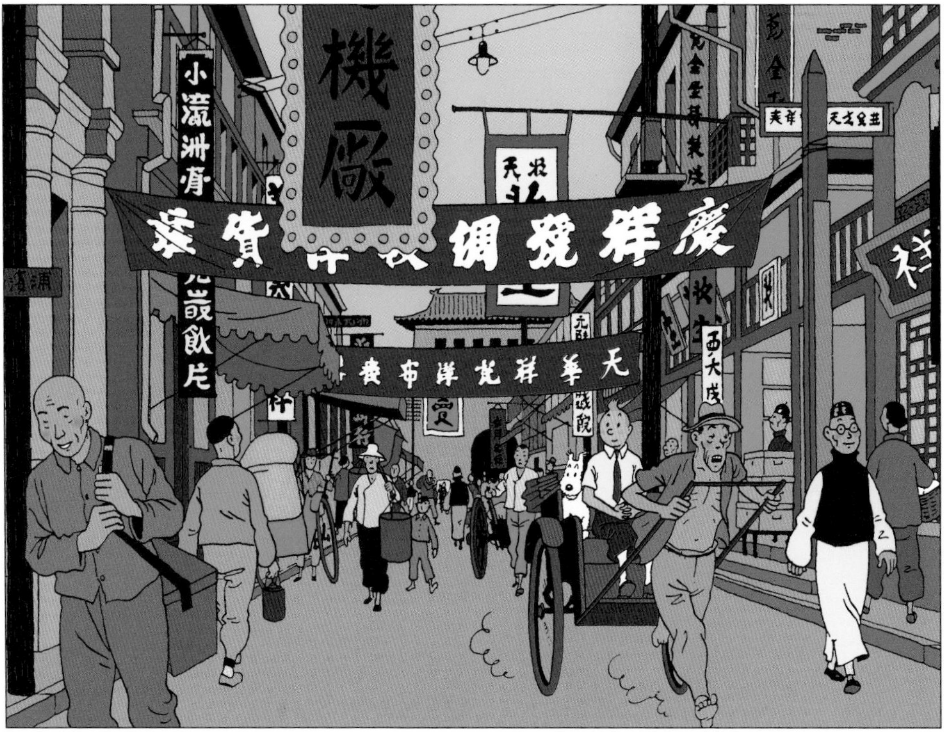

Real Chinese writing

Over the next two pages you can see some of the frames in which Hergé's friend Chang wrote Chinese. The meanings of the words are written out in the list on this page.

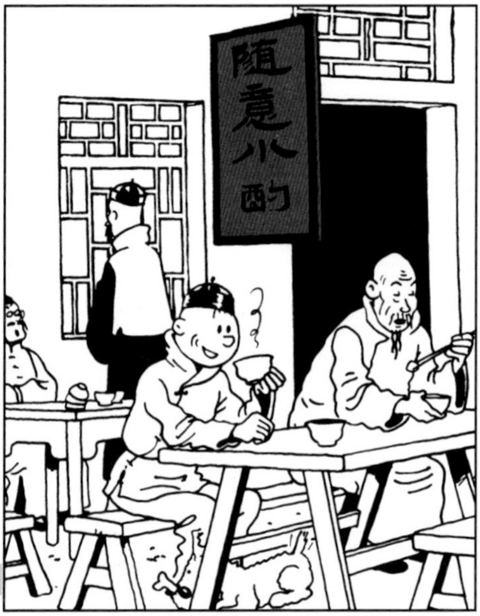

隨意小酌

1

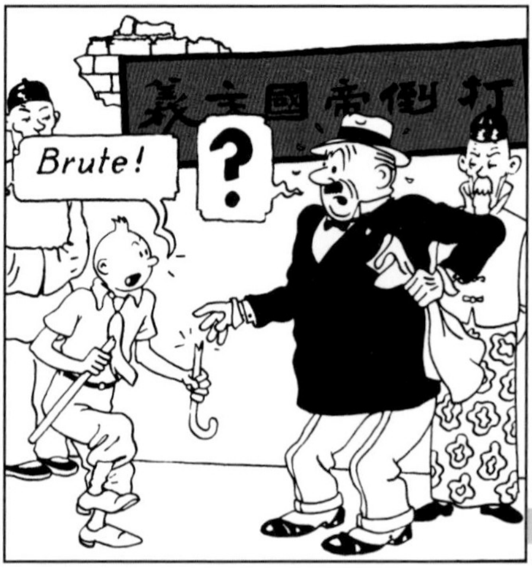

Brute!
?

3

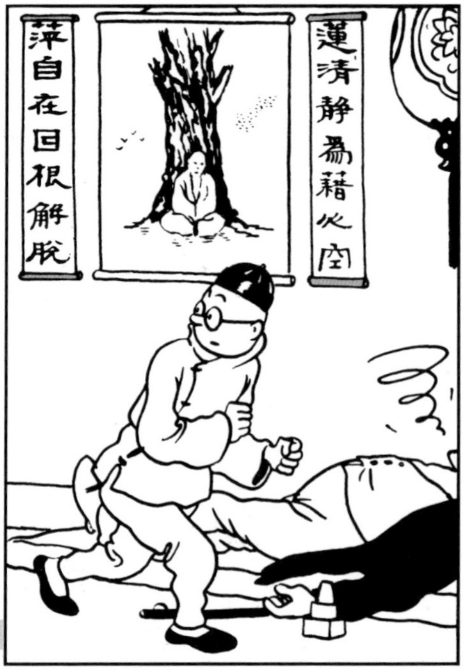

2

1. "Fast food."
2. Left: "The duckweed is free because its roots are not attached." (Moral meaning that true freedom comes from non-attachment to material things)
   Right: "The lotus is calm because its heart is empty." (Taoist maxim advising avoiding desire as a path to happiness)
3. "Down with Imperialism!"
4. "How can you serve your country, however talented you may be, if you are sick?"
5. "The greater the courage required, the keener the heart must become. To become wiser one's conduct must become more disciplined."

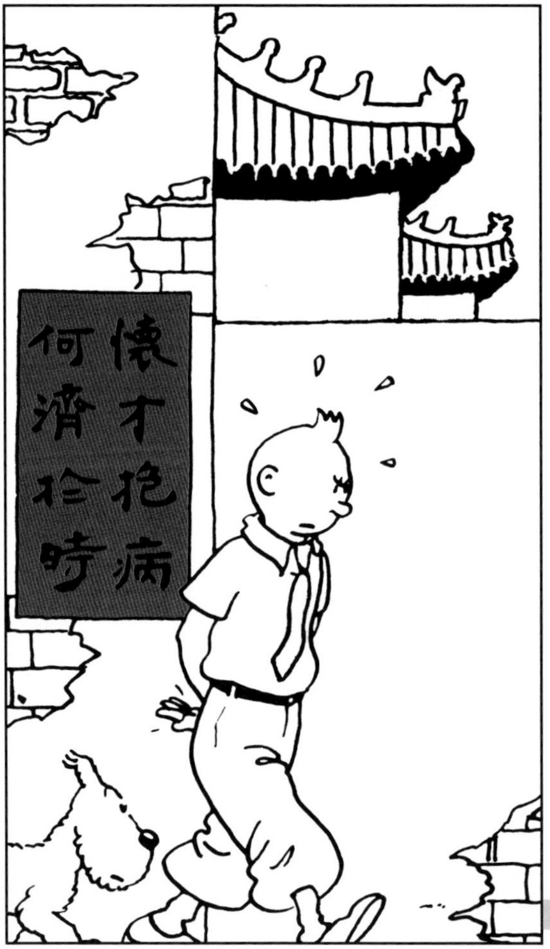
懷才抱病
何濟於時

4

WRITTEN CHINESE

- ★ Written Chinese is made up of symbols, each of which represents a word.
- ★ You need to know about 4,000 symbols to read a modern Chinese newspaper, but in total there are about 80,000 symbols in traditional Chinese!
- ★ Modern Chinese is read from left to right.
- ★ Chinese children can spend up to 5 hours every day practicing reading and writing, learning over 3,000 symbols by the time they are 15 years old.

5

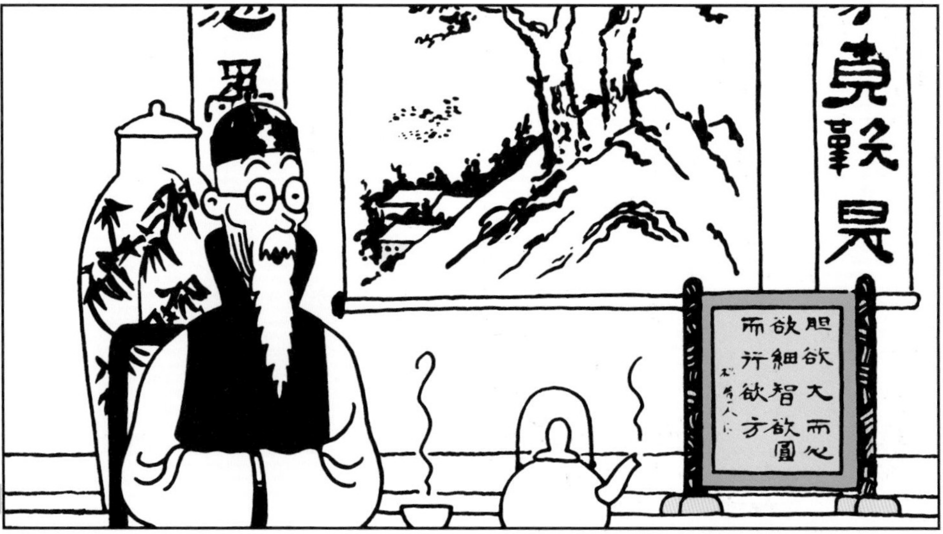
胆欲大而心欲細智欲圓而行欲方

THE CITY GATES

On several occasions in the story Tintin has to trick his way past soldiers to get in and out of Shanghai. Look carefully at the picture below. Can you find the wanted poster on the wall with Tintin's face on it? He had better watch out!

As there are no large gates around Shanghai, Hergé copied gates from the city of Beijing to give his courageous reporter a challenge! Look at the photo on the opposite page, taken from Hergé's archives.

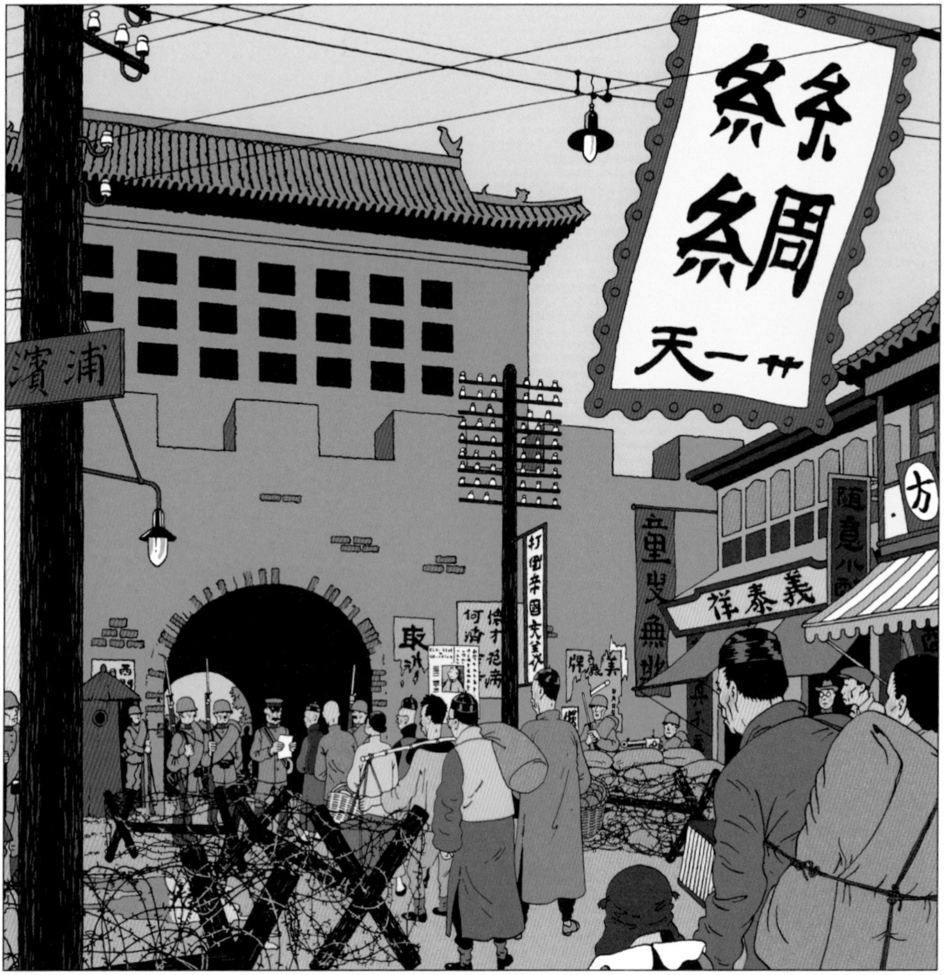
濱浦
祥泰義
方

THE GATES OF BEIJING

★ For hundreds of years Beijing was surrounded by walls with 20 gates.

★ One gate was used by coal merchants; food was brought in by another; the army used yet another gate; and so on.

★ Many of the gates, including the one in this photo, were demolished in the twentieth century to make way for development.

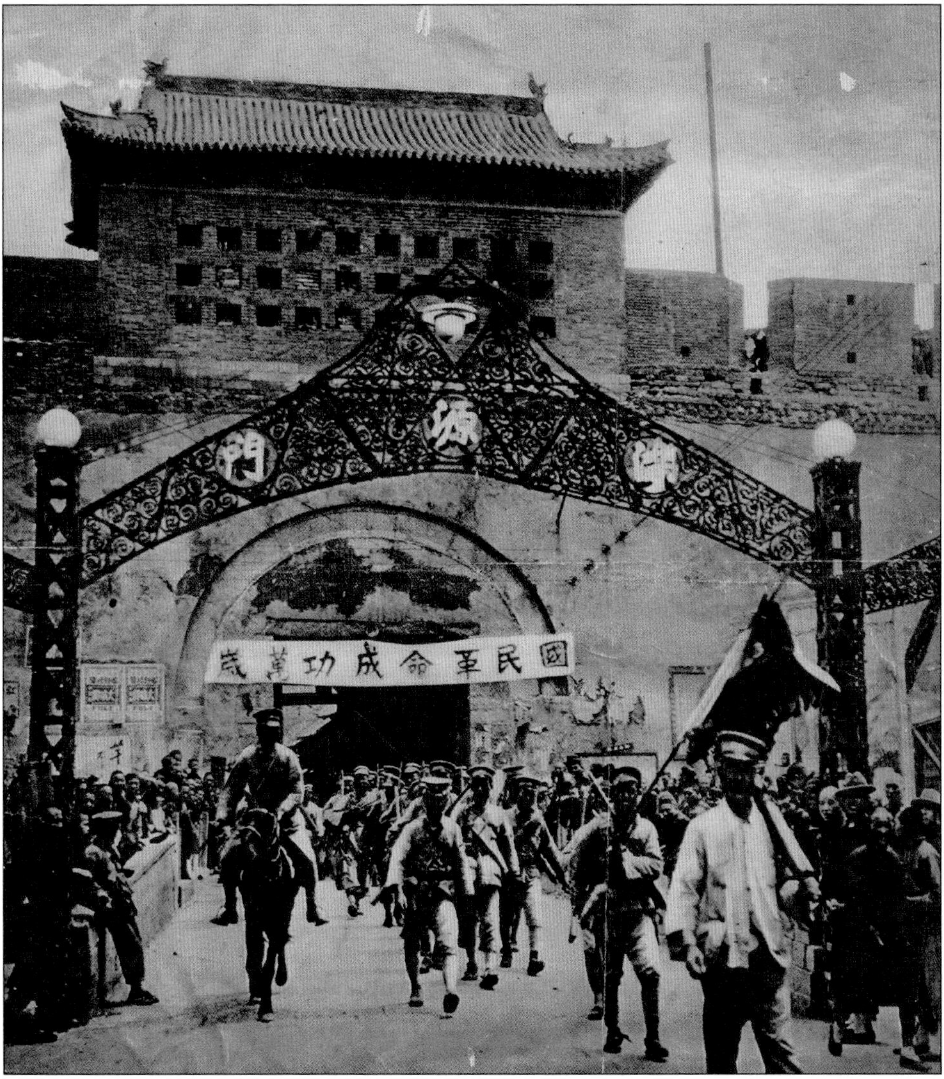

國民革命成功萬歲

CHANG

In *The Blue Lotus* Hergé paid tribute to his Chinese friend Chang Chong-chen by introducing him into the story as a character. Chang is an orphan whom Tintin saves from drowning. They become fast friends, and Chang ends up saving Tintin's life later on!

© Tchang Yifei Archives, Brussels

© Van Parijs

In 1931 the real Chang came to Brussels, Belgium, to study western art and sculpture. After he returned to China in 1936 he became a renowned artist. In 1981, two years before Hergé died, Chang flew back to Belgium from China to be reunited with his friend. They hadn't seen one another for 46 years!

Many adventures after *The Blue Lotus*, Tintin meets Chang one more time in *Tintin in Tibet*.

... *that all Chinese are cunning and cruel and wear pigtails, are always inventing tortures, and eating rotten eggs and swallows' nests* ...

So you see Chang, that's what lots of people believe about China!

They must be crazy people in your country!!

Learning from one another

Chang and Tintin laugh out loud! They have just been talking about the prejudices that people hold against each other. It seems so completely ridiculous!

Tintin explains that in Europe many people mistakenly believe that the Chinese are cunning and cruel. It was all too easy to believe stereotypes in the 1930s, a time when the Internet didn't exist and there were not as many reliable sources of information as there are in today's world.

Look at the picture Hergé drew to conjure up this deceptive image of Chinese people. But of course they are not really like that. Perhaps Tintin and Chang should have a word with Thomson and Thompson!

YOU MUST FIND THE WAY!

Clever Tintin has the villains cornered, but you wouldn't be able to tell by looking at this picture. Just for a moment Tintin wonders if he really does have the upper hand!

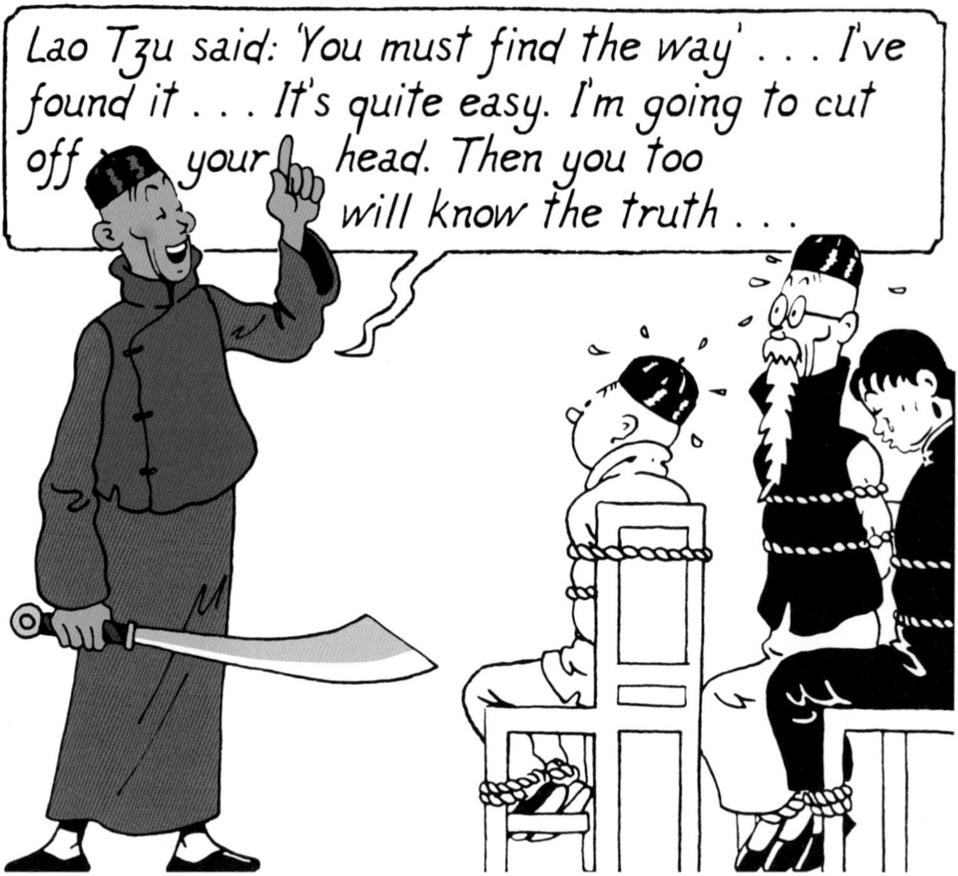
Lao Tzu said: 'You must find the way' . . . I've found it . . . It's quite easy. I'm going to cut off your head. Then you too will know the truth . . .

Mr. Wang Chen-yee's poor son Didi has been poisoned and has gone mad. The sword-wielding philosopher believes he is trying to help people to "find the way," but who is this Lao Tzu that Didi mentions?

LAO TZU

- According to Chinese tradition, Lao Tzu lived in the sixth century B.C.
- Lao Tzu is credited with writing the *Tao Te Ching*, the foundational text of Taoism.
- Taoism is a religion based on compassion, moderation and humility.
- "Tao" means "way" or "path," and refers to the essence of the universe.
- Lao Tzu is often depicted riding a bull, symbolizing the power of a tamed mind.

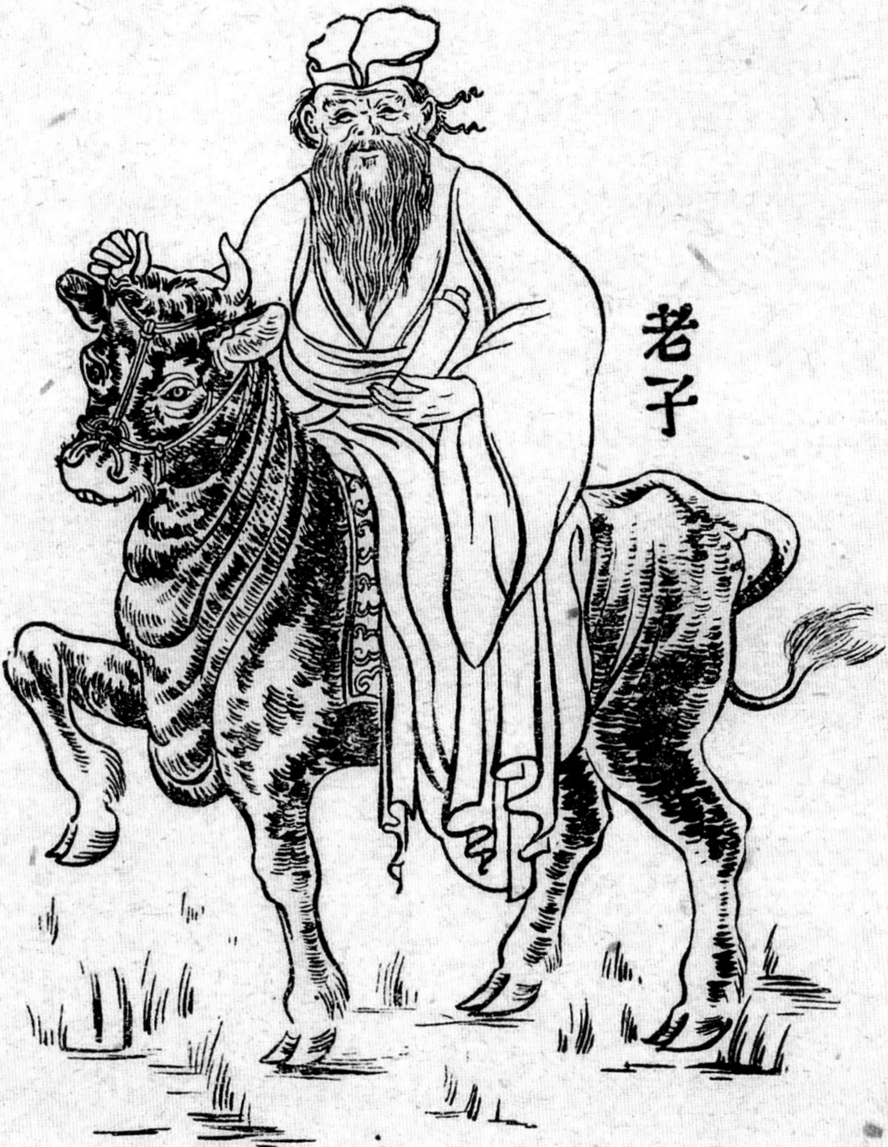
老子

SAVED BY CHANG!

At the last minute, Chang turns the tables on the gangsters! Together with Mr. Wang Chen-yee and the Sons of the Dragon, he rescues Tintin and they bust the gang of smugglers once and for all!

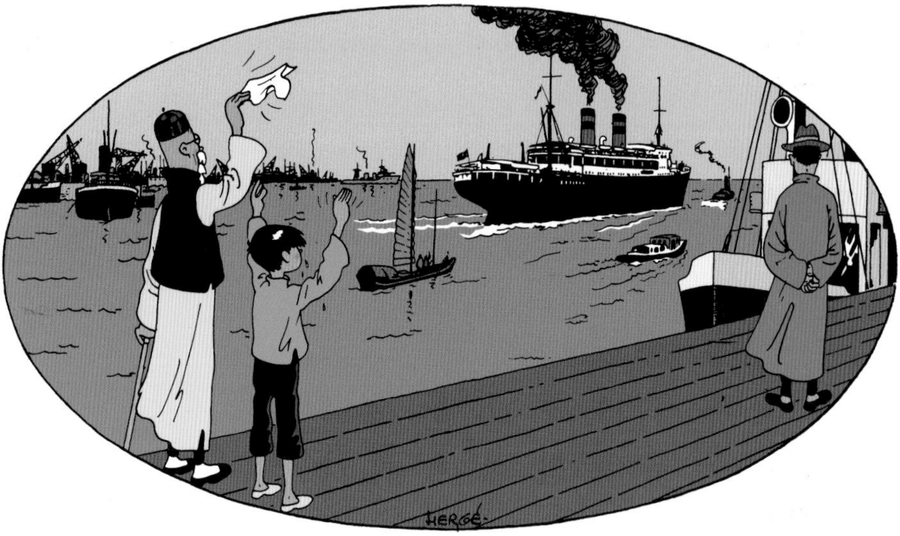
HERGÉ

The adventure is over and Tintin has to go back to Europe. He is sad to leave his new friend Chang behind but they will meet again.

One last thing to discover

It has been great fun exploring the pages of this adventure, but what about the original front cover seen on the right-hand page? Look at this magazine cover from Hergé's archives. The picture inspired the creator of Tintin as he drew the original front cover for *The Blue Lotus*. ▶

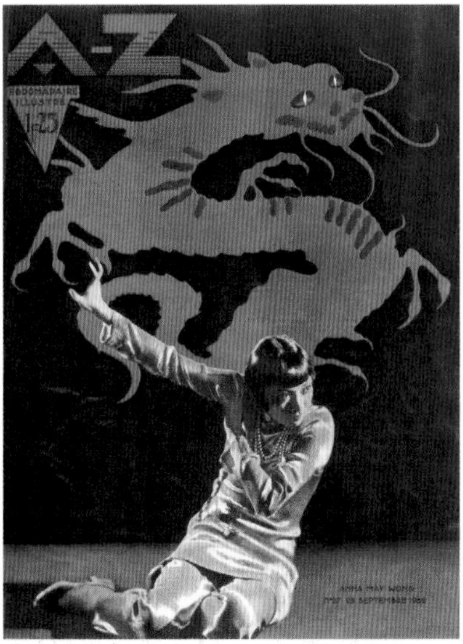
A-Z

TINTIN'S GRAND ADVENTURE

In *The Blue Lotus* Tintin meets Chang and makes a friend for life. At the time Hergé wrote the story, he also made a friend for life! Speaking of the experience much later on, Hergé said: "It was from that time that I undertook research and really interested myself in the people and countries to which I sent Tintin, out of a sense of honesty to my readers." Tintin's adventures would never be the same again!

Trivia: *The Blue Lotus*

Several times in the story the corrupt police chief Dawson is shown in his office. The map behind him shows part of the Soochow Creek, a river running through Shanghai.

The story of The Blue Lotus *so impressed the wife of Chinese Prime Minister Chiang Kai-shek that she invited Hergé to China.*

Roughly speaking, the price put on Tintin's head—5,000 yen—would have been the right amount offered as a reward. It would be about $30,000 today.

Corrupt steel tycoon Gibbons works from his office at 53 The Bund, a famous section of road along the bank of the Whangpoo River. But addresses on The Bund only run to number 52: Hergé put Gibbons at 53 as a joke!

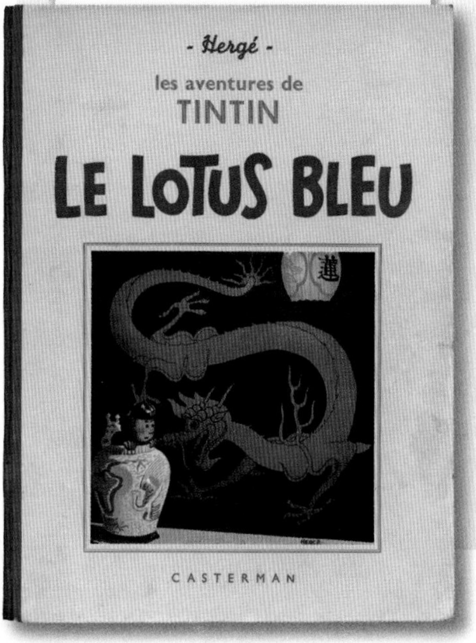

- Hergé -
les aventures de
TINTIN
LE LOTUS BLEU
CASTERMAN

The original cover for *The Blue Lotus* (1936)

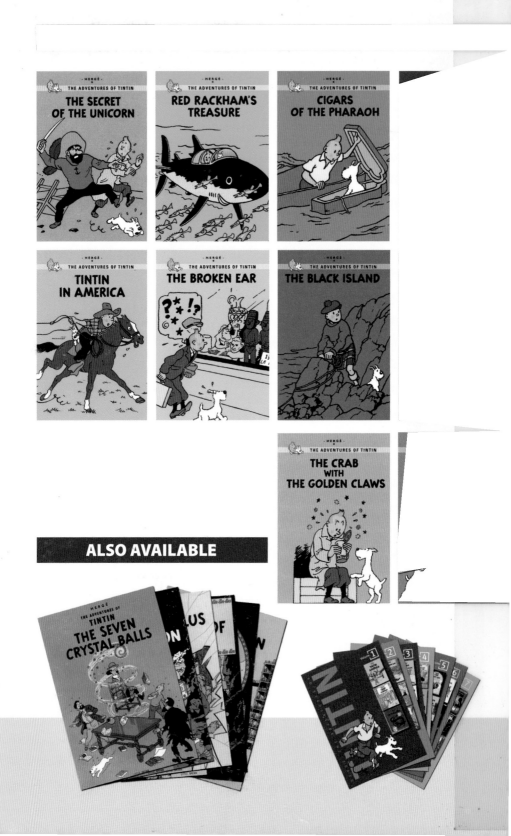

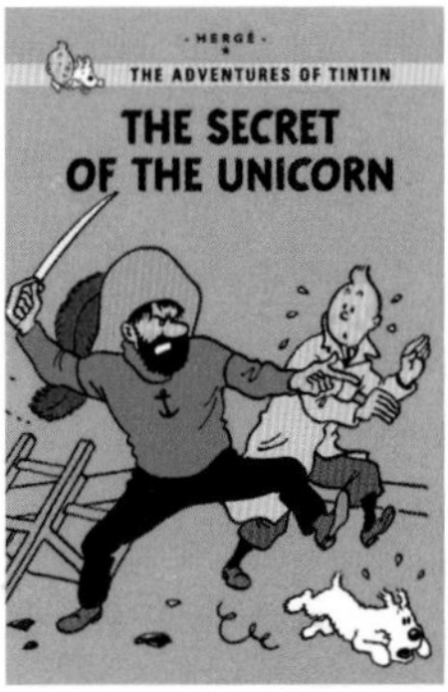
HERGÉ
THE ADVENTURES OF TINTIN
THE SECRET OF THE UNICORN

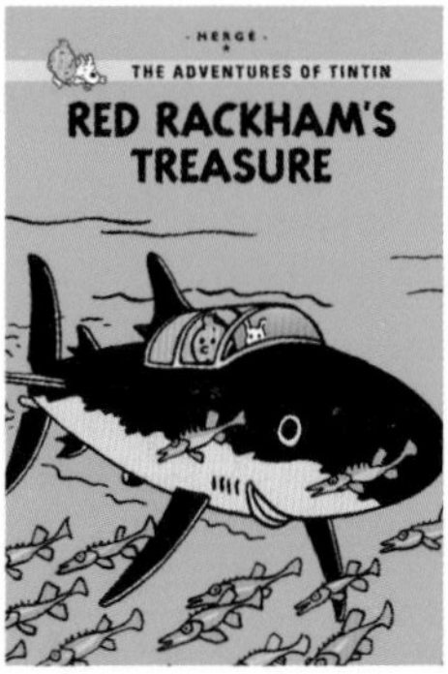
HERGÉ
THE ADVENTURES OF TINTIN
RED RACKHAM'S TREASURE

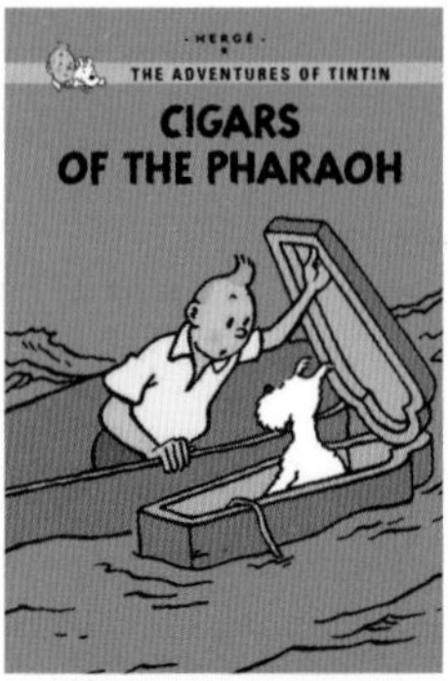
HERGÉ
THE ADVENTURES OF TINTIN
CIGARS OF THE PHARAOH

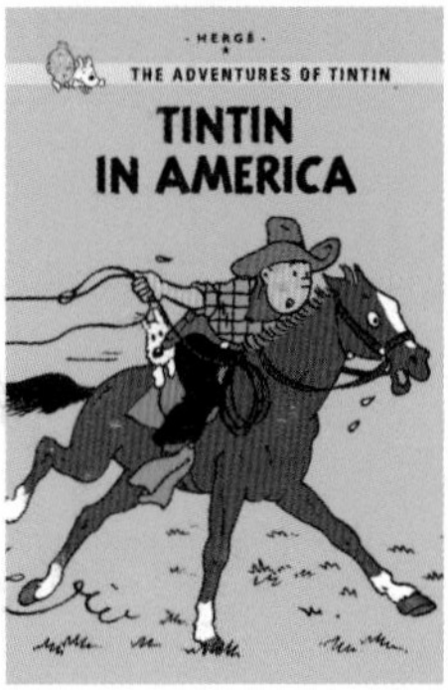
HERGÉ
THE ADVENTURES OF TINTIN
TINTIN IN AMERICA

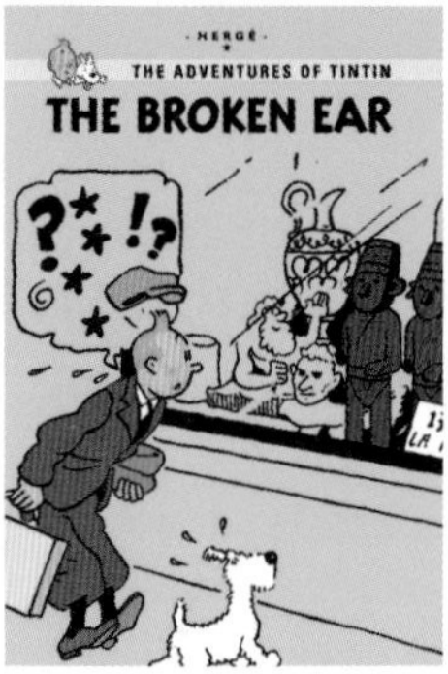
HERGÉ
THE ADVENTURES OF TINTIN
THE BROKEN EAR

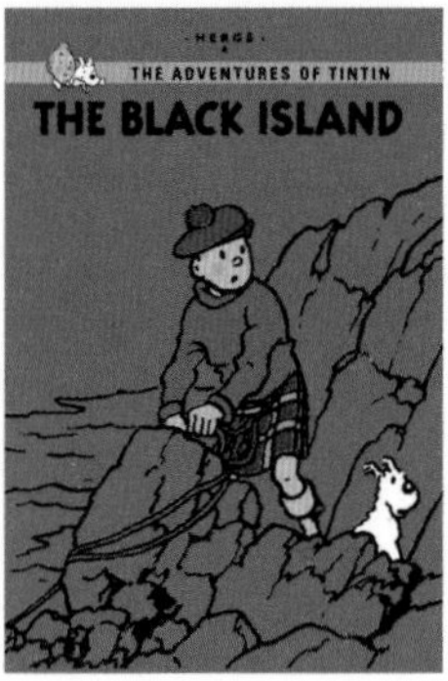
HERGÉ
THE ADVENTURES OF TINTIN
THE BLACK ISLAND

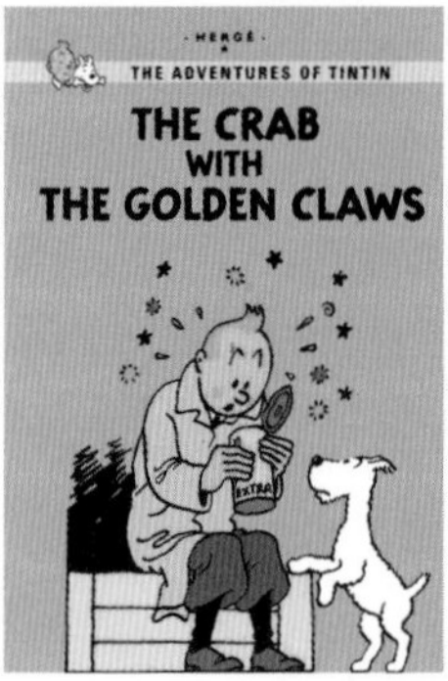
HERGÉ
THE ADVENTURES OF TINTIN
THE CRAB WITH THE GOLDEN CLAWS

ALSO AVAILABLE

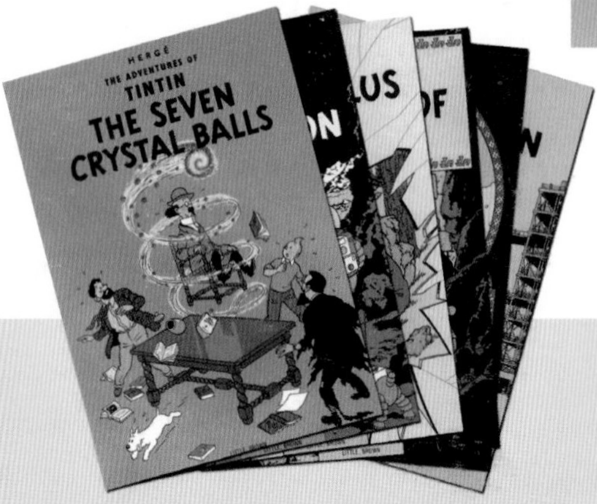
HERGÉ
THE ADVENTURES OF TINTIN
THE SEVEN CRYSTAL BALLS

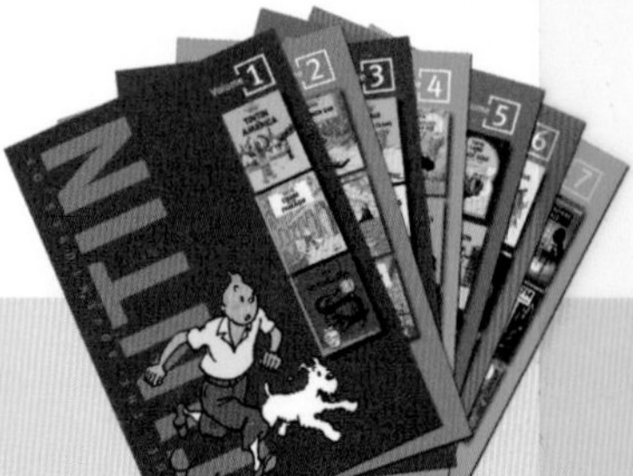

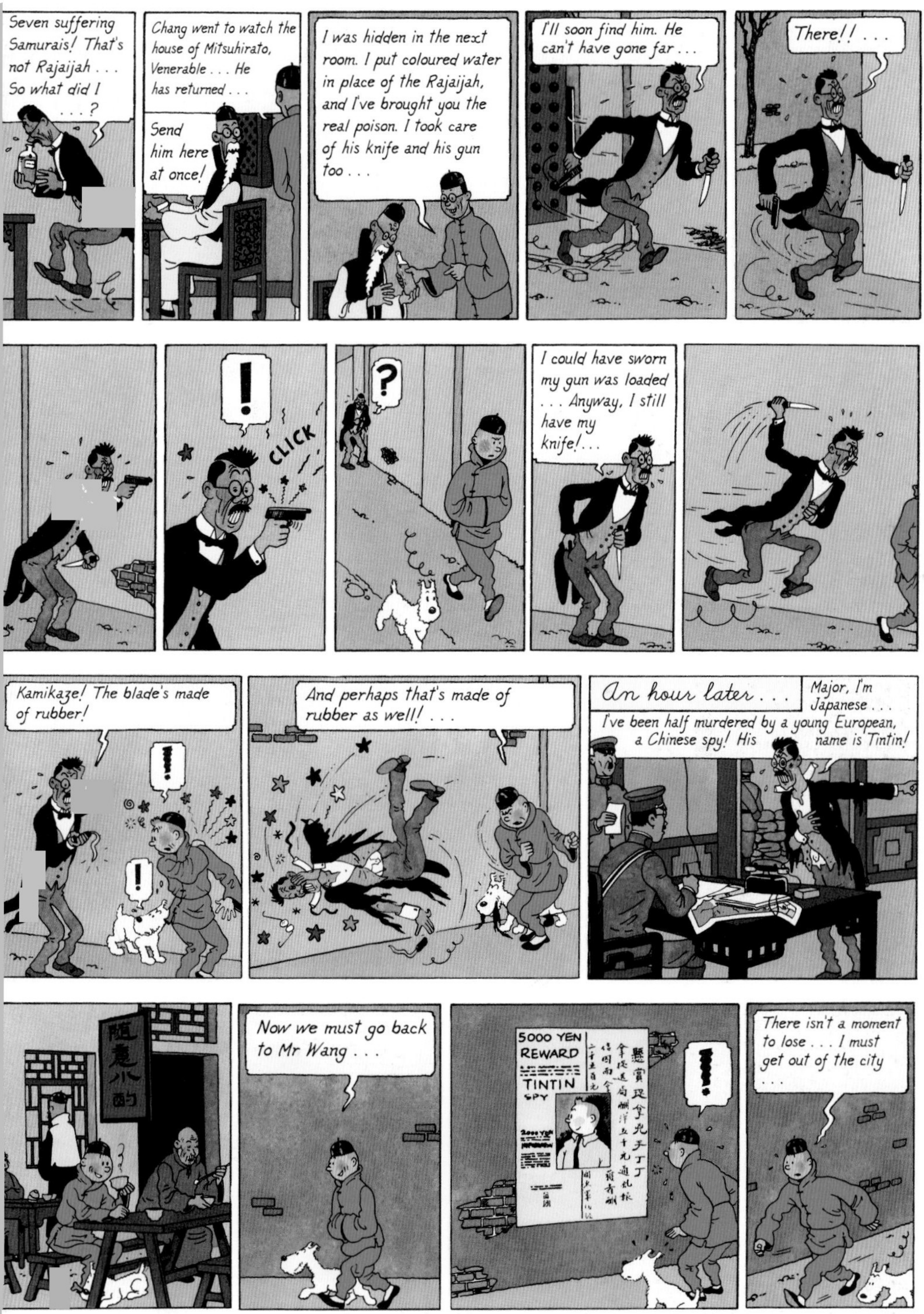
Seven suffering Samurais! That's not Rajaijah . . . So what did I . . . ?
Chang went to watch the house of Mitsuhirato, Venerable . . . He has returned . . .
Send him here at once!
I was hidden in the next room. I put coloured water in place of the Rajaijah, and I've brought you the real poison. I took care of his knife and his gun too . . .
I'll soon find him. He can't have gone far . . .
There!! . . .
!
CLICK
?
I could have sworn my gun was loaded . . . Anyway, I still have my knife! . . .
Kamikaze! The blade's made of rubber!
!
And perhaps that's made of rubber as well! . . .
An hour later . . .
Major, I'm Japanese . . .
I've been half murdered by a young European, a Chinese spy! His name is Tintin!
Now we must go back to Mr Wang . . .
5000 YEN REWARD
TINTIN
SPY
There isn't a moment to lose . . . I must get out of the city . . .